For Homeland

Lalita Gandbhir

ISBN: 978-1-7338357-0-1

Originally published: 2003
Granthali Prakashan

Cover illustration and design by Amit Kaikini
Amit Kaikini's email: youdrawmyattention@gmail.com
Follow @K1llustrator on Instagram

Originally published in the author's native Marathi as "Dahashatwadachi Katha," this novel won the 2003-2004 Maharashtra Government Award for excellence in literature.

Though based on conflicts in India, this novel reflects the stories of displaced men, women, and children all over the world — many of whom I have met in India, the United States, and Canada. This book is dedicated to them.

Refugees

Out of our ancestral homes in the middle of the night

They dragged me, my friends, my neighbors and my relatives,

Drove us out of our village,

And chased us through fields and jungles.

I ran.

My feet bled, I stumbled and I fell.

But I got up and ran again because I heard shots.

I didn't have a single moment

To turn and cast one last glance

At my beloved home and village on fire.

They chased us till we were

Out of our country.

In the strange new land

My friends, relatives and neighbors

Started their search for new homes and horizons

And scattered.

Since that time, tormented, alone and lonely

I struggle to find my home, my village and my country.

CHAPTER 1

"Bijibai, you're all alone here. Please come to my house in town for the night," Bhajan pleaded.

Bhajan had raced a mile in the hot afternoon sun to her mother's rambling farmhouse, making her way over an old dirt road that cut through fields and farmland. Her face was red and her shalwar kamiz was drenched with sweat. She glanced fretfully out the window, scanning the horizon for signs of trouble.

Bijibai smiled indulgently at her daughter, her dark eyes sparkling amidst a web of wrinkles. "I'm an old woman," she said. "No one will hurt me. In any case, Ramlal and our other helpers are on the premises day and night, and we've known our neighbors for generations."

"But you're so isolated here!" Bhajan protested. "There's too much land between you and the neighbors." She anxiously paced the length of the kitchen.

Bijibai cast a loving glance at her daughter. Bhajan was well into middle age now – a grandmother herself – but as vigorous as ever, with an upright bearing and a kind intelligence to her graceful features. "It's all right," Bijibai assured her. "I can ask Ramlal to sleep here tonight, or I can spend the night at our neighbors. I can't abandon the farm while your father and brother are out of town."

Bhajan threw up her hands. "Why did Bauji go away? These are terrible times. He's risking Brijindar's life, and his own."

Bijibai placed some dal and roti into a thali and handed it to Bhajan. "You know your father is like the wind and rain. He'll show up when he wants to. Don't worry, Brijindar is with him. They're big, strong men."

"Big, strong men can't fight guns with bare hands," Bhajan murmured. "And we're Sikhs! Bauji and Brijindar will surely call attention to themselves with their Sikh beards and turbans."

Bijibai ignored her. "Eat. I know you're starving."

Bhajan swallowed a few bites, then turned again to her mother. "I don't think you realize how serious this is. A disaster is at our door."

1

Their family had lived on this sprawling farm in Roha, a small town in Punjab province, for generations. Several families from town had worked for theirs as long as anyone could remember.

Mindful of the townspeople's perception of their riches, neither Bhajan's father, Gobind Singh, nor her mother flaunted their wealth. And their children – Bhajan and her younger brother, Brijindar – had always followed their example.

Bhajan's husband had also grown up on a large farm. He was an ambitious man and had opened a shop in the town bazaar selling material for clothing. They had recently moved to the center of town.

When they first met, Bhajan's mother-in-law had been disconcerted by Bhajan's delicate frame. "How can this fragile girl bear my son's children?" she had wondered. But Ranjit had been born a year after Bhajan and Gurumukh Singh's marriage, and Bhajan's mother-in-law had regained her peace of mind.

Bhajan had waited in vain for more children to arrive. "Don't worry – Ranjit will grow up, and soon enough you'll have grandchildren," her mother had assured her.

Ranjit had indeed grown up, and Bhajan and Gurumukh Singh had found a bride for him. Ranjit and Kuldip now had two young children, Darashan and Rajkumari. Each new addition to the family had filled Bhajan's heart with joy. But while her family had prospered, the political situation in British India had become increasingly unstable. Just the other day, a plan to partition British India into two nations—one Hindu and one Muslim—had been announced on All India Radio. From that moment on, the uneasy peace in Punjab had been shattered.

Before then, Bhajan had heard of occasional attacks on Hindus or Sikhs. But after the announcement, the attacks had multiplied. Hindus and Sikhs stayed in their homes at night, and those living in isolated areas moved to safer, more populated locations. Everyone hoped the storm would pass.

In Roha, families of all faiths had known each other for generations. The community was on edge, but peaceful. Then

2

gangs of strangers had started to arrive. They demanded information from the local Muslims. "Who are the rich Hindus and Sikhs in this town?" "Where do they live?" They threatened to burn the houses of anyone who refused to cooperate. Bhajan had heard whispers of atrocities against Hindu and Sikh families in nearby villages. She didn't know whether the rumors were true, but her family was Sikh, and she knew that that fact, along with their status as prominent members of the community could make them prime targets.

As the whispers of trouble spread, her fears had mounted. Just that morning, she'd heard gunshots and seen smoke on the horizon, impelling her to come check on her mother on this hot afternoon.

Now Bijibai watched as her daughter anxiously picked at her food.

"I must be getting old," she laughed. "My little girl is worrying about me."

Bhajan's brow was still furrowed. "You don't have to come with me now. I'll send a horse and cart for you this evening. And when Bauji and Brijindar arrive, I can ask Ramlal to pick them up at the railway station and bring them to my house."

Bijibai smiled at her daughter's persistence. "Bhajan, I plan to spend the night in my own home."

Bhajan sighed. "All right. Then let me spend the night with you."

Bijibai cast a sharp glance at her daughter.

"I do know what's going on," she said, serious now. "Ramlal's told me about the armed gangs roaming the streets. That's precisely why I don't want to leave. If I'm going to die, I want to die right here in my home. Your situation is different. You have a husband, a son, and grandchildren depending on you. I won't let you spend the night here. Go home."

Bijibai's voice was resolute.

Trying to hide her tears, Bhajan turned to the door. "I'll ask Ramlal to spend the night with you."

Bijibai watched Bhajan go, then wandered, subdued,

3

through the rooms of her expansive ancestral home, letting her hands brush lingeringly over walls, furniture, even well-worn pots and pans – all beloved and rich with memories.

As afternoon faded to evening, Bijibai waited for her son and her husband by the window, gazing into the starry night until clouds moved in and covered the stars. As she fell asleep, she heard the rhythmic drizzle of rain.

*   *   *   *   *   *   *   *

Before sunrise, young Ranga arrived to help Ramlal tend to the cattle. He stepped into the storage shed behind the barn and stopped in his tracks, his eyes bulging with shock and fear. He shot out of the shed and ran toward the farmhouse. Ramlal had just opened the front door, ready to brush *masheri* on his teeth, when Ranga appeared, looking like a ghost, opening and closing his mouth without a sound.

Ramlal took hold of Ranga's shoulders and shook him. "What's wrong?"

Ranga could only point to the barn. Ramlal sprinted toward it, but stopped when he encountered Bijibai immobile on the threshold, a tin bowl of fruit and vegetable peels for her favorite cow in her arms, her face expressionless.

Ranga stepped forward and pointed to the storage shed. Ramlal peered in. Then he screamed and started to weep aloud.

*   *   *   *   *   *   *   *

Back at her own house near the town center, Bhajan had been restless that night, unable to sleep. She rose early and ventured into the kitchen. The cook, who had just arrived, handed her an envelope she had found slipped under the door. Bhajan's hands shook as she tore it open.

"Let last night be a lesson to you. Leave this country now if you wish to save yourself and your family." The signature was the red imprint of a big thumb.

4

Panic rose in Bhajan's chest. "Last night?...What happened last night?"

Suddenly Ranga was at the door, his face ashen.

"Bauji... Brijindar..." he stammered.

"What is it, Ranga?"

"Your father and brother," he choked. "Their bodies were dumped in the storage shed. We found them this morning."

Bhajan gasped.

Tears brimmed in Ranga's eyes. "Your mother is in a state of shock."

Feeling numb herself, Bhajan raced, together with Kuldip, to the family farm. This time Bijibai didn't resist going to Bhajan's home. Her face remained expressionless, her eyes free of tears. She seemed to have lost her powers of speech. The sight of her son's and husband's bloodied bodies had robbed her of her faculties. Bhajan recalled her mother's words: "If I'm going to die, I want to be in my home." Was she witnessing her mother's living death, she wondered, as she and Kuldip pulled Bijibai out her front door.

The funeral that evening passed in a blur. "It's the roving gangs of strangers," Gurumukh Singh said to Bhajan afterwards. "They've killed the richest, most powerful man in town to instill fear. Even the Muslims are terrified of them." He shook his head. "Today Hindus, Muslims and Sikhs alike risked their lives to pay last respects to your father and brother. I don't know if tomorrow they will or can risk being associated with us."

A knock came at the back door. Ordinarily the door would have been left wide open until bedtime. Today Gurumukh Singh had locked it with a metal chain.

"Who is it?" Gurumukh Singh asked.

A child's voice answered, "It's me, Hasan's son."

Hasan was a Muslim whose family had served Gobind Singh's family for generations. Gurumukh Singh opened the door a crack, and the boy squeezed in. "Ammijan wants me to warn you. More men are headed to town, and they have guns and switchblades. She says you must be careful." He squeezed back out and vanished into the rainy evening. Gurumukh Singh closed the door promptly. Hasan's family was risking the gang's wrath, Bhajan and Gurumukh Singh knew, to warn them.

Soon afterwards, another knock came at the door.

"Who is it?"

"Ramlal."

Bhajan welcomed him in.

He stood by the door, shivering from the rain. "Our family is leaving," he said breathlessly. "We've become foreigners in our home. Tomorrow we plan to go to Amrit's parents' home. But first I wanted to pay my respects to Bijibai." He turned to the bench where Bijibai was sitting expressionless, and touched her feet. She didn't seem to notice.

Again he faced Bhajan. He'd seen her grow up and loved her like his own daughter. "Bitiya, these are difficult times. Perhaps God will show us a way out of this nightmare."

"The Gods don't remember us," Bhajan murmured.

Ramlal folded his hands and turned to Gurumukh Singh, who was hovering by the doorway. "Please don't be angry with me for what I have to say. Our town will be part of a Muslim nation soon. They don't want us here. For families like mine, the decision to pack and move is easy. We don't have land or money. But you're wealthy. You own land and have money and cattle. You must remember that your lives are even more at risk for this reason. I beg you to lock your house and go where you will be safe. For now, the goal is survival."

He touched Bijibai's feet again, still receiving no response. Tears rolled down his wrinkled face as he told Bhajan, "You'll have to care for your mother now, Bitiya. I've served three generations of your family and I hope the chain won't break. Maybe we can all return after this storm subsides. If not, only God knows when we'll meet again."

Wiping her eyes, Bhajan said, "Ramlal, this disaster may force us to separate, but our bonds will last forever." She touched his feet. Kuldip and Ranjit came forward and did the same.

Ramlal went to the second floor to cast a last glance at the sleeping children, then returned to the kitchen and opened the back door. Bhajan called out to him. "Ramlal – wait. It's not safe for you out there in the dark. Sleep here tonight, please."

"I can't," Ramlal replied. "We're leaving early in the morning. Besides, I'm old and penniless. No one will bother me."

Bhajan watched him disappear into the night, his gray hair shining in the reflected kitchen light.

It would be her last glimpse of her mother's devoted servant.

Bhajan seated herself beside Bijibai on the bench by the kitchen window and started talking to herself. "Where can we go? Who will care for our cattle and our farm?"

Gurumukh Singh sat down beside her. "Two of my cousins moved to Delhi after high school," he said. "I have their address. We can spend a few days with them, if we have to."

Ranjit, who had been listening from the corner, could contain himself no longer. "This is our land! No one has the right to drive us away. We must fight them!"

He became more animated as he spoke. "I've been talking with other Hindu and Sikh men in town. We've collected weapons. Bijibai's house is like a fortress. We can fight from there."

Bhajan bowed her head. She knew how headstrong her son was. "He's another problem we'll have to face," she thought.

Gurumukh Singh tried to reason with him. "Yes, Ranjit – you can lock yourself in Bijibai's house for a few days, but eventually your water supply will run out. You can't fight an army of men with a few guns and knives. In the long run, what can we do? This is going to be a Muslim country and they don't want us here."

"I don't care who rules!" Ranjit burst out. "The British ruled, and we lived here. The Muslims can rule and we'll continue to live here. I need to find the cowards who killed my grandfather and uncle. I'll strangle them with my bare hands if I have to."

No one spoke. Kuldip started to sob.

Again someone knocked on the back door. "Who is it?" Gurumukh Singh asked.

"Me – Mohammed," a hushed voice answered. Gurumukh

Singh recognized the speaker. It was Siraj Hasan's nephew.

Siraj and Gurumukh Singh had been best friends since childhood. Siraj's father had been a rich merchant until the family had lost their fortune in the paper business. Gurumukh Singh had helped Siraj start a new business selling lumber. Siraj had done well, though the rest of his extended family continued to struggle to make ends meet. Mohammed worked for his uncle.

Gurumukh Singh opened the door. "Uncle talked to the gang leaders," said Mohammed. "They've promised that no further harm will come to your family. But he asked me to bring you these, just in case." He pulled two revolvers from a cloth bag, handing one to Ranjit and the other to Gurumukh Singh.

"Uncle will come by early tomorrow to talk to you."

Then Mohammed, too, hurried out the back door. Ranjit watched him go. "These people may call themselves our friends," he sneered. "But they're Muslims. Can we trust them?"

"We're exhausted," Bhajan said quietly. "Let's sleep now. Tomorrow morning we'll decide what to do."

The men secured the house as best they could, then lay down to sleep on mats near the front and back entrances, revolvers in their hands. Bhajan and Kuldip helped Bijibai up the stairs and settled her on the bed.

Resting on a mattress near her mother, Bhajan tried to clear her mind of thoughts. "I must get sleep to face whatever comes tomorrow," she told herself. But her mind refused to quiet.

"Ramlal is right," she thought. "For now, the goal is survival. We must try to get to Delhi if we can. If Ranjit refuses to come, we'll have to leave without him."

＊　　＊　　＊　　＊　　＊　　＊　　＊　　＊

With the first ray of sunshine, Kuldip came into Bhajan's room. Tears streamed down her face. Bhajan stroked her back. "We'll be all right, Kuldip. We'll find a way through this." But her promise felt empty. She shuddered at the hollowness of her words.

Downstairs, she heard the back door open. She went to the

staircase, Kuldip behind her. Together they listened to the conversation in the kitchen.

Bhajan recognized Sirajjee's voice. "No one will touch your property if you turn it over to me. I promise I'll look after it for you. But it's not safe for you here. Please – collect all the money, jewelry and valuables you can take with you. I'll personally accompany you wherever you decide to go and have my son and nephew guard your home until you're safely on your way. I'll travel with you until you cross to where there are mostly Hindu and Sikh towns."

Before Gurumukh Singh could respond, the back door opened again, and a frightened voice could be heard. "Did Pitajee sleep here last night?" It was Ramlal's son, Ragesh.

A wave of horror washed over Bhajan. Had Ramlal been killed too? Why hadn't she forced him to stay last night? Even his age and his poverty couldn't shield him from this inferno.

There was a flurry of movement, and then she heard Gurumukh Singh's voice. "Ranjit! Where are you going?" Her heart sank. She raced down the stairs.

Ranjit stood half out the door, with Gurumukh Singh grasping his sleeve.

"I'm going to find Dadajee's, Mamajee's, and Ramlal's killers." Ranjit wrested his arm free of Gurumukh Singh's grasp and vanished. Bhajan and Gurumukh Singh looked at each other. For the first time in her life, Bhajan saw her husband looking thoroughly helpless.

Siraj Hasan cleared his throat. "You have very little time," he said. "Please go." He turned to Bhajan. "Your parents' farm belongs to you now. If you turn it over to me, the cattle will survive and your home won't be burned. In the future, I'll try to pay you whatever I can."

Bhajan's mind was spinning. She couldn't speak. "I know this is hard," said Siraj. "You don't have to decide right away. But please think about it. I'll be back soon. In the meantime, you're safe; my son is guarding your house."

The moment he left, Bhajan collapsed on the bench. "I never

wanted to live to see this day."

She heard little feet running down the steps. Darashan ran into the kitchen, a big smile on his face. "Bhajanma!"

She hugged him. "I must live for him and Rajkumari," she murmured.

Darashan nestled contentedly in her arms.

That morning Bhajan gathered up all their jewelry and valuables. Kuldip packed a few articles of clothing and pictures. Gurumukh Singh went to the bank and transferred his funds to a Delhi branch. Then he and Bhajan went to Bijibai's house to collect the valuables there. Siraj Hasan shadowed them everywhere they went. Many of the strangers they encountered said, "Salaam Alaikum." Others ignored them: a few leered. Occasionally Hindus or Sikhs scurried by, merely nodding. No one stopped to talk.

That night Siraj Hasan told Gurumukh Singh, "I have tickets for the train. I'll sleep here tonight and we'll leave early in the morning. I'll be back shortly." He set off, leaving his son to guard the family.

After he left, Bhajan asked Gurumukh Singh, "Where's Ranjit?"

Gurumukh Singh sighed. "I don't know."

Bhajan and Kuldip cooked and packed some food for the journey. The family fed the children and forced themselves to eat a few bites. Several hours later, Ranjit still hadn't appeared. Tears streaked Kuldip's face. Darashan and Rajkumari clung to their mother and grandmother.

At bedtime, Siraj Hasan arrived with two more guns. "I don't know who I can trust these days. Muslims are killing Muslims," he murmured. He waited up with the family for Ranjit. When the children fell asleep, Bhajan and Kuldip carried them to the second floor and helped Bijibai to bed. Then Kuldip and Bhajan waited in the bedroom.

Sometime later, Bhajan heard a knock. She hurried downstairs; Siraj Hasan had already opened the door. A figure outside thrust a piece of paper at him and disappeared into the night. He handed it to Gurumukh Singh, who read it aloud.

"Please don't wait for me. Leave the Delhi address with Sirajchachajee. I'll find you."

The note was unsigned, but Ranjit's energetic scrawl was unmistakable.

Silence filled the room. Then Kuldip spoke, "Please let me wait for him here. You can take Rajkumari and Darashan with you."

Siraj Hasan turned to face Kuldip. "The situation's getting worse by the moment. A pair of Muslims trying to protect their Hindu friends were murdered today. I'm risking my life and my family's lives to keep you safe. I'm not sure I can do it much longer."

"Let's wait one more day," Gurumukh Singh suggested. "I'll try to find Ranjit tomorrow."

Siraj Hasan lowered his voice. "If anything happens to you, the women and children will have no protection. We don't even know where Ranjit is. If you do find him, he won't join you. You saw how angry he was; he's obsessed with the idea of revenge."

Bhajan patted Kuldip. "I'm just as reluctant to leave behind my only son, but we must think of Rajkumari and Darashan."

Her voice was gentle, but Kuldip heard its edge.

"A wife's place is with her husband," she sobbed. "Please, let me stay."

Bhajan continued in the same tone. "We're not moving away for ourselves, Kuldip. If we want to save the children, we must go."

Siraj approached. "Bitiya," he said gently. "You have my word. I'll find Ranjit and try to send him to Delhi. I won't let anyone hurt him."

Kuldip shoved her dupatta into her mouth and ran upstairs.

The next morning, Siraj Hasan, along with his nephew and son, ferried Gurumukh Singh's family to the railway station in a pair of horse-drawn carts. One of the carts belonged to Siraj Hasan. The other, which until now had belonged to Bhajan's parents, would become his upon their departure. Crowds thronged the train, but Siraj Hasan pushed his way through and secured some seats. Bijibai, Bhajan, Kuldip, and the children crammed into them.

11

Gurumukh Singh stood close by, and Siraj Hasan hovered protectively. When the train started to move, some of the women aboard sobbed. Many men jumped from the train to the platform. Some waved frantically at the passengers. Others laughed derisively, shouting, "Go home."

Slowly the crowd relaxed and people began speaking again, in hushed, sober tones. Siraj Hasan found a seat for Gurumukh Singh, who leaned his head back and closed his eyes. Bhajan watched the countryside dotted with smoking homes through her window. She felt anger rising in her chest.

"What right did those politicians have to divide up our country and displace us from our homes?" she wanted to know.

But as the train rolled on, her anger gave way to exhaustion.

She pulled Rajkumari onto her lap and caressed her hair. "Your grandmother lives for you and your brother," she murmured. "Only for you…"

CHAPTER 2

Twenty long years had lapsed since Gurumukh Singh had last visited his cousin, but he managed to find his bungalow. By the time the family reached it, the clouds had dissipated and Delhi was illuminated by the bright setting sun.

At the front gate, the rest of the family hung back as he approached.

Young children were playing in the yard. As he stepped forward, a little girl called out, "Someone's at the door!" A middle-aged woman emerged, cast a glance at the bedraggled family, and shouted, "Go away," before retreating back inside.

Gurumukh Singh hesitated, unsure how to proceed. When the woman peered out again, he blurted, before she could speak, "Jashwant Singh is my cousin."

The woman studied him coolly before replying, "I'll send him out."

Soon Jashwant Singh appeared. "Is that you, Gurumukh?" he asked. "Please come in. We're a bit crowded, but we'll manage."

"We're imposing on them," Bhajan thought, as she followed her husband into the house. "We're unwanted guests."

The moment she was inside she understood why. The home was overflowing with other refugees, their baggage scattered everywhere. Several men occupied the sitting room. The older ones sat on the sofa and chairs; the rest sprawled on the floor. A few young men stood restlessly. The women were in the middle room, a few sitting, others lying on bedsheets, mats, *chataee* – whatever was available. Some had bandages on their arms and legs. One woman had a black eye, another a split lip. An eerie silence filled the home, punctuated only by muffled sounds from the kitchen and the shouts of children outside. To Bhajan, it seemed the house was overflowing with agony.

Darashan tugged at her, interrupting her train of thought. He and Rajkumari wanted to join the children in the yard.

Before Bhajan could speak, an elderly woman said, "Let the children play. The grief in this room is too much for them."

13

Kuldip, holding on to the children's hands, looked at Bhajan, who nodded. Kuldip set the children free and they flew out the door.

Kuldip joined the women in the kitchen, helping to cut vegetables for dinner. No one asked why Bijibai just sat in a corner staring into space. Nor did Jashwant Singh ask why the other men in the family were missing.

The women served supper to the men and children, then served themselves. A few refused food.

At night, everyone laid down wherever they could find space. More families arrived and were somehow accommodated.

The next morning, Gurumukh Singh declared, "We must find a flat as soon as possible." Jashwant Singh said that refugees had so overwhelmed Delhi that there were few flats available for rent. Gurumukh Singh would have to look hard and would need a large deposit. "I still have some money," Gurumukh Singh assured him. "And there's always the women's gold jewelry if we need more funds."

"In that case you're luckier than most of the refugees," said his cousin.

It took several days of searching, but he found two rooms in a five-story tenement. He had to put down an astronomical deposit. "Will you refund the money when we move out?" he asked. The landlord laughed. "We'll decide when you move out. Families in this building live here forever."

Gurumukh Singh hired a taxicab and packed the family's meager belongings in the trunk. The family thanked their hosts, who were relieved to see them go, then crammed themselves into the cab for the ride to their new home.

Gurumukh Singh's cousin's bungalow was located in a recently developed section of Delhi called New Delhi, with tidy streets and newer buildings. Bhajan had hoped to live in the same area, but the taxi instead drove them into congested old Delhi. Bhajan and Kuldip anxiously stared out the taxi windows at the chaos of cramped shops, street venders, and cars, bicycles, and people thronging everywhere. Intrigued by the colorful sights,

Darashan and Rajkumari chattered excitedly and asked questions, which were ignored.

When the taxi pulled to a stop, Bhajan and Kuldip were shocked at the sight that greeted them.

The building must have once been gray, or perhaps off-white. A few patches of paint remained in shaded, protected spots. The rest had peeled off completely save for a couple flakes hanging on tenaciously here and there. A pair of narrow, rickety wooden staircases framed the front entrance.

As the family climbed to their flat, below them they saw an open central square with a slate floor. Four waist-high water taps sat along one side. A line of women bearing metal buckets waited their turn to get water. Around the courtyard were four raised stone blocks. Some of the women were washing clothes on them, beating the fabric with wooden paddles. Open gutters around the perimeter carried the water to drains. A raised platform surrounded the central square, with doors to the ground-floor tenements opening onto it.

A cacophony of noise floated upwards: children's laughter and screams, gossip, shrill arguments, and the sound of water gushing from the taps. The odors, too, were overpowering: soap, rotting garbage, mildew, and urine from the six latrines that lined the building's back.

Gurumukh Singh led the way up the steps. Bhajan, holding onto Bijibai's arm followed, with Kuldip and the two children behind them.

News of the new family's arrival had already spread through the tenement, and people appeared as if from nowhere to gape as they continued their climb. "Refugees!" Bhajan heard one woman say. "Now we'll have to hear them brag about the riches they used to have."

Again she remembered Bijibai saying, "If I'm going to die, I want to die right here in my home."

When they reached the fourth story, Gurumukh Singh led them along the veranda and unlocked one of the doors. Their new home had two small rooms, one facing the veranda, the other

15

facing the road. The noise and smell from the central square flowed in from the window of the first. Dust and blaring music from the shops assaulted them from the other window. There was no bathroom. The men and children could use the open square to bathe, but the women would need privacy. Bhajan knew they would have to build bathroom facilities as soon as they could.

Gurumukh Singh watched Bhajan and Kuldip staring at the rooms in dismay. "I'm sorry," he said. "For now we'll have to manage here."

People continued parading by on the veranda. Bhajan heard more rude comments. Some of the people tried to peek in. She shut both the door and the window, casting the room into dim light. Darashan and Rajkumari clamored to go out and play.

There was a knock, and Gurumukh Singh opened the door. An adolescent girl was there with a friendly smile. "Ma has invited you for a cup of tea," she said, pointing to the adjacent tenement. Then she stepped in, took Darashan and Rajkumari by the hands, and led them next door.

After the shock of the decrepit building, with its shrill noises and unpleasant smells, and the hostility from their new neighbors, this unexpected sympathy from a stranger released Bhajan's tears.

The woman next door soon appeared, introducing herself as Bimala. "Please come in," she said. "The tea is still hot." She had her daughter fetch a chair and set it by the window for Gurumukh Singh. "I'm cooking dinner for all of you," she said. "There's not enough room in my apartment to fit everyone, but I'll send a cup of tea for you now, Saradarji, and my husband will join you in your home for dinner."

Bhajan, holding Bijibai's hand, and Kuldip followed the woman to her apartment.

"Welcome to your new home," Bimala said kindly. "This is my daughter, Binnee."

Bhajan introduced herself, Kuldip, Bijibai, and the children. She was grateful that Bimala didn't shower them with the questions they now routinely faced: "Where are you from?" "What's wrong with Bijibai?" "Where is the children's father?"

16

Bimala told them about the unwritten rules of the tenement: what times different families washed their clothes, which families were friendly, and which to avoid. She offered the women her bathroom facilities until they could set up their own, and said that she would go out with Bhajan the next morning to help her shop.

"I have no words to thank you," Bhajan said through a veil of tears.

"No need to thank me," Bimala said. "A neighbor must help a neighbor."

The next morning the two women went out. Bhajan bought pots and pans, water buckets, a kerosene stove, mats, pillows, bed sheets, and blankets. She watched in amazement as Bimala haggled with shopkeepers, bargaining the prices down steeply, oftentimes by half.

With Kuldip's help, Bhajan set up her new home. She politely refused Bimala's invitation for lunch, sending Kuldip to fetch a bucket of water while she made preparations for a simple meal.

Bhajan had noticed a distinct change in Kuldip since they'd left their home. She moved slowly and obeyed Bhajan mechanically, her face blank. "At least she does what I ask her," thought Bhajan. "And she looks after her children. Without them she might have fallen apart."

She wondered how Kuldip was doing in the quarrelsome line for the water tap. She went onto the veranda to check. There she was in the courtyard, quietly waiting her turn, her eyes periodically glancing at the building's entrance. "She's waiting for Ranjit," Bhajan thought to herself and sighed.

As Bhajan watched, Kuldip filled her bucket and struggled to climb the staircase. She had to stop periodically to rest. "We're not used to carrying such heavy loads," Bhajan thought. "We'll have to get used to hard work."

Gurumukh Singh came in with a newspaper. He scanned the headlines, then cast it aside, unable to read further. It was full of stories of new atrocities in the region from which they had fled. He was glad they had gotten out before the situation had deteriorated even further.

"After lunch I'll go out and try to find a stall," he told Bhajan. "I can start a business selling material for clothing."

* * * * * * * *

Soon after the family's move into their new tenement, India's independence was celebrated with great fanfare. Bhajan and Gurumukh Singh watched the celebrations in detached silence. Kuldip failed to notice them.

Slowly, Bhajan and her family adjusted to life in their new home and established a routine. Though they had to carry buckets of water up multiple flights, their location did have some advantages. The top floor was brighter, and airy. The landlord and his family occupied most of the tenements on that floor, and he permitted women to use his bathroom if they paid a bit more in rent. This meant that Gurumukh Singh didn't need to build a bathroom after all.

Bimala taught Kuldip and Bhajan how to take buses, where to shop, and how to bargain. Before long they were able to shop on their own.

After a time, Kuldip recovered a bit. Her eyes still tended to drift toward the entryway, but she occasionally smiled, and one day, at Bimala and Bhajan's insistence, she even accompanied Bimala to a movie.

As for Darashan and Rajkumari, they adjusted to their new accommodations rapidly. Though they still talked of their father and inquired from time to time when they would be going home, they became fast friends with the neighborhood children, joining in games on the verandas and in the central square.

Gurumukh Singh found a small wooden stall in a narrow alleyway lined with similar stalls and put down a deposit. Most of the owners were refugees like him. He started his business, happy to be among people who understood what he had been through. The competition was stiff and many customers were difficult— haggling relentlessly and even trying to return soiled material. But

18

he persevered, knowing he had little choice if he was to feed his family.

He was an outgoing and optimistic man, and as he threw himself into his business, he began to prosper.

Only Bijibai didn't seem to be adjusting. She rarely spoke, spending her days sitting motionless in a chair. When Bhajan tried to talk to her, hoping for a flicker of response, Bijibai's face remained impassive. Kuldip and Bhajan plied her with food, but she ate very little and lost weight. When she needed to use the facilities, she would rise mechanically and head for the door. Bhajan or Kuldip would drop whatever they were doing to accompany her.

"The murders have unhinged her mind," Bhajan told Gurumukh Singh tearfully.

A few of the women in the tenements gossiped maliciously about Bijibai's state. They would gawk at her when she walked down the stairs, and encouraged the children to yell questions at her.

The building had two types of tenants: struggling lower-middle-class families, who'd lived there prior to partition, and refugees.

Initially the people of Delhi had been sympathetic to the refugees' plight, but over time the influx had created food shortages. Rent, food and clothing prices skyrocketed, causing hardship for families like those in Bhajan's building, who already had difficulty making ends meet. They blamed the refugees for the inflation and were envious of the wealthier ones. They came to dislike all newcomers. In the face of this hostility, the newcomers stuck together, and their clannishness only aggravated the tensions.

One day Kuldip was in the flat, tidying the kitchen, when she heard children fighting. Suddenly a girl appeared in the doorway. "Come quickly, Kuldipchachi! Some of the boys are beating Darashan."

Kuldip sprang to the door to see what was going on.

Darashan was on his back on the second story veranda. Two boys were kicking and hitting him as other children looked on, laughing and clapping. Two women stood nearby, laughing as well. As soon as Kuldip appeared, the women went into a tenement and shut the door. Most of the children ran away. The boys beating Darashan stopped.

"Why are you hitting him?" she asked them, pulling Darashan off the floor.

"He called us names. He cursed us," one answered.

Kuldip held Darashan's arm and helped him to the fourth floor. Inside the tenement she asked, "Is that true? Why did you call them names, Darashan?"

Tears poured down his face. "They said Bijibai is a madwoman."

Speechless, Kuldip stole a look at her mother-in-law, who was watching the scene unfold.

Bhajan couldn't tolerate her grandson's pain. "It's the adults who have encouraged the other children to tease Bijibai," Bhajan said. "He's forced to defend her." She started to cry.

Her tears shocked Darashan. His grandmother rarely cried. To him, she was the pillar supporting the family. He wiped his tears, hugged Bhajan, and said, "Don't be upset, Bhajanma. Bijibai's not mad. She just doesn't talk, right?"

"You're right, said Bhajan, stroking his hair. "She isn't crazy, no matter what those boys say. It's just that what happened back home deeply hurt Bijibai, so she doesn't wish to speak."

"The other children say we're refugees and that we're ruining their lives," said Darashan. "They say we're like a contagious disease invading their homes."

"If you ignore them, their words won't hurt you," Bhajan said gently. "Children just parrot what they hear grownups say."

"If our coming here isn't our fault, whose fault is it?"

"I blame the people who forced us out of our home," said Bhajan. "There's no reason we couldn't have kept living in our home, even if it is a Muslim nation now."

"Are the Muslims to blame, then?"

"Only the ones who forced us to leave."

"Where do we live now?"

20

"In India."

"Will India force us to leave, too?"

"No, it's a nation for everyone."

"But most of the kids here say they're Hindus."

"All of us were Hindus once. Our family is Sikh, but my grandfather was born in a Hindu family."

Darashan was unable to grasp the complexities that Bhajan was trying to explain.

"If we're Sikh, why don't we move to a Sikh country?"

"There is no Sikh country. This is our country now."

"But won't the Hindus force us out?"

"No, Darashan. You don't have to worry about that."

She hugged him again reassuringly, but his eyes were wide. How could they possibly be safe if they didn't have a country of their own?

*   *   *   *   *   *   *   *

One day Kuldip had finished her shopping and was walking to the bus stop when she heard a woman calling her name.

Since coming to Delhi, the family had made no effort to find their relatives. They lived in a shell, not ready to face questions. So Kuldip couldn't imagine that anyone might be seeking her out.

"Someone's calling some other Kuldip," she thought to herself and quickened her step. But the calls grew louder. A woman ran up and hugged her from behind, crying and laughing all at once. "Why are you running away, Kuldip? Didn't you hear me calling you?" Kuldip craned her neck to see the woman's face. Then she dropped her bag of groceries and started to cry too. Her sister, Damayanti, had found her.

Soon Damayanti's husband, Veer Singh, caught up with them. "I didn't know Damayanti could run so fast!" he said. "She couldn't see your face, but she knows her sister. She knows your figure, your hair and how you walk." Veer Singh smiled broadly and added, "Today's a happy day indeed."

The two sisters wept and caressed each other. A crowd of

onlookers started to form around them, but they failed to notice.

"You're alive!" Damayanti murmured.

Veer Singh nudged his wife. "People are gaping at you two," he told her. "We don't live very far. Come along."

Veer Singh collected their bags and Kuldip and Damayanti followed him.

At home, Veer Singh fixed a cup of tea for each sister. "We'll celebrate our reunion with this special tea," he said.

Damayanti asked about Kuldip's family, and for the first time, Kuldip was forced to tell the story, uttering the words she'd been holding back. "We don't know where Darashan and Rajkumari's father is," she confided.

Veer Singh and Damayanti hadn't isolated themselves as Kuldip's family had. In fact, Veer Singh had managed to contact many displaced relatives and friends who had also come to Delhi.

"I must go home now. I'm late," Kuldip said, collecting her shopping bags.

"I'll come along," Damayanti suggested.

Bhajan was overjoyed to see Damayanti, who touched Bhajan's feet and then hugged her, sobbing on her shoulder. Ignoring Bijibai's condition, Damayanti clung to her, too.

*   *   *   *   *   *   *   *

Veer Singh added Ranjit Singh's name to the list of people he would try to find, and asked all his friends who'd met Ranjit Singh to help look.

One day a Sikh hotel owner told him that a Sikh man had rented a room in his hotel and was holed up there day and night, stepping out only occasionally for meals.

The next day Veer Singh settled himself at a table in a restaurant across the street. He waited for four hours. Finally, a Sikh man emerged from the hotel and headed in the direction of the panipuri stand. He didn't resemble anyone Veer Singh knew, but he decided to follow him anyway.

The man wore ripped, dirty clothes that drooped on his

emaciated frame. He dragged his feet and seemed to be pulling his sandals along. He wore dark glasses and had an unkempt moustache and beard.

Veer Singh moved closer until he stood directly across from the man at the panipuri stand. Tears stung Veer Singh's eyes. There was no mistaking that this was Ranjit. But he looked more like Ranjit's ghost.

He quickly walked away. "Ranjit knows that his family is in Delhi," he thought. "And he could easily get their address from his uncle. Obviously, he hasn't tried to contact them. If he's deliberately avoiding them, I can't just confront him. What if he refuses to come along and disappears? How will I find him then?"

Veer Singh could guess what a proud man like Ranjit must be feeling. He had experienced savagery, treachery, physical trauma, and undoubtedly worst of all, a loss of honor. No wonder he was hiding in his room.

The next morning Veer Singh returned with a friend. He hired a taxi and asked his friend Jivan to wait in it. He paid the hotel's overdue bill and went to Ranjit's room and knocked on the door.

"Who is it?" Ranjit asked.

Reluctant to reveal his identity, Veer Singh said, "A friend."

"I don't have a friend," Ranjit responded curtly.

"Please, let me in."

Veer Singh tried the door. It was unlatched and opened easily. A flicker of recognition and joy touched Ranjit's eyes, but it vanished almost immediately. "Get out," he barked.

Ignoring Ranjit's hostility, Veer Singh closed the door behind him. He tried to persuade Ranjit to accompany him to see his family, but Ranjit refused. At length he did agree to visit Veer Singh's friend Jivan's home instead.

In the taxi, Ranjit sat erect and stared straight ahead. Veer Singh opened his mouth to speak, but his tongue failed him. When they arrived at Jivan's home, Jivan decided to take charge.

"Do you want a bath?" he asked Ranjit.

To Veer Singh's surprise, Ranjit promptly consented.

Veer Singh gave Ranjit a set of clothes and a fresh towel.

While Ranjit was in the bathroom Jivan whispered, "Maybe he's been avoiding everyone because he's ashamed of his dirty clothes."

"I don't think so," said Veer Singh. "I suspect loss of honor is the real reason."

When Ranjit emerged from the bathroom, Veer Singh and Jivan could clearly see that his left hand was missing. A scarred stump hung out of his sleeve.

They settled in the dining room. Jivan's wife, Savita, brought them food, then quietly withdrew. Ranjit failed to greet her.

"How's the meal?" Jivan asked Ranjit.

"Fine," Ranjit listlessly responded.

"Better than my wife's food," Veer Singh joked. But still, the conversation stalled.

As they were finishing the meal, Jivan's mother and his two children came in. He'd sent them to his brother's house that afternoon to afford the men some privacy.

Veer Singh promptly touched her feet, and this time Ranjit followed suit. But Jivan was disturbed. "Ma, I told you we wanted the house to ourselves. Please take the children out."

"I know why you want to get rid of me," the old lady griped. "You think I'm nosy and ask too many questions. Now tell me who the new guest is."

Veer Singh and Jivan could only watch dumbfounded as the old woman turned to Ranjit with a barrage of questions.

"Poor child, you're so skinny!"

"What's your name? Where are you from? Who's your father?"

If anyone else had asked such questions, Ranjit would have walked out. But she was an old woman; long-ingrained habits forced him to be respectful.

"Are you married? Do you have children? Where do you live?"

The gray-haired woman reminded Ranjit of his own beloved grandmother, Bijibai. His defenses started to crumble.

Finally she asked the question that Veer Singh and Jivan had been dreading: "How did you lose your hand?"

Ranjit fought to control his emotions. His fist tightened. He clenched his teeth and squeezed his eyes shut. The nightmare returned, as vivid as the day it had occurred.

"He's unconscious. Let me kill him."

"No. Stop! He's Gobind Singh's grandson. Gobind Singh was kind to us. Leave him be."

"We must make him pay for fighting us. I'll take his hand."

Agonizing pain had shot to his brain even in his semi-conscious state. Warm blood had soaked his clothes. Someone had dragged him across rocks, thorny bushes and dirt.

And then...Slow awakening... Gentle sunlight caressing his face, infusing warmth into his shivering body....His grotesque, blood-stained, throbbing arm.... His prayers for death.

A woman's scream.... Two kind men carrying him to a house, washing his wound, changing his clothes.... A trip in a horse cart to the train station... A few rupee notes and a ticket handed to him by one of the strangers.

Raging fever from infection... A ride from the station to a government hospital... Nurses cleaning and bandaging the wound... Delirious days and nights... Discharge with a ticket to Delhi offered by a kind nurse...

A few days spent in a cheap hotel... No more money.... Relentless hunger. The hotel owner demanding payment. Shame and fury. Thoughts of suicide...

The old woman went on firing questions that burst through the shell that Ranjit had erected around himself. Tears began rolling down his face.

"You've been bottling your emotions, Beta," she said. "Even strong men can't bury their misery forever."

Veer Singh finally found his voice. "Ranjit, Darashan is now as tall as Jivan's son." He pointed to the little boy.

Ranjit calmed himself, and Veer Singh told him about old friends and acquaintances, describing the losses they had suffered. Ranjit seemed interested. He asked questions and offered comments, but he refused to talk about himself and what had befallen him back home. He did ask Veer Singh to write his family's and his father's shop's address on a piece of paper.

Ranjit spent the night at Jivan's home, but the next morning he was gone. Savita found a note in the kitchen addressed to Veer Singh. When Veer Singh returned later that day, he read it aloud: "Please don't try to contact me. I have my parents' address. I'll see them when I'm ready. On my behalf, please thank Jivan and his family for their hospitality. His mother helped me. My special thanks to her."

"I think we descended on him when he wasn't ready," said Jivan. "He needs to set his own pace."

"Should we tell his family that we saw him?" asked Veer Singh.

Jivan stroked his chin thoughtfully. "No," he concluded. "They might try to find him and drive him away."

A hush fell over the room. "May I say something?" said Savita. "I think you should tell them. His wife and parents deserve to know he's alive."

"Of course, Savitbhabi," said Veer Singh. "I wasn't thinking of things from their perspective."

Savita smiled. "That's because you aren't a wife or mother," she said gently.

*   *   *   *   *   *   *   *

Early the next morning, Veer Singh mustered his courage and went to see Gurumukh Singh at his tenement. He knew Gurumukh Singh opened his shop promptly at 9:00 every morning and he wanted to break the news to the family in Gurumukh Singh's presence.

Everyone was surprised to see him at that early hour. Kuldip was outside waiting in the line for water. The children were asleep. Bhajan, busy fixing breakfast, welcomed him in. "Please have a seat." She gave him a cup of tea. "What brings you here so early this morning?" Gurumukh Singh asked.

Veer Singh hesitated.

"Go on," said Gurumukh Singh.

"I have news for you."

Instantly alert, Bhajan and Gurumukh Singh asked in unison, "Is it about Ranjit?"

"Yes."

Bhajan and Gurumukh Singh looked at him expectantly.

"I found him."

Bhajan gasped and stood up. Gurumukh Singh was speechless for a moment. "Where is he?" he finally managed, when he had found his voice.

"I don't know. We learned that a Sikh man was living in one of the hotels. I went by and recognized him. Yesterday I confronted him and he agreed to come to my friend Jivan's home and sleep over. He was gone in the morning, but he left this note."

Bhajan and Gurumukh Singh read it.

"We must find him," said Gurumukh Singh.

Kuldip hurried in with the water bucket. Immediately she felt the tension. "What's wrong?" she asked fearfully.

"Veer Singh found Ranjit," Bhajan answered.

Kuldip pushed her balled dupatta in her mouth to stifle her sobs.

Her crying woke Darashan. "Why are you sad, Kuldipma?" he asked, hugging her.

Bhajan answered, "Those are tears of happiness. Your uncle Veer found your father."

Darashan knew this was supposed to be good news, but his father was no longer important to him. He turned to Bhajan. "I'm hungry."

Kuldip asked, "Where is he?"

Bhajan repeated Veer Singh's account and handed Kuldip the note. Gurumukh Singh turned to Bhajan. "I'll try to find him."

"Did he accompany you willingly?" Bhajan asked Veer Singh.

"No. At first he refused to talk to me. I had a hard time convincing him to leave the hotel."

"How is he?"

"He's skinny and…"

"And what?"

"His left hand is gone."

"Gone?"

"Yes, severed. Someone cut it off."

Kuldip started to cry again. Rajkumari woke up and started to bawl because her mother was crying. Bhajan fought to control her tears. With difficulty, she found the right words. "At least he's alive. He can learn to get along without his hand."

She considered Gurumukh Singh's determination to find him.

"My son is a proud man," she said. "He survived cruelty back home. The scorn and insults he must have experienced would hurt him far more than any physical trauma. He vowed to save our homes and our land, and he lost that battle. He's a broken man now. He needs time to heal. He wrote that he'll be back when he's ready. I think we should wait."

Teary-eyed, Kuldip leaned on the door. Rajkumari clung to her.

Bhajan turned to Gurumukh Singh. "Please wait," she told him. "Ranjit will see us when he's ready."

Kuldip started to sob again. "What if he never returns?"

"No one can force a man to do what he doesn't want to," said Bhajan. "If we find him and bring him home by force, he may vanish again. My heart – Ranjit's mother's heart – says we must wait."

And so they waited, haunted by doubts. The children, sensing the adults' tension, stayed away from home, spending as much time as possible with their friends.

Two days went by, and then Ranjit came to the shop. Gurumukh Singh looked at him, locked the shop, and said in a steady voice, "Let's go home."

Ranjit wouldn't meet his father's gaze but simply followed him quietly. Gurumukh Singh stopped at a shoe shop and bought a new pair of sandals for Ranjit. Together they rode the bus home.

As usual, the news of a visitor circulated in the building at once. Men, women, and children gaped at Ranjit. Comments echoed in the courtyard – some caustic, some sympathetic.

"He's so skinny!"

"Is that Kuldip's long-lost husband?"

"The son has returned."

"…Minus one hand."

"Shut up, you idiots. You have no idea what these people had to face."

"One more person in the latrine line."

Thinking Ranjit must be mortified, Gurumukh Singh hurried him into their tenement.

Inside, Bhajan was serving the children food. She gasped and held back tears. She didn't wish to cry in front of the curious crowd on the veranda. Kuldip hid behind the door. Rajkumari and Darashan stopped eating, their eyes wandering from person to person. Then Rajkumari rushed to join her mother.

Ranjit was shocked as well. The two-room tenement, the rude comments, and especially the sight of his mother cooking– a chore that in the past had always been delegated to a cook – dragged him into the new world that he and his family now faced.

Darashan asked, "Who's this new uncle?"

"He's your father, Darashan," Bhajan said in a soft voice.

"Father!" Darashan thought. "This newcomer doesn't resemble my father. My Bauji stood erect, laughed loudly, and walked so fast I had to run to keep up with him." The man in front of him was skinny, dragged his feet, and didn't even have two hands.

Bhajan knew someone had to relieve the unbearable tension. She opened her mouth to say something, but before she could speak, Darashan, blurted, "This man is not my Bauji."

His son's rejection was the last straw. Ranjit started to back toward the door. Gurumukh Singh got there first and blocked it with his body.

Kuldip hadn't slept since Veer Singh's visit. When her husband started to back out of the room, she snapped. Kuldip, gentle Kuldip, slapped Darashan. She lifted her arm to slap him again, but Bhajan pulled Darashan away. "He isn't completely wrong, Beti," she said to Kuldip quietly. Then, hugging Darashan, she said, "Just wait a couple months. He'll be just like the Bauji you remember."

Darashan couldn't hold back his tears. His mother, who never hit him, had slapped him—and all because of this stranger. He blurted again, "Bauji had two hands. This man has only one."

"Let me go," Ranjit begged. "Please move, Bauji. Open the door." Gurumukh Singh refused to budge. Ignoring conventions, Kuldip rushed to her husband and, clinging to him, started to cry.

Bhajan released Darashan and, gently patting Ranjit's arm, said, "Ranjit, Darashan's a little child. You can't let his babble disturb you. This is a golden moment in our lives. Let's be happy. I'll fix you a cup of tea."

Her mother-in-law's soft, soothing words relaxed Kuldip. Waking up to her wifely duty, she said, "I'll make the tea," and started to light the stove. Gurumukh Singh maneuvered Ranjit toward a chair and started to talk about the shop.

Rajkumari gaped uncomprehendingly at the emotional scene and then slipped out to play.

Bijibai, in her now-perpetual fog, failed to even notice that Ranjit was back.

Gurumukh Singh addressed Bhajan that night. "In the state he's in, Ranjit shouldn't be subjected to the cruelty of our neighbors all day. I'll take him with me tomorrow morning." Bhajan agreed.

At the shop the next day, among refugees like himself, Ranjit seemed happier. "Your father needs help," the shopkeepers told Ranjit. "We're so glad you've returned." They didn't ask questions and accepted him as one of their own.

That night, for the first time, Ranjit seemed to relax.

As the weeks went on, he slowly regained weight. Darashan relented and decided that Ranjit was indeed his long-lost father. The neighbors lost interest over time, especially once a new family moved in and they had another target.

Working in the shop helped Ranjit. He didn't have much to say to his family, but as a salesperson he could be his old self.

He learned to measure and cut the material with one hand, holding it down with the stump of his arm – a feat that impressed the customers. Even his visible impairment helped the cash flow, because buyers toned down their haggling.

The business prospered, and soon Gurumukh Singh rented the adjacent stall.

Thrilled to have her husband home again, Kuldip was radiant with joy. Bhajan, too, regained some peace of mind: her son was back and would help provide for the family. But she was keenly aware that Ranjit had withdrawn into a shell.

"Ranjit's a good salesman," Gurumukh Singh commented, "but he isn't interested in ordering material or accounts. He obeys me mechanically."

"Does he mingle with the other shopkeepers?"

"No. He greets them and then keeps to himself."

He needed to talk to someone and grieve, Bhajan felt. Only then would he start to recover.

She tried to ask tactful questions when she and Ranjit were alone. "How long were you back home?" "Where did you cross the border?" But he would refuse to meet her eye or speak.

She turned to Kuldip for help, urging her to try to get him to open up.

But Kuldip only shook her head sadly. "I've tried. He says, 'Don't ever ask me about my life there.'"

Bhajan consoled herself that at least he was back. His children wouldn't be fatherless, Kuldip would have a husband, and she and Gurumukh Singh would have their son. "We've lost a tiger," she thought. "We have a cat now."

One day a neighbor in the tenement became ill, and Kuldip and Bhajan offered to help her to the hospital. Bhajan asked Ranjit to stay home with the children for the morning.

For a while, the children played by themselves, but eventually, tiring of their games, they approached their father.

"Bauji, what happened to your hand?" asked Rajkumari, with childish directness.

Darashan, vividly remembering his father's reaction to

31

comments about his missing hand the day he came home, held his breath and waited for the explosion. But by now Ranjit had grown used to the question. "It was cut off," he answered plainly.

Rajkumari's eyes grew enormous. "Who cut it off, Bauji?"

"Bad, cruel people," said Ranjit, his eyes narrowing.

Looking at the scarred disfigured stump where his father's capable hand had been, Darashan was suddenly overcome with an unfamiliar fury. He clenched his teeth and tightened his fists. How could anybody get away with this?

Rajkumari kept asking more questions "Did it hurt a lot? Did you cry?"

But Ranjit's attention was on Darashan now. "Are you all right?"

Darashan's eyes flashed and his face was flushed. "Bauji," he said in a low voice. "When I grow up, I'm going to kill those bad people who did this to you."

Ranjit Singh stepped back and looked at his son with fresh eyes. "I hope you'll be successful," he said.

Then his own fist tightened. He knelt before Darashan. "Revenge," he whispered. "I intend to get revenge. Do you want to help me?"

Father and son looked into one another's eyes. Something like a promise passed between them.

"Yes," said Darashan.

Gurumukh Singh, stepping in from the veranda, heard only the very end of the exchange. "What help are you demanding from a little child, Ranjit?" he asked lightly.

Neither Ranjit nor Darashan spoke. Not sensing the intensity of the moment, Gurumukh Singh let the topic drop. "I've found a lovely new flat," he announced. "We can move there next week."

Rajkumari was dismayed. "I don't want to move!" she shrieked, throwing herself melodramatically on the floor. "My friends live *here*."

Darashan, too, began to protest. "We want to stay here!"

Gurumukh Singh had expected a joyous reaction. Instead he faced screaming children. "You'll like our new flat," he said. "It's big. It has its own bathroom."

But the tantrums continued.

Returning from the hospital, Bhajan and Kuldip heard Rajkumari and Darashan as soon as they entered the building. They hurried up the stairs, worried that someone had been hurt.

Gurumukh Singh explained what was going on.

"No wonder they're upset," Bhajan murmured. "This has become their home."

She settled down on the floor next to Rajkumari and Darashan. "You can visit your friends often," she promised, "and your friends can visit you."

Gurumukh Singh added, "We can keep renting these two rooms forever and ever. Now let's go visit our new flat. We'll have cutlets, samosas, and ice cream–anything you want."

The bribe worked. Wiping her tears, Rajkumari asked for a balloon in addition to the food. Bhajan asked Bimala to keep an eye on Bijibai for a few hours, and the family headed out of their first tenement in India to visit their new home.

CHAPTER 3

Bright afternoon sunlight shimmered on the window panes as the family stopped, enchanted, in front of their new building. Even Rajkumari and Darashan seemed pleased.

It was a recently built four-story building, with four flats on each floor. Each flat had two balconies, one facing the front entrance, the other facing the side entrance. A lush green lawn formed a large backyard, and bougainvillea climbed bamboo trellises on each side of the front entrance. "It's lovely," Bhajan said.

"Yes," echoed Kuldip, giddy with surprise. The family climbed three sets of stairs. Gurumukh Singh unlocked the door and the children rushed in with the adults behind them.

Airy sunlight filled the flat, which had windows in every room. A lovely sunset was visible from the living room. The children ran ahead, exploring.

"Look – a big kitchen!"

"And a bedroom!"

"No – two bedrooms!"

"Three!"

"And two bathrooms!"

Rajkumari sat down on the floor, softly moving her fingers over the tiles. "How smooth!"

The adults were happy to see the children's reaction. "Hopefully they'll move willingly now," Gurumukh Singh said.

"Here we won't have to live with the constant din of music, traffic, and fights," exclaimed Kuldip, taking note of the peace and quiet. "And we'll have a water tap right in the home. No more trips up and down the stairs with buckets of water."

Gurumukh Singh was pleased to see his wife and daughter-in-law's faces light up. He hadn't seen them so happy for a long time.

Rajkumari and Darashan, exploring the balconies, heard the shouts and squeals of children in the backyard. They turned to Bhajan. "Can we go play?"

"I guess you've had enough of the flat," she laughed. "Go

ahead."

A woman from a neighboring flat came in and introduced herself, inviting the family for a cup of tea and snacks. They followed her to her apartment, and soon more neighbors showed up, drawn by the commotion. Gurumukh Singh met an old acquaintance, and to Bhajan's relief, no one asked questions about Ranjit's hand. The time flew by. Bhajan saw the sun touch the horizon through the apartment's big windows. Suddenly she remembered the hour. "We should be on our way."

"Please don't rush," protested their new neighbor. "Have dinner with us. I'll cook. Kuldip can help me." Bhajan smiled; it was good to see how much the hostess seemed to like Kuldip.

"Thank you for the invitation," said Bhajan, "but I must decline; my mother's at our old home."

"I'll wrap some snacks for her," the hostess said. She turned to Kuldip. "Please ask your children to come upstairs so they can have some sweets."

Kuldip descended a wrought-iron circular staircase to the backyard where a group of children were engrossed in a cricket match. "Darashan, Rajkumari, we have to go!" she called.

"The game isn't even half over," complained Rajkumari, as they followed their mother up the stairs.

Their protests stopped when they reached the neighbor's flat. Their grandfather and father were sitting on a sofa talking to strangers. Darashan was invited to join them. Rajkumari would have preferred to stick with her brother, but Kuldip ushered her into the room where the women had gathered. Soon she was happily munching on sweets as the grownups talked.

"What's upstairs?" she heard Darashan ask in the other room.

"The terrace," someone answered

"Can I see it?" said Darashan.

"Just a peek," said Gurumukh Singh. "Then hurry back."

Darashan shot up the stairs, and Rajkumari raced after him.

The terrace was expansive, with a multicolored, tile floor, arranged in a circular pattern. Next to one wall, pieces of fruit had been laid out to dry on cotton sheets

Rajkumari started to run in circles, following the pattern of the tiles. Darashan was ready to follow her, but then he noticed a girl in the corner, collecting fruits, and he stopped in his tracks.

The girl knelt near one of the sheets, putting dried fruit in a wicker basket. Soft curls of dark brown hair escaped from her pigtails, blowing gently in the evening breeze, framing her delicate face. Thick lashes shaded her eyes. Her red satin dress shimmered in the reflected rays of the setting sun. To Darashan, she seemed not of this earth.

Rajkumari was now pretending to fly like a bird, flapping her arms as she traced the circles of the tiles. The girl stood up and giggled, revealing dimpled cheeks and dancing light brown eyes. Transfixed, Darashan stood rooted to the spot.

Suddenly the girl noticed Darashan staring at her. She sprinted toward him, screwed up her face, folded her arms, and demanded, "What are you doing here? This is *our* terrace."

Flustered, Darashan couldn't respond.

The girl ran to the back of the terrace and jumped onto the wall. She screamed toward the backyard at the top of her lungs, "Hey, look! A neighborhood boy is here on our terrace."

The children Darashan and Rajkumari had just been playing with stopped their game and ran up to defend their territory. But when they saw Darashan and Rajkumari they exclaimed, "Don't you know anything, Maya? These kids are moving into a flat here. This is their terrace, too." They scurried back downstairs to resume their game.

Furious, the girl addressed Darashan. "What's wrong with you? Don't you have a tongue? Why didn't you say you were moving into this building?"

Before he could muster an answer, Kuldip appeared.

"What's your name, you pretty little girl?" she exclaimed.

"It's Maya," Rajkumari declared, adding, "She's fighting with Darashan for no reason."

"Darashan, how can you fight with such a pretty little girl?" Kuldip asked. Giving Darashan and Rajkumari a gentle shove, she said, "Time to go. Everyone's waiting for you."

Darashan quietly followed his mother. Rajkumari protested and had to be dragged. Darashan turned back to glance at Maya, who watched them from the terrace door. She stuck out her tongue.

*   *   *   *   *   *   *   *

Maya was away the day Darashan's family moved in, but she joined the children's cricket game the next day. She was openly hostile to Darashan, telling the captain, "I don't want to be on the new boy's team."

All during the game she criticized Darashan. "You don't know how to bat."

"Run faster, slowpoke."

"I knew you would miss that catch."

Darashan's team captain defended him. "Shut up, Maya. Why are you picking on Darashan?"

In the weeks that followed, Maya and Rajkumari frequently played together, but Maya's animosity toward Darashan was unrelenting. Darashan rarely responded, but his cheeks would redden, and he would glare at the ground.

One day, Maya couldn't play because of a foot injury, so the children assigned her the job of umpire. When Darashan came up to bat, she falsely pronounced him out. "L.B.W.," she called, even though the ball hadn't touched his leg.

Darashan put his bat down, but his teammates protested. "Liar! Darashan wasn't out. You always pick on him."

But Maya didn't let up. "Darashan, you know you were out. Why don't you speak up and tell them so, girly boy."

The insult was too much for Darashan. His pent-up anger boiled over. He picked up a pebble and hurled it at Maya, intending only to scare her. But the pebble struck her eyebrow and she started to bleed.

The rest of the children took off. Maya, Rajkumari and Darashan stood there, rooted to the ground.

"Run, Darashan!" urged Rajkumari, worried on behalf of her

brother. "By the time you come back, maybe Kuldipma won't be so angry."

But Darashan couldn't move. Maya's wound hurt him as much as it had Maya.

Some of the kids shot up to Maya's flat, others to Darashan's. Maya's mother, Meenakumari, ran down to the yard. Kuldip and Bhajan weren't far behind.

Bhajan had brought a wet towel and iodine. She sat down on the grass, pulled Maya onto her lap and started to gently clean her wound.

"It's not Darashan's fault," Rajkumari yelled. "Maya's always mean to him. He wasn't out."

Kuldip, who rarely spanked her children, held Darashan's arm and whacked him. "You've marked Maya's lovely face," she exclaimed. "You must learn to control your temper."

"Come upstairs, Maya, and I'll bandage you up," said Bhajan. In the flat, she applied gauze and tape to the abrasion. Kuldip locked Darashan in his bedroom and told Rajkumari to stop arguing about whose fault it was. "Hitting isn't permitted under any circumstances," she said. She fixed tea for the entire party and served it with refreshments. Soon Maya and Rajkumari were talking and laughing.

That evening Gurumukh Singh and Ranjit encountered Meenakumari and Maya at the front entrance. Gurumukh Singh saw the bandage on Maya's face and asked what had happened.

"She fell," Meenakumari said quickly, but Maya couldn't keep quiet.

"Darashan threw a pebble at me," she said accusingly.

"Are you hurt badly?" Gurumukh Singh asked.

"It's just a little scratch," Meenakumari said, trying to protect Darashan. But the damage had been done.

"I'm sorry, Baby, we'll punish Darashan," Gurumukh Singh assured her.

"Kuldip spanked him and locked him in his room," Meenakumari told them. But already, Ranjit was taking out his leather belt.

When they reached the flat, Ranjit's face was grim. "Where's Darashan?" he demanded.

Kuldip started to cry. She'd seen her husband's rages before.

Seeing the belt in her father's hand, Rajkumari screamed, "Don't, Bauji!"

One look at her son and Bhajan knew that in his anger he could flay the skin off Darashan's back. She blocked the door to Darashan's room. "No, Ranjit. Kuldip has already spanked him. She's decided that he'll be locked in his room after school. That's worse than your belt."

Ranjit opened his mouth, but before he could speak, Maya's father pushed the door open and strode in. He put his hand on Ranjit's shoulder. "Children fight," he said evenly. "Now be reasonable." He snatched the belt away. "Disciplining children is a mother's job. You work all day. You don't need to be worrying about children's fights."

Everyone heaved a sigh of relief.

Inside his room, Darashan heard the whole commotion. His father's belt didn't scare him. He was too busy wondering why Maya's wound made him feel so bad, and why he was so upset with himself for throwing the pebble.

For the next month, he was confined to his room after school. He could only watch the game longingly from his window. Maya noticed him and gestured him to him come down.

When the month was over, Darashan saw that Maya had changed. She no longer picked on him. But he chose to avoid her and didn't speak to her.

One day Kuldip asked Darashan to collect some red peppers that she had spread to dry on the terrace. There he encountered Maya, who was busy collecting her mother's drying cereal. Again, the setting sun illuminated her, and the unsettling emotions he had experienced the first time he saw her flared anew.

Maya approached. "Darashan, I'm sorry."

Darashan was focused on the reddish scar on her right eyebrow. He remembered his mother's words: "You've marked Maya's lovely face in a fit of anger."

"I'm sorry," she repeated. "I was wrong."

He looked at her questioningly.

"Rajkumari told my mother what happened, and she said I was a very bad girl."

Darashan gently touched the scar. "Am I hurting you?" he asked.

"Not anymore," Maya said. They talked a while longer.

The next day, Maya offered Darashan half of a precious Cadbury chocolate that her father had brought for her. Darashan touched the scar again and said, "I'm sorry, Maya."

Maya shrugged her shoulders to indicate that she didn't care, but the guilt was always with him. His mother constantly reinforced it, reminding him of the incident every time he became angry at something else.

One evening, a few months later, Kuldip announced, "Meenakumari's husband is being transferred. They'll be moving soon. It's too bad. I'm going to miss Meenakumari."

"Maya's moving?" Darashan asked, alarm creeping into his voice.

"Yes," said Kuldip. "Maya's father works for the government. Government servants have to go wherever the government sends them."

"They don't have a shop like ours?" asked Rajkumari.

"No, Beti. Maya's father has a salaried job."

Bhajan turned to Darashan. "I thought you didn't get along with Maya. Why are you so upset that she's moving away?"

Embarrassed, Darashan didn't answer.

"Maya admitted she was wrong for calling him out that time," said Rajkumari. "She likes Darashan now."

"But *I* don't like *her*," Darashan said quickly, not wanting his grandmother to know his true feelings.

Bhajan and Kuldip laughed. "You're kids," said Kuldip. "Soon you'll forget each other."

Darashan wasn't so sure.

CHAPTER 4

Gopal Sane was born to a Brahmin family in Rala, a small, green village in Maharashtra.

Though his family had little in the way of material possessions, his world was idyllic.

The entire extended family, including Gopal's parents, grandparents, aunts, uncles, and cousins lived together under one roof, in a home surrounded by blooming fruit trees, a flower garden and a vegetable patch.

Everyone in the family led a busy life, performing such rustic chores as drawing well water, chopping firewood and helping with farmwork during the growing season. The men in the family, in accordance with village tradition, also served as priests for the village temples, earning a small income in the form of petty cash, grain, coconuts and fruits offered to deities by worshippers.

Busy with their labors, the grownups had little time for children, but with so many cousins and other village children to play with, the youngsters were happy to be left to their own devices. They ran wild in the village, swam in the river and wells, and took turns playing with their small collection of hand-whittled toys.

Gopal's favorite playmate was his little sister, Mani, who was two years younger. She had a round face with chubby cheeks, soft curly dark brown hair and big brown eyes. She followed Gopal everywhere. Many of Gopal's cousins were irritated by younger siblings who chased after them. But Gopal was different. He liked having Mani with him. Mani was different, too. She never pestered Gopal like other small children, and obeyed him willingly. The two were an inseparable pair.

One day, one of Gopal's cousins came down with measles. Quickly, the disease swept through the village.

Mani, too, came down with it. Gopal's mother told him that Mani had a fever and was resting in her bed. She instructed Gopal to stay out of the room.

Gopal was unconcerned. So many children had caught

measles and then come back out to play.

But days went by, and still Mani didn't recover. The village medicine man dropped by. Gopal's grandmother stayed in Mani's room around the clock.

Gopal was getting worried. When his grandmother opened the door briefly, he tried to slip into the room, but she pushed him back. "Gopal," she said. "You stay out! Do you hear me?"

Two days later, Grandfather told Gopal's fourteen-year-old cousin Ganga to gather up all the children and lock them in the boys' back room.

The other children didn't object, but Gopal resisted. Two older cousins had to drag him.

When Ganga had closed the door, another cousin, twelve-year-old Meera, spoke up loudly. "I know why they locked us in here. Mani is dead."

"Meera, shut your mouth," Ganga yelled at her.

Meera ignored her. "When someone is dead and the family wants to take the person away," she said, "they lock the children in a room."

Gopal didn't understand the concept of death, but he knew that dead people vanish from the world forever.

He ran to the door, but Ganga held it shut. "Let me out!" he sobbed. "I want to see Mani." The other younger children heard Gopal and joined him.

The racket brought Grandfather to the room. When Ganga opened the door for him, Gopal, who had been standing by the threshold, ran out. Before anyone could stop him, he was in Mani's room.

A group of men and women had circled Mani's bed. Gopal pushed through, and before anyone could act, he was facing Mani, ready to hug her. But one look at her made him pull his arms back.

She lay motionless, her lovely brown eyes closed, her face, arms, and legs, covered with boils. Some of the boils had ruptured, and white fluid that had leaked out lay dried on her body.

The sight repulsed him. "Mani…" he cried. His uncle tried to get hold of him, but he escaped and, crying loudly, disappeared in

42

the backyard. Nobody chased him. They let him go.

Slowly, Gopal crept toward the front. He watched his uncle carry a small figure wrapped in white cloth.

Gopal rushed forward and, hugging his father, asked, "Baba, where are you taking her?"

Grandmother pulled him back. "Gopal, Mani isn't with us," she said. "When she died, her soul flew away. She's happy in God's home."

Nobody could console him. He wept all day. The next day he had a fever. His mother never left his bedside. He cried for Mani throughout his illness. He lost weight, but he recovered.

For several months, Gopal had nightmares, dreaming of Mani's motionless body.

"Why is God so unjust?" he wanted to know. "Why did he take Mani away?"

But with the passage of time, his pain eased, and the peaceful rhythms of village life began to restore him to his old self.

Far from his idyllic world, however, big changes were afoot; India's leaders fought for independence from the British. The revolution shaking the outside world had little effect upon Gopal's isolated village, to which news traveled slowly. Except for a few men from Brahmin families, few adults could read or write. Electric power hadn't yet reached the village, so there was no radio. Occasional travelers or visiting city dwellers sometimes brought a newspaper, and anyone who was literate would read it over and over. Once a week, mail arrived, following a convoluted route. Only a single unpaved road, trisected by two streams and a river connected the village to the outside world. In the rainy season, when the river and streams flooded, the road was impassable. At those times, Rala was like an island. But important news stories eventually made their way through.

One day, Gopal's teacher announced, "Our leaders have been successful. British rule is over. India will be an independent nation soon." Gopal didn't understand the meaning of the announcement, but he was happy that August 15, 1947 – Independence Day – was declared a school holiday.

For a few days, everyone talked about independence, and then life went on as before.

The next big news to arrive from the outside world, a few months later, was Mahatma Gandhi's murder.

As with the news about independence, the villagers registered the information and then went on with their business; it had little to do with their daily lives.

The next day, two bullock carts loaded with men carrying sticks and guns visited the village. Accosting a group of teenage boys, they demanded to see the homes of any Brahmins living in the village. "It's Brahmins who are responsible for the murder of our nation's great leader," they said ominously. "They must pay."

Having made note of the homes the boys showed them, the group trundled away in their bullock carts.

Residents of Rala wondered how Brahmins who never set foot outside the village could be responsible for such a deed.

A few days later, the bullock carts returned at nightfall with re-enforcements. The gang leader went to Gopal's home first, because it was the biggest. A group of village elders pleaded with the ruffians to leave the family alone. But their efforts proved fruitless. The men drove the entire family out of the house.

When Gopal's grandmother refused to leave, they dragged her by force. She tried to go back in, but the gang leader shoved her down. Her head hit a rock, and she bled profusely.

By the light of burning torches, the men ransacked the home, carrying out whatever they could. They found very little money or gold, so they dug up the floor in search of buried treasure. Still finding nothing, the leader slapped Gopal's grandfather. "Where are you hiding your family's gold?" he demanded. Getting no response, the man turned to Gopal's uncle, hit him, and asked the same question.

Uncle, his eyes burning, replied, "We don't have gold."

An elderly man intervened, "Nobody's rich in this village. He's telling the truth."

The leader asked his minions to search the yard and the well. The men did as they were told, but found nothing. Furious, the leader forced the women to hand over the jewelry they wore. Then he had his men carry hay from the adjoining barn into the big room in the middle of the house and set the hay on fire.

Gopal sat and watched, helpless, as his beloved home was devoured by flames. He saw it reflected in his cousin's wide, fearful gray eyes, and heard the wooden beams crack as they caught fire and burned, radiating heat and a golden glow.

At last the looters moved on to ransack other homes, and the young children of the family fell asleep on the bare ground, warmed by the embers of their ruined home. In shock, the adults, too, sat on the ground, their eyes staring vacantly at the remnants of the family homestead.

As soon as the first rays of the rising sun touched the earth, fellow villagers arrived to check on the Sane family.

Other Brahmin families had also suffered, but their homes had been spared. One Brahmin family living on the outskirts of the village was spared altogether, probably because of the sunrise. They invited other Brahmin families for lunch and dinner.

Gopal had lost Mani and now he had lost his home. His childhood was lost that night, too. After that, he rarely laughed and refused to play games.

The next day, Gopal's grandfather thought through how to deal with the catastrophe. He decided that he himself, his wife, his two sons and their wives, along with the family's youngest children would continue to live in the village, making do for now in the back section of the house that the fire had spared. But the older children, including Gopal, would go to live with their uncles in the city. "In the future, when the older children get jobs and start to work, we can rebuild the home. But for now rebuilding is out of the question."

The decision upset Gopal's mother. "Gopal is so young," she thought. "He should be with me." But she didn't have the courage to oppose her father-in-law. When she had packed Gopal's meager belongings and he was ready to leave, she hugged him and wept. "Please ask his uncle and aunt to take good care of him," she begged of Gopal's father, who was to accompany the children to their destinations.

They traveled together to Pune, where Gopal and his two cousins would live. Then Gopal's father left to take rest of the children to Nasik.

Gopal's uncle and aunt lived in two rooms in an old-fashioned building that had once belonged to a rich warrior. Their descendants had divided it into multiple two- and three-room units and rented them to low-income families.

The residence had a large central courtyard with Bakul and Prajakt trees in each corner, and water taps on a stone platform in the center.

Gopal's uncle's apartment had high ceilings because it had once been a stable, but the windows were small and the living quarters dark. A small window near the stove was the only ventilation, so the walls and the bedding were stained with soot of countless cooking fires. In the rainy season, the dirt floor was moist. The home's bedding, which was spread on the floor, absorbed the moisture and smelled of mildew. Accustomed to wide open spaces, fresh air and fresh-smelling clothing, Gopal loathed the dank, cramped quarters.

The family had barely been making ends meet before Gopal and his cousins arrived. Now Uncle had to find extra part-time work to feed the additional mouths. Gopal's aunt found work cooking for other well-off families, while Gopal's older twelve-year-old cousin took over cooking for the family. Her younger brother and other cousins helped as much as they could. Everyone washed their own clothes and hung them to dry. Still, Gopal's uncle faced financial problems because he had to send money orders to the family living in the village until they could get back on their feet.

Finally, desperation drove Gopal's uncle and aunt to send the children to ask for alms.

At first, only the older boys were assigned this humiliating task. But when the food supply proved insufficient, Gopal had to go, too.

Many of the women in the families that Gopal and his

cousins visited fulfilled their obligation of dispensing alms to young Brahmin students only grudgingly, dishing out cruel, sarcastic comments along with the alms.

"Why don't you wash pots and pans for someone and earn some money?"

"People who can't feed their kids shouldn't have them."

"Do you go to school or do you just eat free food and have fun?"

The first day Gopal accompanied his cousin on this chore, he cried the whole way home. He sobbed when he handed the food to his aunt. Her heart melted. "Don't cry," she said. "You need learn to ignore others' rudeness."

By the time Gopal returned to his village for a visit with his mother, he had withdrawn into a protective shell. He was angry and bitter. He rarely laughed, and moved dejectedly, like a lifeless doll.

Dismayed by the change in her son, his mother tried to cheer him.

"How about a nice story?"

"I know all your stories."

"Let me pat you to sleep."

"I'm not a little boy anymore."

She sighed. "You've become so serious. What do you do all day? Bury your nose in your schoolwork?"

"Uncle says if I study hard, I can go to college, get a good job and make a lot of money."

"And what will you do with all your money?"

"Fix this house and buy you nice saris," he said.

"That's very kind of you," she laughed.

"...And find the men who burned down our house and shoot them," he continued.

His mother blanched. She pulled him onto her lap. Tears rolled down her cheeks as she spoke. "Don't be so angry, Gopal. You're only hurting yourself. I wish you could be your old self."

Chastened, Gopal hugged his mother. She smiled and wiped her tears.

47

Though the visit perked him up a bit, he was still inwardly seething. Money and brute strength, his life so far had taught him, were the weapons that mattered. Men who possessed those could do whatever they wanted. The adults in his life had offered him a mantra: study hard, get a good job and make money. He resolved to do just that. And he did get good grades. But physical strength eluded him.

Initially, his uncle had sent him, along with the other children, to a good private school that charged a monthly fee. But just a few months later, his uncle was no longer able to afford the tuition, and the children were sent to a free municipal school serving poorer, mostly non-Brahmin children.

The first day Gopal entered the new school, a group of kids circled him in the yard.

"He's light-complexioned."

"Must be a Brahmin boy."

"Looks like he needs to be put in his place."

The group pressed closer.

But before anyone could lay a hand on him, another boy broke through and stood beside him. "Are you scaring a little kid? Before you touch him, you'll have to deal with me." The boys circling Gopal dispersed.

"I can beat all of them all by myself," the kid bragged. "My name is Khandya."

"I'm Gopal."

"I'll walk you to your class," said Khandya.

As it turned out, they were classmates.

"Sit here," said Khandya, pointing to the desk beside his.

When the teacher arrived, he went over the attendance sheet, calling everyone's name in turn. Students had to stand up when their names were called.

"So, you're the new addition to this brilliant class," said the teacher sarcastically when he got to Gopal.

When the class got going, he directed the first question to Gopal.

"How much is seven times nine?" he asked. All faces turned

to Gopal.

Gopal stood up. "Sixty-three."

"Eleven times six."

"Sixty-six."

"Who taught you your tables?"

"My grandfather."

Now teacher began quizzing Khandya.

"How much is two times six?"

"Fourteen?"

"Try again."

"Ten?"

The teacher punished Khandya, hitting him twice on his hand with a ruler.

At recess, Gopal had Khandya repeat tables after him. And in the days and weeks that followed, Gopal helped Khandya on a regular basis. Khandya's schoolwork improved.

As time went by, Gopal and Khandya became inseparable.

One day Khandya didn't bring a snack with him. "Why don't you have something to eat, Khandya?" Gopal asked.

"My Baba is sick. He stopped working. We don't have any money."

All too familiar with the "no money" situation, Gopal shared his snacks with Khandya for a few days.

Then Khandya dropped out of school altogether.

Gopal had no idea where Khandya lived. He asked the teacher, who shrugged his shoulders. "Kids drop out of municipal school all the time."

Without his best friend, school became a lonely place. He began to wonder if he would ever see Khandya again.

One afternoon, taking a shortcut on his way home, Gopal cut through a narrow alleyway in a bustling section of town. A dingy door was propped open midway down the block. As he passed by, he idly peered in, and then stopped in his tracks.

"Khandya?!"

There was his friend, cleaning dishes in a hotel sink.

Gopal rushed to him. "What are you doing here? Why aren't

you in school?"

"Baba died. My mother told me to quit school and find work."

Khandya didn't seem to care, but Gopal was upset. "My parents don't have money either, but I'm in school."

That night he approached his uncle, "My friend Khandya's mother doesn't have money, so she made him quit school," he said. "He washes dishes in a hotel now. *We* don't have money, either, but you haven't asked us kids to do that. Why not?"

"I'm guessing your friend isn't Brahmin," said his uncle. "Am I right?"

"How did you know?"

"For non-Brahmins, education often isn't important," said his uncle.

"It's not fair," Gopal thought. Khandya's caste was determining his education, and Gopal was losing a beloved friend because of it. "Khandya will never get a good job now."

After a couple of months, Gopal went to the hotel where Khandya worked. "He doesn't work here anymore," the hotel owner told Gopal.

"Where can I find him?" Gopal asked.

"I fired him. Khandya is a thief. We caught him stealing food."

"My friend is not a thief!" cried Gopal vehemently.

"Kids like him are thieves, son," said the hotel owner. "I suggest you forget him."

"No – I'll never forget him!" said Gopal. As he walked away, his eyes brimmed with tears.

After that, every time Gopal saw a little boy washing dishes, he thought of Khandya, his best friend.

Gopal started to participate in school activities. He debated students from other schools and won. When he received a scholarship reserved for gifted fourth-graders, the headmaster of his school sent a note to Gopal's house, asking his uncle to come in for a talk.

"Your nephew is very smart," the headmaster told his uncle.

"He should be attending a better school. If you agree, I can contact a school for boys and make the necessary arrangements. The scholarship he won will cover his tuition."

Gopal's uncle happily consented, and Gopal entered the fifth grade in a new school.

Gopal had been looking forward to it, but the boys there had already formed tight cliques. No group would accept the shy and introverted Gopal.

Two of the boys recognized Gopal. "He used to visit our home to ask for alms," they announced to the rest of the class. After that, he was mercilessly teased.

"Scholarship boy."

"Beggar."

"Municipaltiwala."

When he received the highest marks on the first quarterly examination, the other kids tormented him even more.

Gopal kept to himself, swallowed the insults, and never complained.

One of the boys, Arun, who had recognized Gopal from visits to his home, asked his mother, "Aie, do you remember a boy named Gopal? He used to come to our home to ask for alms."

"A very fair, gray-eyed boy?" Mother asked.

"Yes. He's in my class now. He transferred from the municipal school. He receives a scholarship."

"He must be very brilliant," said Arun's mother, Vijaya. She thought for a moment. "I'd like to meet him. Why don't you invite him to play after school?"

"I can't."

"Why not?"

"The other boys tease him and call him names. If I invite him here, they'll tease me too."

"That's nonsense. When a poor boy does well we should encourage him – not ostracize him. Invite him and see what happens."

Arun mustered his courage and asked Gopal to walk with him to his home.

Reluctant to visit a home where he'd asked for alms, Gopal

hesitated. But he was curious and walked with Arun to his home the next day.

Arun's mother Vijaya's appearance, manners and outfit impressed Gopal. She wore a five-yard sari of soft pink silk with a matching blouse. Her short hair was tied back in a ponytail, and she had makeup on her face. Gold bangles jingled on her arms.

"Gopal, I remember you," she said. "You're taller now. You can call me Aunty Vijaya."

Her smile and soft voice helped Gopal overcome his reticence.

Gopal compared her to his own mother and aunts, who walked barefoot, wearing dark-colored old-fashioned saris.

More shocks awaited Gopal.

When he had come to Arun's bungalow before, he had been so engrossed in his own shame that he hadn't paid attention to the surroundings. Now he took in Arun's home with amazement.

The living room, with a luxurious cushioned sofa and chairs, was decorated with colorful paintings. A coffee table held a flowerpot with fresh flowers. A cook served Arun and Gopal refreshments in a glass dish with a cup of milk.

"I want you to finish all the refreshments," Vijaya said. "Then you can finish your homework. Afterwards you can play."

Gopal had seen big homes in his village, but those had been filled with extended families. Arun's home was different – a big home for a single family.

Arun and Gopal ate and then finished their homework, which they showed to Vijaya. Pleased, Vijaya said, "Gopal must have helped you, Arun. Usually you spend a long time struggling with your studies."

Gopal and Arun looked at each other. "Go out now and play." They joined a cricket game in a playground across the street.

Arun found that he enjoyed Gopal's company and invited him to come over again. Vijaya encouraged the friendship, hoping that a smart friend might help her sports-crazy son buckle down to his studies. As the boys spent more time together, Arun started to receive better grades, and Gopal learned new sports. Gopal, an expert swimmer, accompanied Arun to swimming lessons.

Now that Gopal had a friend, the other children accepted him. Arun's family treated him like a nephew. Slowly, Gopal's inferiority complex abated, and his bitter memories retreated to the background.

Gopal started to spend his evenings at Arun's and often slept there.

In the high school matriculate examination, Gopal placed first in the region. Arun received first class.

Just about the time Arun passed the matriculate examination, his father was transferred to Delhi.

Afraid that Arun would be lonely in a college in Delhi, Vijaya suggested, "Let's take Gopal with us."

"Do you think Gopal's family would consent to that?" Arun's father asked.

"You could visit his uncle and see what he says," said Vijaya.

Mr. Varavadekar visited Gopal's uncle with a box of sweets, a celebration for Arun's and Gopal's success. Mr. Varavadekar praised Gopal and then put forth his proposal. "The government has decided to transfer me to Delhi. We want Arun to move to Delhi, too, so he can go to college there. But he would miss Gopal, who's been such a good influence on him. I have a request for you. Let us bring Gopal with us. He has a scholarship. His housing will be free. Any other expenses are nominal. Together Gopal and Arun will be happy."

Uncle was aware that Gopal spent a lot of time at Arun's home, but the proposal astonished him. "I must talk to Gopal and his father," he said.

"Is this something you'd like to do?" he asked Gopal that night.

Gopal thought it over. Money and political power were centered in Delhi, he knew. And Delhi, unlike Pune, was cosmopolitan. He would meet people from all over India.

"Yes," he told his uncle. "I'd like to go."

Gopal's uncle wrote to Gopal's father about the proposal.

"For all intents and purposes," Gopal's father replied,

"you've raised Gopal. You know the Varavadekar family better than I do. You may decide what he should do."

Gopal's Uncle gave it serious thought. After much soul searching, he concluded that an education in Delhi was too good an opportunity to pass up.

When Gopal left for Delhi, the entire family showed up at the Pune station to bid him good-bye. He touched everyone's feet. They waved to him from the station until they could no longer see his window.

Gopal waved back with a sense of elation. He looked out the window without really seeing. At last, it seemed, his ambitions were within reach.

CHAPTER 5

The college restaurant, housed in a two-story cement building across from the college's front entrance, was a favorite student hangout. From early morning to midnight, noisy students monopolized the outdoor seating area.

Darashan and his college friends had adopted a corner table as their own. After a session of table tennis or cricket practice, the group automatically headed to the restaurant. Today they arrived, put in their orders for tea, toast and omelets, and settled in to discuss the important events in their young lives.

Of this group, except for Gopal and Arun, none of them had known each other before enrolling at the college. Darashan and Bhushan had happened to sit next to each other when they attended their first lecture and discovered a common interest in sports.

Unlike many of his high school friends, who were studying science with a vocation like medicine or engineering in mind, Darashan already had his line of work cut out for him in the family's clothing business.

"Why waste the tuition money when I know I'll just have to help with the business?" he'd asked Bhajan.

"Don't think like that," she'd said. "College will make you a better businessman. We live in a cosmopolitan city. You'll understand your customers better, and if you ever have to deal with foreigners, an education and the ability to speak English will help you."

Bhushan, who planned to join his family ventures after his college education, was in the same boat.

Soon Darashan learned that it wasn't a bad boat to be in. There were many pretty faces to look at, since the liberal arts classes he took were mostly filled with girls. He also had plenty of free time for sports and to meet interesting students from other regions of India.

After their first class Bhushan had introduced himself and said, "I want to join the cricket team."

Darashan had exclaimed, "So do I."

At team meets, Bhushan and Darashan had struck up friendships with other sports enthusiasts. George and Arun played cricket, Gopal played badminton, table tennis and was a good swimmer, Jitendra played cricket and tennis, and Ikbal was a good runner. And so, their group had coalesced.

"Look, there goes Ranee," announced Jitendra now, pointing to the street.

Everyone except Gopal stood up to stare at a pretty girl on the sidewalk, passing by the restaurant hedge. When she disappeared from view, everyone settled down. A waiter arrived with their food.

Bhushan sighed, "She's lovely. Looks like Meenakumari."

"She does," Darashan agreed.

"She does not," Arun insisted.

"Soon her parents will marry her off, "Bhushan sighed again.

Jitendra laughed, "Don't worry. I'll find you a beautiful wife."

Arun's eyes widened, "How? Do you have a stock of beautiful girls?"

"Yes," Jitendra told him. "Actually, my mother has a huge supply on her list. Arranging marriages is her hobby."

"Will she find a good-looking girl for me?" Bhushan asked.

"Well, she says if you want a pretty bride, you must first look at yourself in the mirror. You should be handsome, otherwise a girl will turn down your proposal."

Arun stood up, "I am tall, dark and handsome."

His friends and customers at the tables nearby turned to look at him. Some chuckled.

"Me, too." Darashan stood up and customers turned to look at him too. A group of girls at the next table eyed them all coyly.

George shook Jitendra and asked, "Will your mother find brides for me and Ikbal?"

"She doesn't have a supply of Muslim and Christian girls," said Jitendra.

"We're willing to marry pretty Hindu girls," said Ikbal,

laughing.

The waiter returned to clear their plates and the group gathered up to go.

When Gopal had first moved with Arun to Delhi, he'd been uncomfortable with Arun's family's lifestyle. But the cook, maids, gardener and chauffeur treated him like a member of Arun's family. When Gopal tried to wash and iron his own clothes and sweep his own room, Vijaya had objected: "Gopal, you study and have fun. You're one of us now."

Gopal also tried to resist the pocket money the Varavadekars gave him, but Mr. Varavadekar told him, "You're our adopted son. Please accept the money. You're going to need it."

Arun spent all his pocket money, but Gopal managed to save a little. His family also sent him money orders periodically because his older cousins were working, so his family had money to spare. He saved it all and bought gifts for his family when he visited them in Diwali and summer vacations.

The Varavadekar family's affection and the way they treated him touched Gopal's heart. He saw that his family's economic class truly didn't make any difference to them.

He was hopeful that his cosmopolitan new life in Delhi would enable him to put his past behind him. And indeed, with each passing day, the scars of his childhood seemed to fade.

But as he soon discovered, old wounds could not be so easily buried.

One Sunday evening Arun, Darashan, Gopal and George were aimlessly strolling in old Delhi when they heard a series of blood-curdling shrieks. The noise seemed to be coming from a whitewashed building with barred windows. The front door was slightly ajar.

Let's go!" Arun cried, and the group rushed in.

They followed a narrow stone path to the back of the building where it opened into a courtyard. There they encountered a horrifying sight; a woman ablaze, her arms flailing, flames leaping from her clothes and hair. "Call an ambulance!" someone called.

As the four friends watched in shock, a woman rushed forward and sprayed the burning figure with water while another doused the flames with a blanket. In the corner, a pair of young children cowered.

The flames at last extinguished, the burned woman fell to the floor moaning.

Gopal struggled to breathe. Long-suppressed images of the night, years ago, when his family home had burned came unbidden to his mind.

Now an older woman, sobbing hysterically, came charging into the courtyard with a comb in her hand. Her long graying hair hung loosely down her back.

The crowd parted to let her through. A man murmured, "Poor mother! After Pakistan she has to suffer this."

At Gopal's side, Darashan blanched at the mention of Pakistan, and his hands curled into fists.

The old woman let out a heart-wrenching wail as she crumpled to the ground and tried to hug her daughter.

Gopal watched the unfolding scene as if in a nightmare.

Now a wild-eyed man carrying a dripping gasoline canister approached and stood menacingly over the women.

"My wife takes up with my best friend?" he spat. "This is what she deserves!" His eyes were bloodshot, and he reeked of liquor.

The older woman moved protectively toward her daughter.

"Get away from her!" the man snapped, shoving her brutally back. "She doesn't deserve your help."

Suddenly, like a flash, Darashan had pushed through the crowd and was pummeling the man in a frenzy of punches and kicks.

Before he knew what he was doing, Gopal had joined him, striking the man again and again with a fury that felt boundless. Tears streaked his face.

"Have you lost your minds?" screamed Arun.

"What are you doing?" shouted George. "The police will arrest you."

With help from a handful of bystanders, George and Arun managed to restrain their friends, while someone helped the other man to his feet.

An ambulance arrived and hurried away with the burned woman.

Soon afterwards, a pair of policemen carted away the woman's husband.

Arun turned to Darashan and Gopal. "What got into you two? You would have killed that man if we hadn't stopped you."

Gopal was still breathing heavily. To his surprise, he saw that Darashan's face, too, was streaked with tears.

"It's like you couldn't control yourselves," said George, watching Darashan's retreating back.

His fists still clenched, Darashan turned and stalked away.

"Darashan's family migrated from Pakistan," said Arun. "He may have witnessed atrocities at the time of partition. Maybe that's why he reacted the way he did."

"What about you, Gopal?" George asked. "Was there something like that that happened to you?"

Gopal still couldn't speak. Like Darashan, he turned, fists still clenched, and walked wordlessly away.

CHAPTER 6

"Darashan, a lovely new table tennis star is playing tonight," announced Bhushan one morning several weeks later. "Do you want to watch? I hear she's quite good."

"Have you seen her play?" asked Darashan.

"No, but I will tonight," said Bhushan.

"I'll join you," said Darashan.

The sports hall was a large, wide-open building with a sloping metal roof supported by poles. For today, a tennis table had been set up at the center.

That evening, when Bhushan and Darashan entered the hall, a group of girls was already gathered by the table. Bhushan asked a couple of students which one was the new star player. One of the students pointed to a girl in the midst of the group. Darashan spotted a pretty face for a moment before it vanished in the crowd. He had an odd sense it was a face he had seen sometime before.

When the game started, floodlights illuminated the table, and Darashan could see the new player clearly. He struggled to recall where he had seen her. "What's her name?" he asked Bhushan.

"Maya Khanna."

"Maya..." Darashan's mind flew back to the evening he had first laid eyes on his old childhood playmate. He remembered each and every moment he had spent with her, but couldn't recollect her last name. Could this be her?

He watched the girl, hardly registering the game.

Suddenly there were shouts, clapping and whistles. The game was over. Maya had won.

Darashan stood where he was, scanning the crowd.

"Let's go," said Bhushan.

Darashan ignored him.

Bhushan grabbed his arm. "The game's over. What's wrong with you, Darashan? Did you take hashish this evening? You're not yourself."

"I must take a closer look at Maya," mumbled Darashan.

"What do you mean by a closer look?" asked Bhushan.

"I want to see if she has a scar on her eyebrow."

"A scar on her face? Now I know you must be drugged. Let's get out of the sports hall." Bhushan tried to pull Darashan away, but Darashan refused to budge. By the time they reached the table, Maya had disappeared.

"You search the front of the college," called Darashan. "I'll cover the back. Look for Maya. See if she has a scar on her eyebrow."

Bhushan laughed aloud. He watched Darashan leave. He had no wish to find Maya. Instead he went to the front entrance, where a lively group of students always loitered, watching passersby, and laughing and talking.

Darashan searched the entire college and finally returned to the sports hall. It was deserted now except for a lone girl standing by the door. Darashan knew who she was. His heart started to pound. He shivered. He collected his courage and walked to her.

"Congratulations," he said, glancing at her right eyebrow.

"Thanks," Maya responded.

Darashan said, "I must apologize again."

Surprised, Maya asked, "What for?"

Darashan smiled, "I was young and you were mean, but that's not an excuse. How can I compensate you for the scar on your face?"

Maya stared at him. "Darashan...*Darashan*...are you Darashan?"

"Yes."

Her face lit up and she smiled.

"You're taller and a little more mature," said Darashan. "But other than that, you look the same. Didn't you recognize me?"

"How can I recognize you? Your face is covered with a beard and moustache now! But as soon as you talked about the scar, I knew exactly who you were."

Wordlessly, they gazed at each other. Darashan remembered that evening when he had gently touched the reddish scar on Maya's eyebrow. He wanted to touch it again, but was afraid of

61

offending her.

Maya smiled. She lifted Darashan's right hand and moved his fingers over the scar.

She spoke first, "I may not have recognized you, but how can I forget you? I think of you every time I look at myself in the mirror. When people ask how I injured my face, I tell them about our fight and have to admit I had lied. Now tell me, did you forget me?"

"How could I forget you? Every time I step onto the terrace I remember the first evening I met you. Whenever I'm too quick to anger, Bhajanma and Ma remind me of our argument and point out that I'm responsible for the permanent scar on your face. Maya, I want to tell you…" He stopped to find the right words. "I'm willing to pay any penalty for my crime. Feel free to punish me."

Maya smiled. Her eyes twinkled. It was her old mischievous smile. "She smiled like this so many times when she was young," Darashan thought.

She said, "So can I throw you in prison if I want to?"

"Yes. I'll be your prisoner. I will be at your mercy," Darashan said.

"Well, I reserve the right to throw you in prison. I'll wait for the right time."

"When will that be?"

"I'll let you know."

Bhushan appeared in the doorway. Tired of waiting for Darashan, he had come back to find him.

"Who's this?" asked Maya.

"Bhushan, meet Maya," said Darashan.

"And look. Here's the scar." Darashan pointed to the scar on Maya's eyebrow.

Puzzled, Bhushan said, "Yes. I do see the scar."

Darashan tried to explain, "I threw a pebble at her."

"No, not a pebble…a rock," Maya corrected him.

"What? You hit her with a rock?" Bhushan looked even more puzzled.

Now Maya launched into an explanation. "He did throw a

rock at me."

Darashan interrupted her. "She lied. She said I was out. L. B. W."

"I wanted revenge," Maya said.

By now the trio had exited the hall and were standing by the entrance.

A car drove up. "Daddy, look who's here." Maya hurried to her father. "I ran into Darashan. He's still acting like a six-year-old."

"Darashan!" exclaimed Maya's father. "You look just like your Bauji now." He shook Darashan's outstretched hand. "Maya's mother is planning to visit your family. We have pleasant memories of the time we spent in your building. Would you like a ride home?"

"No, thank you. I'm planning to spend the night at my friend Bhushan's home. But I'll tell Ma and Bhajanma that you're in Delhi. They'll be thrilled to hear it."

Darashan stared at the car until it disappeared from sight.

"Well, I see what's going on," Bhushan said. "Too bad I didn't throw a rock at a lovely girl when I was young. You hit a girl and she loves you. What luck! Where is that magic rock? I must try and see if the trick works for me."

Meenakumari and Maya visited Bhajanma and Kuldip after a few days. Kuldip and Meenakumari were happy to see each other again and immediately started to plan outings.

Soon Darashan introduced Maya to his friends.

Maya usually stayed late after college hours to practice badminton and table tennis. She also participated in the drama club and had roles in plays. Darashan, who usually stayed late for his games, accompanied her home. Once when he had another commitment and couldn't chaperone her, he asked Gopal to accompany her.

The next day Maya asked, "What's wrong with Gopal?"

"Why? What happened?" Darashan asked.

"Nothing happened. That's the point. He won't come near me. He keeps a distance of two feet between us as if I'll shock him if he moves closer."

Darashan laughed, "You may not know this, Maya, but pretty girls are electric and can shock men. Men die of heart failure caused by such shocks."

"And he doesn't utter a word. I have to repeat a question three times before he responds in monosyllables. How long can I talk by myself?"

"That shouldn't be an issue for you, Maya. Your mother told my mother that you started to talk at the age of six months and haven't stopped since."

"Oh, shut up," Maya said. "I don't talk that much! Besides, what can I say to your friend? He doesn't answer me."

"Beautiful girls leave men tongue-tied. Lots of men don't know what to say to a girl like you."

"Why? Don't I have brains?"

Darashan pretended to ponder solemnly. "I don't know what Gopal thinks, but I have serious reservations about your brain power."

Irritated, Maya said, "I don't want another chaperone if you're not free. I can ask Daddy to pick me up. If he's busy, I can go home by myself. I don't want that walking statue to escort me home."

"You don't understand, Maya. I want Gopal to walk you home precisely because he is an emotionless statue. Someone else may try to steal you. I don't have to worry about Gopal. I trust him completely."

Maya's eyes widened. "You don't trust your other friends? Just him? Why?"

"He's not interested in girls."

"Really?"

"Really."

"Darashan, I have to rush. Let Gopal accompany me if he wants to. I'm intrigued. He's a fascinating character."

Maya walked away. Darashan couldn't understand her logic. "Girls are strange," he thought to himself. "She wants to study Gopal's character because girls don't interest him."

One evening Maya waited for Darashan. The sports hall was almost deserted. The sun had set and in the twilight Maya could see a few stars twinkling in the sky. She gave up and decided to go home by herself. But then she noticed a man walking toward her.

"Gopal?" she said to herself, surprised.

"Maya, where is Darashan?" Gopal asked. "Is he coming?"

"He didn't show up. I can go home by myself. What are you doing here?" Without waiting for a response, she started walking at a fast clip.

Gopal followed her. "It's late. It's not safe for you at this hour."

"Why are you here so late?" Maya asked.

"I was in the library studying communism."

"Then why did you come to the sports hall?"

"I thought Darashan might still be practicing table tennis. I wanted to practice, too."

"Really and truly, I can go by myself." Maya didn't believe Gopal. "He was checking on me," she decided. It occurred to her that she was being curt. She glanced at his face, but couldn't read any emotion.

"Please let me escort you. Darashan will be upset if I let you go by yourself."

"He thinks of me as his best friend's property," she thought. The idea irritated her, but at the same time she was thankful for his company. Delhi's streets could be dangerous for a young girl alone at night.

She didn't utter a single word during their entire walk. When they reached her home she glanced at him and saw that he was watching her. She failed to understand the expression on his face. Maya was accustomed to men's eyes caressing her body. But Gopal's expression wasn't lustful. Her beauty didn't seem to attract him. He never tried to talk to her or impress her with witty jokes like other men. She couldn't fit Gopal into any worldly parameters of male types she knew.

As time passed, it became clear that Gopal had willingly taken the responsibility of guarding her upon himself. If Darashan was late or failed to show up, he would appear from nowhere and walk her home; if Darashan showed up, he went away. "He's like my bodyguard," she told people jokingly.

Meanwhile, Bhajan had noticed Maya and Darashan's friendship. She wondered if they were in love. Concerned, she tried indirectly to warn Darashan.

"I know that Sikh-Hindu marriages are common," she said one morning before Darashan had left for class. "And I know lots of Hindus don't even think of Sikhism as a separate religion. Plenty of Hindu families raised their oldest sons to be Sikhs, after all. And I know it's unlikely there will ever be a Hindu-Sikh conflict. But situations change. Who ever thought my father and brother would be ruthlessly murdered in our own town? From the day of that attack, to the day she died just a few years ago, your great-grandmother Bijibai was never the same."

Darashan listened quietly.

"And do you remember our Muslim neighbors in Pakistan?" she went on. "Your grandfather's best friend took over our home and land. He said, 'Someone will invade your home and force you out, so why don't I take it?' He promised he would compensate us, but we never heard from him. My own son–" Bhajan was starting to get emotional. She stopped herself and concluded simply, "In choosing a marriage partner, it's safest to stick to your own people."

Bhajan never mentioned Maya or the fact that she was Hindu, but she didn't need to.

Darashan said, "A married woman should be loyal to her husband and his community."

"I know," said Bhajan, "but blood bonds are tenacious. Remember – a Hindu woman married to a Sikh could be suspect in both communities. Her children raised as Sikhs may have divided loyalties."

Darashan didn't ask any more questions and Bhajan didn't raise the topic again.

As for himself, Darashan resolved that he loved Maya and would marry her if she too loved him and consented. "We'll just have to face the consequences if the political situation changes," he decided.

After a few days, Darashan invited Maya for a cup of coffee. At a cubicle in the college restaurant he recounted for her the conversation he'd had with Bhajanma.

Maya asked him to please repeat the conversation again. She listened carefully and then was subdued for the rest of the evening.

Maya had assumed that Darashan would marry her even though he hadn't proposed. Bhajanma's warning unsettled her.

After a few days, Maya told Darashan of a conversation she'd had with her father. "My daddy reads the newspapers all the time and knows a lot about politics. I asked him whether Hindus and Sikhs would ever be enemies. He said he doesn't think so, but Sikhs do have grievances. The Sikh leadership may have conflicts with the Indian government, but I don't think Hindus and Sikhs would ever hurt each other."

Darashan asked, "Maya, why are you thinking about this issue so earnestly?"

Maya was annoyed. "I'm not a young girl and can't run around with you anymore."

Darashan demanded, "Why not?"

"You should be able to guess the answer."

Darashan laughed, "Maya, are you laying the foundation for a Hindu-Sikh war? If a Hindu-Sikh war starts, we'll convert to Christianity."

"You're not funny," griped Maya, and vanished into the ladies lounge.

Maya had been in the habit of meeting Darashan every morning outside the ladies lounge to plan the day. But she stopped meeting him there. Finally Darashan managed to stop her one evening outside the sports hall. "Stop – please. Maya, why are you avoiding me?" he asked.

"Leave me alone," said Maya. "I can't be seen in public with you. I'm a grown woman now."

"All right. Then we'll book a room at a hotel."

Maya walked away. He ran behind her. "Maya, what's my

crime? What can I do to correct the situation? Announce our engagement?"

Maya stopped. "Engagement? You haven't even proposed to me."

"Well, I thought we had an understanding. I wanted to take you to a romantic garden and ask you to marry me. You ruined my plans. You forced a proposal out of me in public. What's the big rush?"

Maya ignored his question. "Darashan, you're graduating this year. What are your plans after graduation?"

"You're supposed to act happy, dance joyfully at a moment like this."

Maya looked levelly at Darashan. "Answer my question."

"How sad! No romance for me at this magic moment. Maya, when I graduate, I'll help my grandfather. We have a family business. You already know that."

"Yes. I do know that."

"Now are you happy? Any more questions?"

"No. No more questions for now."

"But I have a question. Do you accept my proposal?"

"I was planning a romantic answer in a romantic garden," Maya said. Her eyes twinkled.

"And I'll wait for your romantic answer, but I must warn you…"

"Warn me?"

"Yes. If we announce our engagement to our families, they'll want us to marry right away. Not that I mind that idea, but I want you to graduate."

Maya said, "I do, too."

"Right now you're a free bird. But once you're married you may be constrained."

"That's true," said Maya.

"That's why I wasn't rushing to propose and announce our engagement."

"Very thoughtful of you."

"I thought everybody knew our plans anyway."

"I thought so, too, until Bhajanma warned you against marrying me."

"What do you mean?"

"I couldn't confidently assume, 'Darashan will marry me.' And you hadn't asked."

"Ok, then – let's announce our engagement tomorrow. Forget your degree."

"I haven't accepted your proposal, remember?" Maya said, laughing.

"Maya, since you're talking like a businesswoman, you should know that I want to open another branch of the business in Indore and also start a business selling tractors."

"That's fine with me."

"We may have to relocate. Are you willing to move?"

"I've spent all my life moving."

"While I pined for you!" Darashan said.

"Liar," Maya laughed. "I'll talk to my parents and they'll talk to your grandparents and parents."

"Send them soon before another boy hooks you."

Maya, suddenly serious, asked, "What will you say if Bhajanma raises the Hindu-Sikh issue?"

"I'll say that Hindu-Sikh makes no difference to me."

"And is that true?"

"Until Bhajanma pointed out the differences in our backgrounds, I hadn't even thought of it."

"If anyone brings up the difference, we'll say, 'Hindus and Sikhs are the same people.' And we are."

"Will I see you tomorrow?" Darashan asked.

"Yes. Remember when we first met here, you promised me that I could punish you for throwing that rock?"

"Yes, I did."

"I had planned the punishment," Maya giggled.

"Is marriage the punishment?"

"Yes."

"So, I'll face your wrath all my life."

"If you talk like that, we're through!"

"No, no, no. The punishment thrills me."

"Well, I must go home now. Walk me home, please."

Maya and Darashan walked companionably side by side, each engrossed in their own thoughts.

CHAPTER 7

In her early years everyone loved Rajkumari and spoiled her. They scolded and sometimes spanked Darashan when he teased her. Yet she sensed Darashan had priority over her.

At times the daily exchanges her mother had with Darashan about his homework bothered her.

Darashan would have a snack when he returned home from school, and then Kuldipma would insist, "Darashan you must finish your homework first, and then you can go out to play." She would sit down with him, read his books and help him. She rarely asked Rajkumari about her homework.

Kuldipma did routinely scan and sign Rajkumari's monthly report card. But she asked Darashan to show his card to Gurumukh Bauji, the most senior member of the family, who read it carefully and never failed to comment.

She asked Kuldipma, "Why do you sign my card and send Darashan to Bauji?" Her mother answered, "He's older."

But as she grew older, she learned that the age wasn't the only factor determining Darashan's status in the family.

Rajkumari had attended many wedding celebrations when she was young. She loved the festive atmosphere, the fancy clothing, the jewelry and the feast. She especially liked the elaborate outfits worn by the brides.

One day after the family had returned from a wedding celebration, she said to Kuldip at dinnertime, "*I* want to marry. Can I?"

Kuldip solemnly replied, "You must study now. According to custom, my family married me off right after high school graduation. But times have changed. You must graduate from high school and then college."

Rajkumari didn't like the response. "I don't *want* to go to school. I want to marry," she wailed.

"Of course you'll marry," said Kuldip. "But first you must study and have fun in school and college."

"Fun! School isn't fun." Rajkumari puffed her cheeks and

71

narrowed her eyes. "Teacher makes us sit still. We can't talk or laugh. We have to study. Nobody wants to go to school. Marriage will be fun."

Annoyed, Kuldip raised her voice, "Many girls don't have the chance to go to school. They have to stay home and help their mothers cook and care for little brothers and sisters. We send you to school but you're not interested."

Rajkumari pouted. Her eyes brimmed with tears.

Bhajan tried to put things in perspective for Rajkumari. "You know, Rajkumari, after marriage you'll have to go and live with your husband's mother and father."

"By myself?" Rajkumari wiped her tears, "Why?"

"All girls have to go to live with their husband's family after marriage."

"Why can't he come to live with us?"

"He can for a few days, but then he'll have to take you back to his family."

"That's not fair."

"Yes, but that's our custom."

"Can I come back to live with you after marriage?"

"For a few days, yes, but then you have to go back because you'll belong to your husband's family. Your Ma and I had to move to our husband's after our marriages."

"You mean you didn't live with our family when you were little?"

"No. I lived with Bijibai and your Ma lived with her Ma."

Rajkumari stopped eating. She thought for a while. If that was what happened to girls after marriage, nice clothes and jewelry hardly seemed worth the price. "Not fair," she muttered, and dropped the subject.

A few years later, Rajkumari watched with interest as Bimala and her husband, who lived next door, were trying to arrange a marriage for Binnee.

A prospective groom and his family were coming to visit Binnee's family.

Kuldip told Rajkumari, "I'm planning to help Binnee's

mother cook for guests. You can join us if you wish." Rajkumari went along willingly and helped Kuldip and Binnee's mother prepare a feast of samosa, kachori and gulab jamun. Then she accompanied Binnee to the store to buy additional sweets. After they returned home, she helped Binnee sweep and mop the stone tiled floor and laid down a borrowed red and green carpet. She went with Binnee to some neighbors in the tenements to borrow a coffee table and more chairs. The neighbors willingly lent the items and teased Binnee about the impending visit. Binnee blushed.

While Binnee prepared for the visit, Bimalaaunti lectured her continuously.

"Don't look at anyone directly."

"Speak softly."

"Don't laugh loudly."

"Even if they ask rude questions, don't get angry. Girls must learn to swallow their anger and pride."

"Get up and serve more food if anyone's plate is empty."

"Don't touch your hair."

Binnee had been Rajkumari's role model. She always ranked first in her class. She participated in sports, and could cook, sew, and knit. Bhajanma and Kuldipma often praised her. "She's a model daughter. And so modest! She's not light, but her features are lovely. She has all the qualities her in-laws would desire."

Binnee's mother's barrage of instructions angered Rajkumari. "Any man should be thrilled to have someone like her."

"If they ask rude questions, why do you have to put up with it?" she asked Binnee. "Why can't you be yourself and tell them what you what you really think?"

Binnee sighed. "Because I'm a girl." Her eyes filled with tears.

"What if the groom is ugly and old?" Rajkumari asked. "Will you refuse to marry him?"

"No, I can't. My parents are poor and I'm a burden. They worry about my future all the time. I'll have to marry any groom who will accept me."

"What about your brother, Bhagawan? Don't your parents

73

worry about him?"

"No – he's a boy. He'll get proposals, choose his wife and receive a dowry." Binnee paused in her preparations and turned to Rajkumari, "I have advice for you. Fix your own marriage – a love marriage so you won't be humiliated like me." Rajkumari solemnly nodded.

She then watched Binnee put on make-up and fix her hair.

Binnee's father ironed the only suit he had for the occasion. Bimalaaunti carefully chose a nice sari, somewhat old-fashioned, pressed it, and handed it to Binnee.

She had an eye on Binnee's make-up. "Keep it light, Binnee. We don't want you to look like a movie actress." Then she tried to rush Binnee. "Hurry up. Sometimes guests arrive early." Binnee put on her sari and looked at her reflection in the mirror. Finally she turned to her mother. "I'm ready."

Kuldip and Bimalaaunti had already filled individual plates with snacks and arranged them in the tray. By five o'clock, apart from the last-minute chore of boiling water for tea, everybody was ready to receive the guests, who were expected at six.

Kuldip went home, but Rajkumari, interested in the proceedings, wanted to stay. "You can be at Binnee's after the guests arrive," Kuldip agreed, "but you have to follow the rules. You must wait in the kitchen and keep your mouth shut. And you can come home only after the guests leave."

The guests arrived at seven. Rajkumari and Binnee settled themselves in the kitchen and watched the events unfold through a small crack between the door and the wall.

"Please, come in. Make yourselves comfortable," said Binnee's father, pointing to the chairs. The men seated themselves. Binnee's mother addressed the women. "Please," she said, pointing to the mat on the floor. The women sat down. The conversation turned to politics, food prices and education. Binnee's mother offered them glasses of water. Binnee's parents seemed to be saying "Yes" continuously. Bimalaaunti laughed constantly, and her husband was ingratiating. Rajkumari had never seen the pair act this way.

Eventually Bimalaaunti asked Binnee to join the group. Binnee carried the tray of refreshments into the living room, set it on the coffee table, and touched everyone's feet except the groom's and his friend's. Then she handed plates of food to the guests and sat down on the carpet, her eyes fixed on the floor. The guests began to ask Binnee questions.

"What school did you attend?"

"What were your grades like?"

Binnee produced the report cards she'd stacked near the back wall in case the groom's family wanted to see them. Bimalaaunti handed them to the oldest male guest, who handed them to the groom, who passed them to his mother. She glanced at them and commented, "Smart girl."

Then she asked Binnee to read aloud from an English book the groom had brought with him.

After half an hour, Rajkumari, who was still watching the proceedings through the crack in the closed door, couldn't bring herself to watch any longer. She wrapped her arms around her knees, stared out the window and waited for the guests to leave, regretting her decision to stay. But she had to wait. Her mother had ordered her to stay in the kitchen while the guests were in the living room.

Stuck there, she daydreamed of her own future. She tried to imagine herself dressed up for a similar exhibition, her parents and grandparents ingratiating themselves like Binnee's parents. The idea horrified her.

"I'll arrange my own marriage," she vowed. "And if I can't arrange my own marriage, I won't marry at all. I'll never allow anyone to humiliate me like this."

The guests left and Rajkumari darted out of the kitchen.

Binnee caught her arm. "Wait. Why are you rushing?"

"I want to go home."

"I'll pack some sweets for your family," Bimalaaunti told her.

Binnee said, "Please help me clean up." But Rajkumari was in a dark mood. She ignored Binnee, took the package Bimalaaunti handed her and ran out.

When she got home, she handed the package to Bhajan, who opened it and offered Rajkumari a piece of burfee that she liked.

"I don't want it," said Rajkumari, bitterly.

"What's wrong?" asked Bhajan, surprised.

Rajkumari shrugged.

"Did you see the groom?"

"Yes. He was ugly."

Perplexed, Bhajan pulled Rajkumari aside, "Why are you upset, Rajkumari?"

"I don't know."

"If something's bothering you, we can talk about it. Please don't go around insulting the groom."

When Kuldip returned from an errand, she asked the same question. "Did you see the groom, Rajkumari?"

"Yes. He was..." Rajkumari looked at Bhajan. "He was all right."

Rajkumari calmed down after a couple days and decided perhaps she had more to learn about the business of marriage.

"What was your marriage like?" she asked Bhajanma.

"We had a ceremony like everyone else."

"Yes, but who fixed it?"

"My parents."

Rajkumari heaved a sigh. "How?"

"They talked to your grandfather's parents."

"Did they come to your parents' house to see what you looked like?"

"No, they knew who I was."

Bhajan's answer was a relief to Rajkumari. At least Bhajanma hadn't faced the humiliation of being looked over like Binnee. It also meant there were more ways of fixing a marriage.

"Do parents always fix marriages?"

"Most of the time. But nowadays, some college-educated girls and boys fix their own marriages. Those are called love marriages."

"In that case, I want a college education."

Bhajan laughed, "Fine with us."

The next day, Rajkumari visited Binnee, who was in tears because the groom's family had refused the match.

A few more prospective grooms and their families looked Binnee over. Finally, a groom and his family agreed to marry her. After protracted discussions about a dowry, gold jewelry for Binnee and payment for the wedding festivities, Binnee's marriage was fixed. A priest picked an auspicious time for the ceremony.

Rajkumari attended the wedding with her entire family. When the ceremony was over, Binnee had to leave for her in-laws' home. She hugged her mother and sobbed. Binnee's mother, aunts, cousins, and numerous related and unrelated guests all cried. Kuldip cried, too, and even Binnee's father wiped tears.

Rajkumari looked on in dismay. "Why do girls have to suffer like this?" she wondered.

After a year, Binnee had a little baby boy. She seemed happy. She had forgotten the insults she had suffered and the pain of moving out of her parents' home.

Rajkumari loved Binnee's cute cuddly baby with soft skin and big black eyes.

But it still seemed unfair that Binnee had to be humiliated like that and move away from her beloved parents to win her prize baby.

"Why do women have to marry?" she asked Bhajanma.

"A husband supports his wife," Bhajanma answered.

"Why can't women earn money and support themselves?"

"That's just how our society is, Rajkumari. But the situation is slowly changing."

When Rajkumari asked her mother the same question, Kuldip had a different answer. "Women can't do men's work. They have to depend upon a man, so they must marry."

Rajkumari next queried her father, who said, "A woman's job is cooking for her family and raising her kids. A woman needs to learn to read and write and learn English so she can read telegrams. Don't worry. We'll find you a husband as soon as you graduate from high school."

Her grandfather, sitting nearby, heard the exchange, as did Bhajan, who was aware of Rajkumari's feelings on the subject. She worried that Rajkumari might say something impertinent, infuriating Ranjit Singh, so she quickly said, "Rajkumari, why don't you ask your grandfather the question?"

"If a woman doesn't marry," Gurumukh Singh said, "she has to live with a male relative – like her father or brother."

"I don't *want* to live with Darashan and his wife. I'll find a flat for myself."

Gurumukh Singh laughed. "Really! I know only one woman who lives by herself. She's not married and is a doctor. She has a hospital where she delivers babies."

Rajkumari was thrilled. Finally, here was a route to independence.

"What do I have to do to be a doctor?"

"You must study hard," Gurumukh Singh told her. "Admission to medical school isn't easy. You need to do very well in school and college."

Rajkumari went to her room. Lying on her bed, she mulled over the conversation. Then abruptly she jumped up, opened her schoolbook and began to study.

Two months went by. Rajkumari brought home her report card. Before dinnertime she handed it to her mother for her signature. Kuldip glanced at it and was shocked. "Is this really your report card, Rajkumari?" Kuldip asked.

"Yes," Rajkumari said, feeling triumphant.

Kuldip turned to Bhajan, "Look at her marks! Amazing!"

"Let me see," Darashan pulled the card out of his mother's hand and read it. "She studies day and night. No wonder she has top marks and is first in her class. I'd be first if I studied hard."

Kuldip was annoyed. "What's wrong with studying hard? You play all the time. Do you want her to play day and night like you?"

"I don't need to. I'm going to be a famous cricketer," Darashan announced.

"That's an awfully ambitious goal, Darashan," Gurumukh

Singh commented.

Rajkumari started to fight with Darashan. "Study hard and then let's see if you can do as well as I have."

"I don't need to." Darashan glared at her.

"Be quiet, you two," said Ranjit Singh.

"I think I know why Rajkumari is studying so hard," said Gurumukh Singh. "She wants to be a doctor."

"A doctor?!" exclaimed Kuldip, thrilled that her daughter would have such aspirations.

"Yes. A doctor, so she can live independently," said Gurumukh Singh. "Am I right, Rajkumari?"

Rajkumari didn't respond.

Kuldip wondered – could a woman become a doctor and still marry and have children?

"That's a great idea," said Darashan, forgetting his jealousy. "We'll have a doctor right in the house. We won't have to pay someone to treat us if we get sick. We'll save money!"

Ranjit Singh normally ignored dinnertime small talk. But now he banged his fist on the table. "My daughter will marry after graduation. Her parents and grandparents will find a husband for her."

Rajkumari, her eyes on fire, flashed her father an angry glance. She stalked out of the room. "I'll eat with Bhajanma," she hissed.

Gurumukh Singh was annoyed that Ranjit Singh had ruined a pleasant evening and interrupted the jovial conversation. "Ranjit," he said." Rajkumari is young and immature. Let her dream for now. We can worry about medical school when she's older. She's doing well in school. Don't discourage her."

Bhajan foresaw trouble. Rajkumari could be argumentative and rebellious, and never obeyed orders unless she believed they were fair. With any luck, Rajkumari would mellow with time and forget about a medical education. After all, Bhajan knew Ranjit Singh would never yield, even if Rajkumari succeeded and achieved her goal. She also knew that Rajkumari wouldn't give up easily.

"Father and daughter are alike," she observed to Gurumukh Singh that night.

That year Rajkumari was first in her class.

And several years later, in her last year of high school, she ranked seventh in the entire district in the matriculate examination. Her name was published in the newspapers, and she received a scholarship for a college education. Neighbors poured in to congratulate her the night the result was announced. The family and neighbors celebrated with a spontaneous party.

In her interscience examination, she did extremely well, ranking second. The moment of decision had arrived, and Rajkumari had made up her mind.

She casually informed Bhajan and Kuldip, "I plan to apply for medical school admission."

Bhajan and Kuldip were thrilled. But Bhajan asked Kuldip not to say a word to Ranjit Singh. "I'll speak to Rajkumari's grandfather first," she said.

"Let me think about it," said Gurumukh Singh.

The next morning he visited a doctor he knew to learn more about a medical education. The information he received upset him. When he returned home in the middle of the day, Bhajan and Kuldip were surprised to see him. "Why are you home?" Bhajan asked. "Are you sick?"

"I need to talk to you," he said

Kuldip stopped cooking in the kitchen and stood behind the door to listen.

Bhajan settled down on the couch. She could guess what this was about.

"Do you realize what medical students have to do?" he asked.

"They do whatever they have to in order to become a doctor," Bhajan answered.

"Medical students dissect dead bodies." He looked at Bhajan for a reaction to his words.

She was unperturbed. "What's wrong with that? She dissected frogs in college. A doctor needs to operate on live people.

They need to practice on dead people first."

Behind the door, Kuldip shuddered.

"And she'll have to work with boys," he added.

"Doctors work with other doctors. It only makes sense."

Bhajan's calm responses and rational thinking irked Gurumukh Singh. He continued his argument, "She'll have to touch men's bodies." Surely these words would bring Bhajan to her senses, he thought.

"When a mother cares for a baby she touches him," said Bhajan. "A doctor's touch is like God's touch. Anyone who thinks that touch is immoral is a wicked person."

Kuldip, hearing the conversation, was impressed. Kuldip herself felt utterly incapable of arguing about anything with anybody.

Gurumukh Singh was bewildered by his wife's answers, but he went on: "What about her marriage? What if her husband's family doesn't approve of her profession?"

"She shouldn't marry into a family that doesn't approve of her profession."

"Will we find a husband for her?"

"Yes, we will. I know several married lady doctors. Besides, Rajkumari wants to be independent."

"What do you mean?"

"She wants to support herself."

"She does? Why?"

"Rajkumari observes the world carefully. She's seen widows suffer in our society, and she's seen that no matter how well a husband treats his wife, there's a difference between her own money and the money her husband gives her."

"All these years, have you been uncomfortable living off my income?"

"I would have liked to have my own resources," replied Bhajan. "But when I was young, I had no choice. Women of our class didn't work outside their homes. I had to walk the path society laid down for me. If *I* had the opportunity, *I* would study medicine."

Gurumukh Singh sighed, "I've spent my entire life with you, but I feel like I hardly know you. It turns out you think of yourself as a dependent person."

"That's the reality," Bhajan said matter of factly. "And I accept it. I like to think I have a right to your income."

Gurumukh Singh laughed. "I'm pleased to hear that. I suppose Raj wants financial independence."

"Yes. And she doesn't want an arranged marriage. She says she doesn't want to exhibit herself."

Gurumukh Singh sighed again. "I guess we'll have to postpone her marriage. For now I won't think about it."

His tacit approval pleased Kuldip and Bhajan.

Bhajan asked Kuldip to talk to Ranjit Singh that night about Rajkumari's plans, so that he would have time to get used to the idea.

Terrified, Kuldip informed her husband of Rajkumari's plans, begging him not to oppose them before at least talking to his father and mother.

"I don't need to consult anybody about my daughter's future," Ranjit Singh bellowed. "The answer is no." Everyone heard him.

The next morning he confronted Rajkumari. "You have your mother and everyone else wrapped around your little finger. Why do you think a girl like you wants to be a doctor?"

"Why do *boys* study medicine?" Rajkumari countered. Her angry voice and sharp words matched those of her father.

"I plan to arrange your marriage," said Ranjit Singh. "A woman's place is in her home."

"I don't *want* to marry."

"It's not your decision."

Kuldip and Bhajan were quietly listening.

"That's what you think." Rajkumari's voice was low, her eyes on fire. "It's my decision. I have a scholarship. I can pay my own way. I don't need your help."

Bhajan saw that the situation was rapidly deteriorating. She stepped forward, "Rajkumari, please go to your room," she said.

Ranjit Singh, Bhajan knew, still lived in the past, the time of his glorious youth in Pakistan. He hadn't noticed that society had evolved. These days, girls traveled by themselves, attended college and worked in offices. But as far as he was concerned, a woman's place was in her home.

She turned to him now. "Ranjit, times have changed. We live in a different society now. Please don't try to stop Rajkumari. Maybe someday she'll be a famous doctor."

Used to winning family arguments, Ranjit Singh refused to yield. "Rajkumari will not study medicine," he declared. "Those are my final words."

Bhajan tried again. "She's a smart girl. If you restrict her choices, she'll be unhappy for the rest of her life. You're her father. You must think of her future."

"I am thinking of her future," Ranjit Singh said, "I know what's best for her."

Kuldip heard the exchange and started to cry.

In her room, Rajkumari began to think about her next move. She knew her father would never yield and that her grandparents and mother would end up reluctantly withdrawing their consent. The family wasn't going to let her to study medicine after all. At dinnertime that night everyone was quiet. Palpable tension filled the room. Rajkumari retired to her room immediately afterwards.

Darashan followed her and closed the door. "They're being unfair, Raj. I don't know how to help you. I would if I could, but I don't know how. I'm afraid even God isn't going to be able to change our father's mind."

Rajkumari started to cry, and Darashan quietly withdrew, closing the door behind him.

The next morning, after the men had left for the day, she turned to her mother and grandmother. "What's your decision?" she asked.

Teary-eyed, Kuldip said, "Rajkumari, your father is a strong-willed man."

Bhajan couldn't bring herself to look at Rajkumari. "It's disgraceful," she thought. "Not one of us can stand up to Ranjit's irrational behavior."

"Study something else," she advised Rajkumari. Overnight, she'd thought of a few famous and educated women in different fields. She offered them as role models. "Queen Vijayadevi is a famous leader," she pointed out. "And Premkumari is a College Dean. Or how about Snehalatadevi? She's a famous mathematician."

Rajkumari smiled cynically. The smile touched Bhajan's heart. "I'm sorry, Rajkumari. I'm helpless. Ranjit is so stubborn!"

A short while later, Rajkumari exited the apartment without a word. Bhajan and Kuldip let her go. "She needs to calm down," Bhajan thought to herself. "She's probably just going to visit a friend."

CHAPTER 8

Rajkumari made her way to a nearby shop in a bustling commercial district.

There, busily entering figures into a columned notebook, she found the proprietor—her family's old acquaintance Balavant Singh. A glass cabinet near the entrance displayed rolls of elegant clothing material. A few rolls lay open on the countertop. The shop's walls were lined with shelves bearing colorful rolls of cloth as well.

Like Rajkumari's family, Balavant Singh was a refugee. He and his grandmother had lived near Rajkumari's family when each had moved to Delhi from their homes in Pakistan. He'd visited Gurumukh Singh's shop shortly after his arrival. "I need a job," he'd said. "Any job will do."

"How old are you?" Gurumukh Singh had asked.

"Fourteen."

"You should be in school."

Fighting tears, he'd protested, "But I must support myself and my grandmother."

"Don't you have any other relatives?" Gurumukh Singh had asked.

"No. Just an uncle in Punjab. He sent us money, but we've spent it all. My grandmother had to sell her jewelry. We have nothing left."

Gurumukh Singh didn't ask what happened to his parents or the rest of the family. He understood that like so many others, they must have been killed at the time of the partition.

Gurumukh Singh offered Balavant Singh a part-time job in his own shop and referred him to another shopkeeper who needed help. Then he dragged the reluctant boy home with him for the evening meal.

There Balavant Singh answered Bhajan's questions in a soft voice, never speaking unless spoken to. Young Rajkumari badgered him with questions.

"How old are you?"

"Do you play sports?"

"What school do you go to?"

"Do you have a brother or a sister?"

When he mumbled his responses, she ordered him to speak louder. Finally, Kuldip told her to leave him in peace.

"My grandmother will be waiting for me," he said after the meal. Bhajan packed up some food for him to take home to her. He thanked her and went on his way.

When Gurumukh Singh told Bhajan about the boy's reluctance to accept the invitation for dinner, Bhajan observed, "He thinks a meal at our home is charity. He'd rather just get an advance."

"He has an uncle in Punjab," said Gurumukh Singh. "I wonder why they aren't living with him."

"His grandmother must have her reasons," said Bhajan.

When Balavant Singh first visited Gurumukh Singh he'd been a sad, skinny boy. As time passed, he gained weight, but the sad expression never left his face. He rarely smiled, and spoke only when absolutely necessary.

Eventually he learned the business and managed to rent a small stall of his own. He stopped working for Gurumukh Singh, but before leaving he told Gurumukh Singh, "I'll never forget what you've done for me and my grandmother. If you ever need help, please call me. I'll be at your service."

"We're happy to see you succeed," Gurumukh Singh replied. "Keep in touch."

When Bhajan heard a couple years later that his grandmother had passed away, Gurumukh Singh and Bhajan paid him a visit and offered their condolences.

Bhajan decided he must be lonely. "He's still young," she told Gurumukh Singh. "But in a few years I'll try to find a bride for him."

She didn't forget him. When he reached his early twenties, she sent for him. He came by with a package of sweets. After a few preliminaries, she said, "I'm pleased to hear you're doing so well. You have your own shop now. But you need a wife so you can have a family. Do you want me to find a bride for you?"

Balavant Singh was touched. "I'm not quite ready for marriage yet," he said. "But I'm grateful for the offer. I'll contact you when I'm ready."

He never came back. But one day he spotted Rajkumari shopping with a friend near his store. He stopped her and inquired about everyone in the family. Rajkumari told him everyone was fine and went on her way.

At dinnertime that night, Rajkumari mentioned the meeting.

"Is he married?" Kuldip asked. "Does he have a wife?"

She shrugged her shoulders. "He didn't say anything about a wife," Rajkumari answered. "Why should I worry about his wife?"

Gurumukh Singh laughed, "Because your grandmother and mother have decided that he needs a bride."

Rajkumari snickered. "He's old. He must be married."

"He's probably in his twenties," Bhajan said.

"That's ancient," Rajkumari told her.

"Are you saying I'm ancient?" Darashan asked.

"You sure act like you're ancient," said Rajkumari.

"You won't be sixteen forever," said Darashan.

Everyone laughed and the discussion ended.

The next day Balavant Singh visited Gurumukh Singh in his shop. After a long pause, he blushed and struggled to find words.

"Go on," Gurumukh Singh encouraged him.

"I wish to marry your granddaughter," he finally blurted. "I have money. My uncle is rich. My grandmother always refused his help because he married a woman she didn't approve of. But after her death, he came over and made amends."

"Now he visits me when he can. He tried to arrange a marriage for me, but I refused."

His eyes downcast, he said, "I hope you'll accept my proposal."

Gurumukh Singh was taken aback by the unexpected proposition. "I must consult my family," he said.

Balavant Singh agreed. "I live in just one room, but I can

easily buy a flat and offer Rajkumari all the comforts a woman could want. She can continue her education, too, if she chooses."

That night after dinner, Gurumukh Singh presented the proposal to the family.

Darashan laughed. "Good!" he said. "Get rid of her. He won't accept any dowry, so we'll save a lot of money."

"No!" shrieked Rajkumari.

Bhajan thought it over carefully. "He's too old for Raj," she said. "Also, he's a quiet, subdued man and he doesn't have any close family. He's not right for our bubbly, outgoing girl."

"You're right," said Darashan, winking at Rajkumari. "She needs a man who will beat her."

Kuldip told him to be quiet.

"What do you think, Ranjit?" Bhajan asked her son.

"He's too old for her," Ranjit agreed.

"As a courtesy, I'll invite him for a visit," said Gurumukh Singh.

"Fine. But I won't be here," announced Rajkumari. "I'll go visit a friend."

The next week Balavant Singh visited with a box of sweets. Bhajan and Kuldip had prepared special snacks for him, and Gurumukh Singh stayed home to welcome him. Bhajan asked Balavant Singh about his uncle's farm, which he described in detail.

"Our farm was just like that," Bhajan sighed. Gurumukh Singh discussed business with him until at last he brought the conversation around to the topic at hand. "Rajkumari is still young and immature," said Gurumukh Singh. "I'm afraid we've decided to decline the offer." Balavant Singh didn't express any emotion. After thanking the family for considering his proposal, he left.

Kuldip and Bhajan were sad. "He's so handsome!" Bhajan said. "I could easily find a lovely bride for him."

"He has money, too," Kuldip added.

"He still has that sad expression, though," Bhajan observed.

"A wife may change him," Gurumukh Singh said.

A week later, Gurumukh Singh invited Balavant Singh for a cup of coffee." My wife and daughter-in-law will be happy to find a bride for you," he said.

Balavant Singh shook his head. "No. Other women don't interest me."

Gurumukh Singh told Bhajan what Balavant Singh had said.

"He's a unique man," said Bhajan. "I'm impressed. He'll make a wonderful husband."

After a few months, Rajkumari and Darashan ran into Balavant Singh on a shopping expedition and were embarrassed. But Balavant Singh showed no sign of bitterness and asked about the family.

That night Darashan told the family of the meeting and teased Rajkumari. "That man pines for you, Raj. Romeo didn't love Juliet as much that guy loves you. Don't torture him – marry him."

Rajkumari made a face and Kuldip told Darashan to shut up.

Since then Bhajan had heard through acquaintances that Balavant Singh was still single – turning down all proposals put forth by other families.

Now here was Rajkumari turning up on her own in Balavant Singh's store. When he had recovered from the shock of seeing his beloved unexpectedly before him, Balavant Singh offered her a chair and went next door to order a Mangola. He didn't ask questions, and instead waited for Rajkumari to speak. She just sat there, holding the Mangola bottle and stared at the floor.

Finally, she stammered, "I'm ready...I mean, I will..." She broke off.

"Say what you want, Rajkumari."

"I want to marry you," she said in a barely audible voice.

Balavant Singh was stunned. He wasn't sure he could believe her. "Why, Rajkumari?" he asked, trying to contain the joy overflowing from his heart. "Why have you changed your mind?"

"Two conditions," said Rajkumari. "I'll marry you if you allow me to study medicine, and if we can get married right away. And don't tell anyone. If my father finds out, he'll kill us."

"I'll marry you tomorrow, if you want," said Balavant Singh. "But tell me – have you resolved to walk away from your family because they won't allow you to study medicine?"

"Yes." She started to cry.

"Will you be happy with me?"

"I'll be very unhappy if I don't study medicine," Rajkumari sobbed.

"Don't cry, Rajkumari. I know you don't love me, but I love you, and couples do learn to love each other after an arranged marriage. You'll learn to love me, and smart as you are, you'll make a wonderful doctor."

Rajkumari wiped her tears and tried to smile. "I've already filled out the forms to apply to medical college. I'll drop them off this afternoon."

"Come to the shop early tomorrow morning."

"I will. Now I must go. I don't want anyone to see me."

The next day Balavant Singh anxiously waited for Rajkumari. "Will she change her mind?" he worried, his eyes focused on the road.

His heart beat violently when he saw her turn the corner onto his street. He closed the shop and asked the shopkeeper next door to accompany him to the courthouse for a registered marriage. Surprised, the shopkeeper told his assistant that he would be gone for a few hours.

The trio went to the courthouse in a taxi. Wordlessly, Rajkumari signed all the papers and mumbled responses to any questions directed at her. The shopkeeper witnessed the marriage, and after the formalities were completed, congratulated the couple. Balavant Singh wondered what he should do next. The shopkeeper suggested a lunch to celebrate the marriage, but Rajkumari politely declined.

"You two can celebrate. I don't want anyone to see us and tell my father." Then she turned to Balavant Singh. "Please come to my home tomorrow morning at 10:30. Make sure the men are out of the house. We have to go away. We can't let my father find us."

"Don't worry," Balavant Singh assured her. "I'll find a discreet location for us to spend a couple of weeks. No one will find us. We can go away for a whole month if you want."

Rajkumari thanked the shopkeeper, waved goodbye and

was gone.

She went home. There she packed a small bag and hid it under her bed. At dinnertime she talked about a yellow sari she wanted to buy, and said she'd like to go shopping with a friend. Kuldip and Bhajan looked at each other and smiled. They were pleased to see her talking and acting like her old self again.

The next morning Gurumukh Singh and Ranjit Singh had their breakfast and left for the shop. Then Darashan, late as usual, rushed out.

From a taxi parked on a nearby street, Balavant Singh watched them leave. The prospect of facing Rajkumari's mother and grandmother terrified him. "What will I say?" he fretted. "I married your daughter and didn't bother to inform you?"

After sitting paralyzed for a long while in the car, he at last forced himself to mount the stairs to Rajkumari's apartment and rang the bell.

Rajkumari opened the door. "Please, come in," she said.

"Is that your friend, Rajkumari?" asked Bhajan from the kitchen.

Kuldip peered out from the kitchen. "It's Balavant," she said, surprised.

"Balavant! At this hour?" Bhajan pushed away the dal she was washing, and was about to step into the living room to welcome him, but before she had a chance, Rajkumari dragged Balavant Singh into the kitchen. "I married Balavant yesterday," she announced in a dry, emotionless voice.

Kuldip and Bhajan froze. Words failed Bhajan. Kuldip's eyes brimmed with tears. Finally, Bhajan said, "You are your father's daughter."

"My father controls all of you," said Rajkumari. "One man's whims rule this family. I've found my way out. I know Ranjit Singh will try to shoot Balavant when he learns of our marriage. Please stop him. That's all I ask."

She fetched the bag from her room and, dragging Balavant Singh with her, marched out the door. Balavant Singh paused at the threshold and turned to Bhajan, "Majee, I apologize for marrying

91

your grand-daughter secretly. I didn't wish to hurt you, but Rajkumari…" he tried to find the right words.

Trying to compose herself, Bhajan asked, "Where are you going?"

"I won't tell you," said Rajkumari, curtly. "We need to hide from Ranjit Singh."

Kuldip started to cry.

Walking down the stairs, Rajkumari kept her eyes focused straight ahead, not turning back to look at her mother and grandmother who were standing outside the apartment door to watch her go.

"Wait!" Kuldip suddenly cried, and began to run after them.

Bhajan blocked her path, "No – it's too late. She may be our daughter, but she's Balavant's wife now." Kuldip turned sadly back.

Back in the apartment, Kuldip picked up the phone.

"No," said Bhajan.

"But what shall we do?" exclaimed Kuldip. "We need to inform the men."

"No. Give Rajkumari and Balavant time to get away. Ranjit must not find them today."

"But how long can we hide the truth?"

"I'll call Rajkumari's grandfather."

Bhajan dialed the shop number. Gurumukh Singh answered. "I have to visit a doctor," she said. "Please come home."

"Can't Kuldip go with you?"

"She's sick too."

"You were fine this morning."

"Please come home."

Gurumukh Singh gave up. He turned to his son, "Your mother is sick. I have to take her to a doctor."

Busy with a customer, Ranjit Singh nodded.

When Gurumukh Singh arrived, one look at weeping Kuldip and Bhajan's stricken face told him there was bad news. "What happened?" he asked.

"Rajkumari married Balavant Singh yesterday," said Bhajan.

"They've left the city."

Overwhelmed, Gurumukh Singh sat down on the sofa.

"She's gone," said Bhajan. "We need to deal with Ranjit now."

The door flew open and Darashan rushed in. "I forgot an important paper," he said. He stopped in his tracks when he saw everyone's faces. "Why are you all so upset?"

"Rajkumari married Balavant yesterday," Bhajan told him.

"What?!"

"They went away this morning."

Darashan held his head and began pacing the room. Suddenly he exploded, "She didn't want to marry him! Bauji drove her to it because he wouldn't let her study medicine. What kind of life will she have with a husband she doesn't want?"

"It will be like an arranged marriage," Kuldip said.

"To an unwanted husband."

"It will work out."

"One crazy man runs this family," Darashan raged. "I failed her, too. We both could have walked away. I could have supported her."

"Darashan, stop it," Gurumukh Singh said.

"Rajkumari is gone. What's done is done." Bhajan said.

But Kuldip snapped at Darashan. "Your sister deserted the family and married a man without our permission. Our community will laugh at us. What about our *ijjat*? Instead of blaming her, you're blaming your father. He had her best interests at heart."

"Oh, so now the issue is Bauji – as usual. He's ruined Rajkumari's life, but everyone's wondering how to pacify his wounded ego. And who cares about our *ijjat*? Is our family's honor really more important than your daughter's happiness?"

"He's right," thought Bhajan.

"Just tell him she got married and there's nothing he can do about it," said Darashan. "I'll try to find them. Let's bring them home and then marry her off with a proper ceremony. Balavant is a nice man. He'll try to make her happy."

No one responded.

"Say something."

"Darashan, your father isn't going to accept her decision so easily."

"This is an unbalanced, dysfunctional family."

"Darashan, stop," Bhajan said. "Stop cursing your father. He has a right to do what he did. Most families don't allow their daughters to attend college at all, let alone medical school."

"She's right, Darashan," said Gurumukh Singh.

"I'm going to find her," declared Darashan.

He stormed out of the apartment, letting the door bang behind him.

He searched the railroad station and bus stands. Then he went to Balavant Singh's shop, which was closed. He saw the neighboring shopkeeper and inquired about the couple. At first the man refused to say anything. But when Darashan told him Rajkumari was his sister and that he desperately needed to find her, the shopkeeper started talking. "They went away. Balavant Singh's new wife is afraid of her father; she thinks he might harm them. You must have a crazy family. What's so bad about Balavant Singh? He's one of the nicest men in the world. Your sister is lucky."

"Where are they?" Darashan asked.

"Nobody knows. They didn't tell me and I didn't ask."

"Are they in Delhi?"

"No. They went to some other town."

Darashan thanked him. Next he tried the building where Balavant Singh had been living. The room was padlocked, so he knocked at the adjacent flat. "Balavant has left town for a few days," said the old lady who answered the door.

Defeated, Darashan went to Bhushan's home and slept there.

That evening he called Maya and told her what had happened. "Why didn't she talk to me?" Maya asked. "Maybe my father could have convinced your father."

"Even God wouldn't be able to convince my father," Darashan said. "He's a stubborn, irrational man. Everyone in the family humors him."

"How can you speak like that about your father?" asked Maya.

"Maya, I've just lost my beloved sister. My father's not going allow us to see her after this."

"I'll visit her and so can you, as long as your father doesn't know."

Late that night Gurumukh Singh came home by himself with an anxious look on his face. "Where's Ranjit?" Bhajan asked.

"I don't know," said Gurumukh Singh. "After we closed the shop, I told him about the marriage. He went berserk. I couldn't reason with him. He kept shouting, 'Where is she? Where is her husband?' He was so loud a crowd collected around us. Finally, he broke through the crowd and ran off. I couldn't stop him."

"I'm glad Darashan's not home," Bhajan said. "He might try to argue with Ranjit, which would be a disaster."

Fearfully, the family waited for Ranjit Singh. Two hours later, he burst through the door, his eyes burning red, a murderous expression on his face. In his hand was a revolver.

He approached Kuldip and shook her by the shoulders. "Tell me, woman – where is your daughter? She and her husband will pay for disobeying my orders."

Kuldip sobbed, "I don't know. They're not in Delhi."

Ranjit Singh started pacing back and forth, "You spoiled her. You encouraged her to disobey me."

"She's your daughter, headstrong like you," thought Bhajan.

"Please—sit down and have some dinner," she said and went into the kitchen.

"I'll deal with my daughter first," Ranjit Singh spat.

Bhajan served the food and set it on the table. "Eat, Ranjit and then we can talk."

When Ranjit Singh smelled the food, hunger overpowered him. He sat down.

"I'll go see a lawyer tomorrow," Gurumukh Singh said after dinner. "We'll see if the marriage is valid."

"Rajkumari's of age. She's legally married," Bhajan said.

"After this episode, no one else will marry her."

Ranjit Singh looked at her and in a cold voice declared, "I will deal with my daughter."

For the first time since Ranjit Singh's escape from Pakistan, Gurumukh Singh stood up to his son. "Ranjit," he said calmly. "You will have to shoot me before you hurt my granddaughter or her husband."

Bhajan stepped forward. "Me, too."

Ranjit Singh glared at his parents, threw the thali against the wall and, rambling incoherently, stalked out of the apartment, slamming the door behind him.

In his fury, Ranjit Singh had left the revolver on the table. Bhajan took it into her room and hid it there.

Ranjit Singh returned late that night and slept on the sofa.

The next morning, the men breakfasted wordlessly and went to the shop. Nobody talked about Rajkumari.

After the men had left for the day, several women from the building dropped in.

"What happened last night?"

"What was all that screaming about?"

Kuldip was glum, her eyes red and swollen, but Bhajan told the truth.

"Rajkumari got married yesterday."

"Without your permission?"

"Yes."

"Is he of a different religion?"

"No."

"Was it a Love marriage?"

"No."

"Is she pregnant?" one woman whispered.

Bhajan couldn't help laughing at the notion. "No."

"Then why?"

"She wants to go to medical college."

"So? What's wrong with that? Our Rajkumari a doctor! We'll be so proud of her."

"Her father didn't want her to study medicine, so she

married Balavant Singh. He loved her. In fact, he had brought a proposal earlier, but we refused. He has his own shop."

"Our Rajkumari must have a wedding! Let's celebrate. I know a hall…"

As the women chattered on, it dawned on Bhajan that times were indeed changing.

Men from the building visited that night. They, too, seemed perplexed by the outrage against Rajkumari.

"I wouldn't allow my daughter to study Medicine either, but once she gets married, her husband will decide what she can and can't do."

"Think of the money she'll make. I wouldn't mind sending my daughter to medical school if she could get in."

Ranjit Singh was speechless.

Darashan showed up after the neighbors had gone. He had hoped everybody would be in bed, but the family was still awake, sitting around the table. An open box of sweets lay on the dining table. He held his breath.

Ranjit Singh stood up. "Darashan, Rajkumari is dead to our family. I won't allow her to set foot in our home and I forbid you to visit her."

Darashan quickly glanced at the faces in the room. His mother was wiping tears. Bhajan nodded imperceptibly. "I won't," Darashan muttered.

Bhajan breathed a sigh of relief. For now the issue was resolved.

The next morning, after Gurumukh Singh and Ranjit Singh had left, Bhajan said to Darashan, "Disowning Rajkumari is the best solution for the time being. It breaks my heart, but at least this pacifies his rage for now. You can visit her. Just be discreet. For now we have no choice."

"Yes, you do," Darashan countered. "Stand up to your son."

Bhajan ignored him.

"After she returns with Balavant Singh, please visit Raj and tell her that her mother and grandparents send her their blessings."

Kuldip cried as she heard Bhajan's words. "She'll finish her education and will be a doctor someday," Bhajan went on. "That thought is a ray of sunshine in this darkness."

Kuldip smiled, though her face was still tear-stained.

Bhajan fetched the revolver from her room and handed it to Darashan. "Get rid of this," she said.

Four weeks later, Darashan and Maya visited the lady's hostel at the medical school. Darashan waited in the visitor's room and watched as Maya disappeared into the depths of the hostel. Girls walked in and out, eyeing him curiously. After what seemed an eternity, Maya reappeared, dragging Rajkumari with her.

"Here's your beloved sister," she announced and vanished into the hostel again, calling behind her, "when you want to leave, send for me. I'll be playing table tennis."

Darashan had difficulty meeting Rajkumari's eye.

"How can I face her?" he wondered. "Instead of standing up to my father and arguing on her behalf, I acted like a spectator. The fact is I'm a weakling."

Rajkumari stood erect and proud. She had changed in just one month's time. A thoughtful expression had replaced her usual cheerful, mischievous demeanor, and instead of two loose braids, she wore her long hair in a single tight braid down her back. The girl who usually chattered continuously had uttered not a single word. She faced Darashan and was quiet.

For the first time in his life, Darashan was tongue-tied.

With effort, he lifted his eyes to her face. Trying to compose himself, he offered her a package, "This is from Ma and Bhajanma."

"Tell them I don't need anything."

"Raj, they'll be hurt if you refuse refreshments they made for you. They know you don't need anything, but they want you to have it."

"I can't accept it." Tears brimmed in her eyes.

A few giggling girls glanced at the pair and walked away.

"Raj, no one is angry with you. It's just that..." Darashan groped for the right words. "Raj, the family failed you. *I* failed you. I should have..." He broke off.

"What could you have done? You have no income. You

couldn't support me, Darashan. I'm not angry with you."

"You have every right to be angry."

"No. I blame myself. Girls are supposed to be obedient, not ambitious like me,"

"Raj, can I visit you sometimes?"

"Of course! I want you to visit."

Darashan asked the question that had been plaguing him. "Rajkumari, are you happy with Balavant?"

Her face crumpled. "He's very happy," she said. "He'll do anything for me. Not many girls find a doting husband like mine. I'll get used to married life."

She looked at Darashan with concern. "Is there any danger that Ranjit Singh will try to hurt Balavant?"

Darashan noticed that she referred to her father by his name, Ranjit Singh. He was no longer Bauji to her.

"No," said Darashan. "The family has agreed to disown you. He's promised that he won't hurt you or your husband."

"Raj," he went on. "Ma and Bhajanma want to see you. Can they visit you here in secret?"

"No," said Rajkumari. "You blend in here, but they wouldn't. Someone would snitch. Balavant is planning to buy a flat. They can visit me there."

Darashan was relieved. He had feared Rajkumari might refuse to see her mother and grandmother, which would have devastated them.

Maya reappeared with a young medical student. They were laughing and talking. "I'm playing with a champion today," the student boasted. Then she asked Rajkumari, "Are you related to your visitors?"

"This is my brother."

"And future sister-in-law?" The girl winked.

"Ask *them*," Rajkumari replied, playfulness returning to her face for a moment.

Darashan and Maya were embarrassed. Maya blushed.

"I hope your future sister-in-law will visit often," said the student. "She can teach us to play table tennis."

"She's welcome any time," said Rajkumari. "She can spend the night in my room."

"Your brother is spoken for," said the student. "Do you have any other handsome brothers who aren't already taken?"

"No," said Rajkumari. "But I have cousins."

"Make sure they're like your brother and husband," said the student. She turned to Maya. "Balavant Singh is a wonderful husband. We all want husbands like him. Rajkumari, is your brother nice like him?"

"Maya should answer that question," Rajkumari said.

"I'll let you know after our marriage," Maya said, and the three girls giggled.

One of the girls spied the package lying on the table. "I'll take this," she said. "Please bring more – we need food!"

"Save a little for me," said Rajkumari.

Darashan was relieved that, even if only indirectly, Rajkumari had accepted the package.

Promising Rajkumari he would visit again soon, Darashan left with Maya.

"All of the girls are so proud of Rajkumari," Maya commented as they headed out. 'She has guts,' they say. Everyone thinks she's so poised and elegant."

Darashan was sad. "She looks different," he said. "She walks and talks like an older woman. So serious! She rarely smiles. She's so unlike the sister I used to have."

"The old Rajkumari will come back," Maya assured him, though in fact she wasn't sure.

The next day Darashan and Maya visited Balavant Singh in his shop. He welcomed them gladly. "It's nice to have relatives again," he said. "I hope your parents will forgive me for the sake of their daughter, and that we can be part of the family."

"You are part of the family. It's just that…my father…"

"I know," Balavant Singh said. "Someday he'll change his mind."

"Bhajanma and Kuldipma send this package. They plan to visit you soon."

"Balavant Singh is so happy!" Darashan told Bhajanma and Kuldipma that evening. "He looks younger, and he talks and smiles. He worships Rajkumari."

Kuldip and Bhajan were relieved to hear the news.

A few months later, Gurumukh Singh visited Balavant Singh's shop. Balavant Singh touched his feet, and Gurumukh Singh blessed him and handed him an envelope containing 10,000 rupees and a few pieces of jewelry for Rajkumari. "I am grateful," said Balavant Singh. "I'm sure Raj will be pleased with the jewelry."

Balavant Singh searched for a suitable place for them to live. Eventually he located a two-room flat close to the medical school and his shop. After Rajkumari had moved in, Bhajanma and Kuldipma visited for the first time.

Kuldip hugged her daughter and wept. "I don't know when we can welcome you back in our home."

"Don't worry," said Rajkumari, pulling away to fix tea.

Kuldip and Bhajan had brought packages of food. "This is all we can do for you," they said apologetically.

"That's plenty," said Rajkumari. "I never have time to cook."

After that, Kuldip and Bhajan visited often and learned to keep track of Rajkumari's erratic schedule.

Rajkumari had mixed feelings about their visits. Each time they came, the wound she had suffered started to throb again. She tried to act like her old self, but she couldn't be the loving, bubbly daughter of the past. Only with Darashan could she be herself.

Kuldip barely noticed, but deceiving Bhajan was harder. One day Bhajan said, "Rajkumari, we were unfair to you. Can you ever forgive us?"

"I'm not angry," Rajkumari mumbled, and quickly changed the topic, bustling out of the room to fetch a glass of water.

Rajkumari also had to put on an act at night. "I love you," she would murmur, but she couldn't control her body.

"Relax Rajkumari," Balavant would say. "I'm not a lion or tiger. I won't hurt you."

Some nights and weekends she had to stay at the hospital,

and when she was home she pretended to be asleep when Balavant Singh came home. He would pat her hair and murmur, "You're mine, but I'm still waiting. I hope someday you'll really love me."

Rajkumari resolved to love him, but wondered, "Do I even know what true love is?"

Soon Darashan and Maya's wedding was celebrated. Large numbers of people attended and the festivities lasted for days. Rajkumari and Balavant Singh weren't invited, but Balavant Singh dropped off a gift after the event was over.

One day Balavant Singh received a telegram from his uncle's neighbor. "Your cousin has been killed in a truck accident."

Balavant Singh rushed to Punjab.

He returned, despondent, two weeks later. "My poor uncle," he said. "My family disowned him because he married a girl from a family they hated. He had to move with his young bride to another village. Then, after years of hoping, they finally had a son. Now this tragedy happened. My uncle and aunt are devastated."

Balavant Singh and Rajkumari had visited his uncle's home shortly after their marriage. Rajkumari had enjoyed the visit – wandering in the village and on the farm, trying to milk the cows and drive a tractor. The farm had reminded her of Bhajanma's description of the home their family had been forced out of in Pakistan. Balavant Singh's uncle and aunt had adored her. "I wish I had a daughter like you," his aunt had told her.

"You do have one. I'm your daughter," Rajkumari replied.

"Yes. You are," said his aunt. "Visit us often."

Their son, Balavant Singh's young cousin, looked up to him and had been impressed with Rajkumari, for her plans to study medicine.

A couple months after his cousin's death, Balavant Singh received a letter from his uncle:

```
Dear Balavant:
     I no longer have the energy to work my land.
My friends advise me to sell it, but I can't bring
myself to do so. My land is like my mother.
     You are the only relative I have. You will
```

inherit my estate.

I want you to come to live with me. We have a big house, and farming is in your blood. I can teach you the art and science of farming.

I won't be angry if you decline, but if you don't come, I'll have to sell the land.

I know your wife will be a doctor soon, and she may wish to practice in a city near her family. But please know that people in my village would welcome a lady doctor with open arms and worship her like a goddess.

If you do decide to move to my farm, it is my hope that you will have a son as soon as possible. My brother's grandson is my grandson, too. I want to see an heir to my land before I die.

My blessings to you and your wife,
Chachaji.

For Balavant Singh this summons brought back a flood of childhood memories that he had long sought to suppress. He recalled his old home near the family farm, with its ripening wheat gently swaying in the wind, and his younger siblings chasing him through the fields.

He remembered, too, waving goodbye to his parents, brothers and sister, as he set off with his grandmother for a short visit to relatives in another village. Then he remembered that terrifying night, being awakened by his grandmother as she urgently shook him, telling him they had to run – that there was no time for explanations.

He recalled his relatives and fellow villagers walking quietly in the dark, trying to stay hidden from dangerous strangers. Burning village homes glowed in the dark and lit the sky. He could smell the smoke.

He remembered their arrival at the train station, pushing and shoving to get on the train. And he recalled that on the train, he and his Grandmother had met a neighbor from his home village who, hiding in the garden, had witnessed an attack on Balavant's family. The man had barely just managed to escape to save himself. Halting after every word, he had described the attack in awful detail.

Balavant Singh tried to stop the tears streaming down his face. He forced his eyes open, so that the past would stop dancing before his eyes.

He read the letter again and spent the next few days deep in thought. He had opened a shop to support himself in Delhi, and his business had succeeded. But his heart was elsewhere. "I didn't know it until the opportunity presented itself," he thought, "but farming is my calling." He'd loved his uncle's farm. He wanted to go back to the land.

"But what about Rajkumari?" he wondered. Balavant Singh had no idea how she would react to the suggestion. She seemed such a city girl.

When Rajkumari returned home that evening, she was surprised to see him. "Why are you home so early?"

"Sit down, Raj. Read this letter," he said. "I'll fix you a cup of tea."

Rajkumari washed her hands and settled down to read the letter. Her eyes widened. She finished it and turned to Balavant Singh. "What have you decided?"

"I want to go," he said. "My heart is in farming."

She jumped up, hugged and kissed him and then held his hand and danced in circles, pulling him with her until he was dizzy. Her face beamed with joy. "I want to go, too," she exclaimed, jumping up and down like a child.

Her reaction thrilled Balavant Singh, but he was cautious. "Raj, please don't be rash. Think for a few days. You have no idea what village life is like."

"That may be true, but I've heard detailed descriptions of my own family's life on our farm in Punjab. I used to dream of moving there when I was a little girl. Besides, I'd like to practice medicine in a village where my services are really needed."

"But what about your relatives? Your mother and grandmother? Do you really want to move away from them?"

"Other than you and your uncle's family, Darashan and Maya are my only relatives in this world."

Balavant Singh was dismayed. "Rajkumari, how can you be so vindictive? Your whole family loves you dearly. You may not respect your father, but I do. He lost his hand trying to save his home. I know all too well about attachment to the home. We're all victims of the time period we live in, Raj. Please, don't resent your family."

"You have a bigger heart than I."

Balavant Singh sighed. "I wish you would learn to forgive."

She changed the subject. "If I intend to establish a village hospital for deliveries, I'll need a postgraduate degree and surgical experience, which means I'll need to be in Delhi a while longer."

"And I'll need at least six months to sell my business. After that you can live in Delhi for a few years. But Rajkumari, there is another issue..." He hesitated.

"What is it?" Rajkumari said impatiently.

"You read my uncle's letter. He wants an heir to carry his name."

Balavant Singh anxiously scanned Rajkumari's face.

Rajkumari thought for a moment. "That's not impossible. I'll just have to free myself for a month or two after graduation for childbirth."

Balavant Singh's face was glowing. He hugged Rajkumari. "I'll raise the baby on the farm. He'll have a childhood like mine."

Rajkumari laughed. "I've never seen you so happy in my life."

Hugging her tighter, he said, "I never thought I'd see a day in my life when I would have everything I wished for...you, a child, a farm... I'm bursting with joy."

"Maybe I can learn to love this man," Rajkumari thought. He was so giving, and so undemanding, unlike other husbands.

When Rajkumari told Kuldip and Bhajan about her plans, Kuldip protested, "You're moving away from us."

"Yes," said Bhajan, "but she's going to Punjab, her home. She'll have a farm, she'll build her own hospital and she'll have family — Balavant's uncle and aunt, who were lucky to have moved to Indian Punjab before partition. Hopefully, she'll let me come visit her and bathe all the newborn babies."

"Bhajanma, you're dreaming," Rajkumari laughed. "Yes, you can visit me! Please, don't let your son stop you."

Balavant Singh sold the business and moved to his uncle's home, while Rajkumari moved to a ladies' hostel, where Balavant Singh visited her as often as possible.

Rajkumari graduated at the top of her class, and a year later she gave birth to a baby boy. Ecstatic, Balavant Singh named him Balbir.

Darashan announced the news of Balbir's birth at dinnertime. "Rajkumari had a baby – a boy."

The news stunned Ranjit Singh.

As far as he was concerned, the family had no contact with her and he wanted to keep it that way.

Kuldip started to cry. "She's so alone. She needs help."

Gurumukh Singh had planned his next move. "I'm an old man," he declared. "I intend to see my great grandson."

"Maya and I can bring him here," said Darashan. "That way no one has to see Rajkumari."

"I want to see him too," Bhajan said.

Ranjit Singh refused to speak.

The next evening, he faced a roomful of neighbors cooing over the baby.

"Forgive your daughter, Ranjit," an elderly man said. "You're lucky to have a grandson. Enjoy him."

Ranjit Singh glanced at the sleeping baby and sat watching the commotion.

Kuldip cried continuously. Exasperated, Ranjit Singh said, "Go. Stay with your daughter and help her, woman. I can't stand your tears."

Kuldip smiled, packed a small bag and moved in with Rajkumari for a short time to help her. Periodically she would bring the baby home. Ranjit couldn't help noticing how happy everyone was when the baby visited. He relaxed a little.

Rajkumari finished her graduate studies in two years, and soon afterwards Balavant Singh sold their flat in Delhi. They put the funds toward the clinic they planned to build in Punjab. Rajkumari contacted an architect and developed a design for the hospital and dispensary. She sold her furniture, donated her pots and pans and bought the surgical instruments she would need.

Bhajan cried when the time came to bid good-bye to her granddaughter and great-grandson. Gurumukh Singh and Kuldip accompanied Rajkumari to her new home, and Darashan and Maya promised to visit as soon as possible.

As for Ranjit Singh, he refused to see his daughter off, and Rajkumari shed no tears as she waved good-bye to her family.

CHAPTER 9

Gopal returned home after his final college examination. He was confident that he would graduate with high honors. Now he had to sort out what he would do next.

Gopal's mother didn't mince words in laying out her dreams for him. "I want you to earn a graduate degree so you can find a government job with a good salary," she said.

"Aie, I don't need a graduate degree to achieve my goals," he protested. "I went to Delhi seeking power. Now I know better. Power doesn't interest me anymore."

"You don't have to go back to Delhi," said his mother. "You could stay in Pune with our family and go to school here."

"It's not the living arrangement that's an issue," he said. "It's that a graduate degree won't help me achieve my goals."

"But everyone says if you have more education you'll make more money."

Gopal sighed. His mother could barely read and write. She'd spent her entire life in a village. How could she possibly understand?

"Aie," he said. "I don't want a regular job."

"Do you mean that you want to come back to the village? You know our farm can't feed many people."

"No, I don't want to live in the village."

"Then how will you feed your wife and children?"

Now Gopal dropped another bomb. "I don't wish to marry."

To his surprise, his mother laughed. "Are you planning to be a *sannyasi*, then, and cover yourself with ashes and beg for food?"

"No, I want to be a social worker. And I believe a social worker shouldn't marry. A wife and children shouldn't be dragged into the kind of life I intend."

"And what kind of life is that?"

"A life of sacrifice, poverty, scarcity..."

His mother looked at him now with concern. "Gopal, I know you were far too young when your grandfather had to send you away to Pune. And I know you ended up having to beg for food.

108

But you shouldn't let the trauma of that experience drive you now to make a rash decision."

"That experience taught me that money and power are important," said Gopal. "But then I went to Delhi and changed my mind. I learned that money and power won't make me happy. I want to uproot evils like the caste system and classism from our society."

His mother shook her head. "If your goal is to uproot the caste system, you'll need a hundred lives to do it."

A tear slipped from her eye and she wiped it away. "Your brother isn't smart like you. I had hoped you would be a big boss some day and fulfill my dreams."

She smiled at him through her tears. "But whatever you decide to do, I hope it brings you happiness."

Gopal was amazed. She wasn't even educated, and yet she understood. Society dictated that parents could decide what their children should study. But his mother wasn't seeking to exercise that right.

His father, on the other hand, wasn't so understanding. "I'll throw you out of the house!" he raged. A pair of letters from Arun's father, Mr. Varavadekar, aggravated the situation. To Gopal he wrote:

"I consider you Arun's brother and my son, and I wish only the best for you. I am dismayed to learn of your plans. Please finish your postgraduate education before you follow your dreams. Don't drop out now."

To Gopal's father he wrote:

"Gopal is still young and idealistic. He doesn't know what he is running away from. I hope you can make him understand the right course of action."

Gopal's father read Gopal's letter as well as his own. Spurred by Mr. Varavedekar's concern, he harangued Gopal day

109

and night. Gopal began to think about moving away.

Then he received a postcard from Arun: "Gopal – Darashan, George and I are coming to visit you. In fact, we may arrive before this postcard."

Sure enough–before he'd even finished reading the card, two boys rushed to his house, shouting, "Gopaldada, some friends of yours are at the bus stop!"

Mr. Varavadekar had been so upset with Gopal's plans that he'd decided to send Arun to talk some sense into him. "Force him to come back with you," he'd urged. "An intelligent student like Gopal needs rational arguments to convince him. His father is probably just badgering him. We need to make him recognize that he'll be more useful to society as an educated man."

"I'll go if you want me to," Arun had said, "but I'm not sure I can bring him back."

"You should think positively," said his mother.

An idea had occurred to Arun. "Darashan is in Bombay visiting George. He went to see movie stars and the ocean. Maybe I'll ask them to join me."

"That sounds like fun," said his mother, "but don't forget the purpose of your visit."

"George and Darashan can help," Arun insisted.

"I hope so," his mother said. She thought for a moment. "Gopal is from a conservative Brahmin family. They may not welcome non-Brahmins into their home."

Arun laughed, "Gopal doesn't believe in the caste system."

"Yes, but his family probably feels differently," she said. "At least drop him a postcard so he'll be prepared."

Arun had done as she said.

At the bus stop in Gopal's village, Darashan was causing a stir with his tell-tale Sikh turban and beard. No Sikh had ever set foot in the village of Rala before as the guest of somebody's family. Children crowded around the three friends, and adults gaped from a distance.

Amused, George laughed, "I feel like a celebrity."

"I feel like a monkey in a zoo," said Darashan.

News of the guests' arrival spread like wildfire, and throngs of villagers came out of their houses to watch.

Gopal laughed when he saw his friends surrounded by a crowd of children leading them to his house.

"Join the circus parade!" called George.

"This isn't a show," Gopal shouted to the children. "It's time for you to go home."

"Let them be," said George. "They're watching a free movie."

Arun recalled his mother's warning and stopped outside the house. "Gopal, are you sure it's OK for us all to go in?"

Gopal looked at him quizzically before realizing the reason for Arun's hesitation. "Of course you can come in. Just remember, no one's allowed in God's chamber. And please remove your shoes."

Everyone obeyed. Darashan and George were impressed with the front porch that ran the entire width of the house and with the wide swing in the middle of the adjoining room. "Nice to have a swing like this," Darashan said, settling down onto it.

Gopal's mother called out, "Have your guests wash themselves and I'll send out snacks."

They walked to the back courtyard and Gopal poured water on their feet.

"This is the real India," Darashan said. "Our house in Pakistan must have been like this. Now I understand why Bhajanma and Ma miss it so much."

The group seated themselves on a mat. Snacks arrived, and a few kids joined them. It suddenly occurred to Gopal that while a Sikh visiting the family might not be an issue, having a Christian in the house might be another matter. He slipped into the kitchen and whispered to his grandmother, "George is a north Indian Brahmin. His real name is Joru."

"All right," his grandmother responded warily. "Just keep everyone out of God's chamber."

For the next several days, the visit proceeded with no discussion of Gopal's future. Gopal and his friends swam in the

111

river and visited a fort and some temples nearby. They even tried to milk a water buffalo.

On the fourth day, a postcard arrived from Delhi, reminding Arun of his mission.

Arun looked at Gopal sheepishly, holding up the postcard. "I'm supposed to drag you back to Delhi," he said.

"Why would he ever want to go back?" asked Darashan, looking around at the lush greenery. "Life in the village is wonderful."

"If you don't come back with me, my father will just send me back again to fetch you," said Arun.

"So? It'll be a good excuse to visit Gopal again. I'll come with you," said Darashan.

"Why are you bugging Gopal, Arun?" George asked. "Everyone should be free to spend their lives however they want."

"It's my father who wants him back," Arun said. "I'm just the messenger."

"My father's bugging me, too," Gopal told them. "He says I'm a fool for wanting to be a social worker."

"He's right," said Darashan. "Why don't you join Bhushan and become a politician? You can help me in the future when I need permits."

"Permits for what?" George asked.

"How should I know what permit I'll want in the future? It never hurts to have government connections."

Gopal's father had kept himself in check since the guests had arrived. But now the postcard from Arun's father got him going again. He asked Gopal to see him in his room after dinner.

This time, though, Gopal had a strategy. "I'm going to apply to graduate school in Pune," he told his father. "I'll leave with my friends."

In truth, however, he had decided to join the Communist Party.

He had been attracted to communism's tenets when he'd studied the subject in school. Since then, China's invasion of Indian Territory had given him pause, but he would base his life on the ideology's teachings, he decided – not on one communist country's aggressive actions.

Now he just needed some practical experience. He would find a job and a place to live in Bombay, and would join the Party there. After that he could sort out what to do with the rest of his life.

He traveled to Bombay with his friends. On the train he divulged his plans. "You're insane," said Arun. "My parents aren't going to be happy."

"Gopal's a lost cause," groaned George.

"Don't worry," Gopal reassured his friends. "If I decide I hate this life, I can just go back to school next year."

From Bombay he wrote a letter thanking Mr. Varavadekar for his help and interest, and apologizing for disappointing him. He wrote a similar letter to his father and promised to write again.

George asked his father to help Gopal find work. "Gopal, you are an intelligent idiot," George's father said. But he found him a position as a clerk for a shopkeeper he knew. Next, Gopal asked George to help him find accommodations he could afford on his meager salary.

"Do you really want to live like a poor mill worker?" George asked. "You're going to be miserable."

"I'll be glad to live like a mill worker. I need that experience."

"Nobody needs that experience," George insisted. "Though maybe the experience will shake the idealism out of your rotted brain."

George asked for advice from his servant, who directed him to a five-story tenement where a cot was advertised for rent.

George and Gopal went to see the room, located in a run-down area of Bombay.

The building's paint was peeling, and a rickety wooden staircase led to a series of one-room apartments on each floor. Entire families lived in some of the rooms, originally intended for a single person. Children freely wandered in and out of the rooms and played in the verandas and the street. The bathroom facilities consisted of two water taps enclosed by a low concrete wall and four latrines on each floor, located at opposite ends of the building.

Gopal and George knocked on the door of the fifth-floor room that had been advertised. A mill worker, who was half asleep, let them in. He promptly agreed to rent Gopal a cot, accepted one month's rent of 25 rupees and was asleep in a few minutes. The room contained three metal cots set against the wall. Each occupant's clothing hung on a rope tied to nails on the wall. A naked bulb hanging from the ceiling lit the room. Dirty teacups and dishes were heaped in a corner.

George vehemently protested. "You can't live in this hell-hole. I'll share my room with you. My family won't object."

"I'm broke," Gopal said. "I'll be earning 200 rupees a month. I can't afford better accommodations. Besides, I want to live like the poor."

Gopal borrowed money from George and bought a cheap, cotton-filled futon, two bed sheets, a pillow and a pillowcase. Then he moved into his room. He tied a rope across the wall beside his cot to hang his clothes, stored his toothbrush and soap in a basket in one corner, and shoved his small suitcase under the bed. He was all set.

For breakfast, he had tea and toast at a nearby stall. He managed to find a South Indian restaurant that served inexpensive vegetarian food and ate his lunches there. At night, the kindly shopkeeper provided him home cooked food.

The older women in the tenement liked Gopal. Some of them hoped he would marry their daughters, though they knew such a match was unlikely. Gopal didn't announce his caste, but his last name, his speech, and his complexion made clear that he was a college-educated Brahmin. There was much speculation about why he was living there.

Sometimes he played cricket on the road with the tenement children. The kids were thrilled. He brought them small gifts, like balloons, and helped them with their schoolwork. His neighbors appreciated his help and began calling him "Big Boss."

George often invited him for outings. Every time they met,

George hectored him about his living arrangements, warning that the filthy conditions put him at risk for cholera and tuberculosis.

Gopal wrote to his family and told them of his resolution to join the Communist Party. His mother mailed him postcards from time to time, but he never heard from his father.

His brother and cousins visited and were dismayed by the way he lived. "Don't you remember our Uncle's home in Pune?" Gopal reminded them. "We once lived like this with bed bugs and filthy latrines."

"Yes," they agreed. "But we had no choice then. Now you do."

Gopal laughed. "I choose to live here," he said

His cousins and brother went away shaking their heads.

CHAPTER 10

Balavant Singh hurried into the new addition to Rajkumari's maternity hospital. The work was almost finished. A painter stood by with paint cans and brushes.

"Green or blue?" Balavant Singh asked.

"We already painted one of the rooms blue," the painter reminded him.

"Paint this room light green then," said Balavant Singh. "Do you need more help to get the work done in time? Our guests will be arriving in just a couple days."

Before the painter could respond, Rajkumari bustled in. She panted as she spoke. "Darashan just called. He's arriving tomorrow with a flock of relatives from Delhi." She glanced at the work in progress.

"Do you like the colors we've picked?" Balavant Singh asked.

Rajkumari waved her hand dismissively. "Whatever you choose is fine. It just has to be finished in time for the opening ceremony."

"Don't worry, Doctor," one of the painters said. "We'll be finished by sundown tomorrow."

"Leave the painting to me," said Balavant Singh. "You work on sorting out where your relatives will sleep."

She settled onto a stool and frowned.

"What's wrong?" Balavant Singh asked.

"I didn't want to put on a major show. We didn't celebrate when we opened the hospital in the first place, so why are we celebrating for one wing now? This is all because Bhajanma insisted on an opening ceremony."

Balavant Singh turned to her crossly. "All she said was that you've been talking about this new wing for a long time and she was glad to live to see it finished. She just wanted a little ceremony and to get the whole family under one roof for a joyous occasion. The fact that the rest of the world heard about it and invited themselves isn't her fault."

Rajkumari opened her mouth to speak, but Balavant Singh went on.

"Bhajanma never asks anyone for anything, though God knows, she has a right to. She loves you and is proud of your achievements. For once in her life, she's requested a get-together and here you are moaning and groaning about it!" He stalked out of the room.

Chastened, Rajkumari looked around at the room's chaos of brushes and paints.

Balavant Singh was right. The hospital staff had gotten wind of their little family event to mark the opening of the new wing and had simply presumed they would be invited. Then the townspeople had heard about it too, and started to call: "My son and daughter were born in your hospital. Of course we're coming!..." Then medical consultants in the city decided to rent a bus and make the trip with their families. The last straw was the Health Minister, who had telephoned and insisted he wanted to cut a ribbon and make a speech.

To top it off, Balavant Singh and Balbir were throwing themselves into plans for the day. They talked about it incessantly, wrote lists, ordered more and more food, planned for bigger and bigger ceremonial *mandap* and failed to notice Rajkumari's annoyance.

With a sigh, Rajkumari hoisted herself off the stool and went to look into sleeping arrangements for the guests.

Balavant Singh found her almost right away. "Maya called. Her friend, Devaki, is coming. She wants to write about your life. I said she could interview you the day after the opening."

"All right," Rajkumari said wearily. "If there's time for that."

"Varsha also called," said Balavant Singh. Her friend, Rati, will be joining us as well."

Rajkumari threw up her hands. "It's hopeless!" she exclaimed. "From here on out I'm just going with whatever happens. This whole function is beyond my control."

Balavant Singh laughed. "For once in your life you're talking some sense!" He put his hands on her shoulders. "Now smile and welcome your guests with a happy face."

When Darashan arrived with his family, Rajkumari sparkled. Darashan and Maya, together with their son Mohan, their daughter Varsha and her friend Rati, got to work right away helping Balbir and Balavant Singh.

Workers set up a *mandap,* erecting poles covered with colorful strips of cloth, over which they stretched a canopy to shield guests from the sun. They also erected a stage, decorated it, and set up loudspeakers and folding chairs. Rajkumari and Maya ordered what seemed like mountains of food for breakfast, lunch, and dinner for the many guests. Balavant Singh had arranged for a team of cooks to prepare the food, and Balbir had a list of volunteers to serve it. Rajkumari and Balavant Singh's younger son Charan, who was in college, arrived that evening, along with a host of relatives from Delhi. Men and boys slept wherever they could find space on mats that Balavant Singh had borrowed from the townspeople, while women and children slept in bedrooms.

The next day, dressed in finery as if for a wedding, Rajkumari, Balavant Singh, Balbir, Charan, Darashan, Maya, and Mohan welcomed the guests. Varsha and Rati ran around with cameras and giggled.

The ceremony started on time. Balavant Singh said a few words of welcome. Then the Health Minister cut the ribbon to the new wing, and Rajkumari led a tour, explaining how the different rooms would be used. In a series of speeches, the Health Minister and several of Rajkumari's colleagues spoke at length – lauding Rajkumari as an inspiration to women, and expressing gratitude for all she had done to improve health conditions in the region. Rajkumari was overwhelmed. She was only doing what she had always wanted.

With the speeches over, Rajkumari readied herself to approach the microphone. But Balbir said, "wait," and grabbed it first. "Now Rajkumari's grandmother will say a few words," he announced.

The audience started to clap.

Maya helped Bhajanma climb the steps. With her gray hair,

white sari and blouse, Bhajanma was a contrast to her lovely daughter-in-law in her colorful blue sari. Her peaceful, wrinkled face was radiant and joyful. Maya supported her. Balbir held the microphone. In a clear voice, Bhajan began, "My granddaughter built this hospital with her husband's help. It has prospered beyond everyone's wildest expectations. I am proud of her and so is our whole family. I am gratified and pleased that all of you have joined our family for this happy occasion. Thank you."

Everyone including the health minister stood up and clapped for such a long time that Rajkumari wondered when it would stop. Finally Bhajanma raised her hand and the crowd quieted.

Darashan glanced at his father who was looking on impassively, his arms at his sides, refusing to clap. "Bhajanma had to know that her son wouldn't approve of her speech," Darashan thought. "But for once in her life, she didn't care." Before he could ponder the issue further, Rajkumari was on the stage.

"My grandmother has stolen the spotlight," she joked. "Her thanks are sweeter than mine. Just the same, I want to thank the Health Minister, my consultants, the doctors, my staff, the cooks, the volunteer helpers, the townspeople and all our guests for joining the celebration."

Balbir winked at his father, who smiled knowingly.

When the speeches were over, the guests moved to the food stalls.

A crowd surrounded Bhajanma. Many men and women touched her feet and asked their children to do the same.

Sitting in the front row, Maya's friend Devaki wrote notes on her pad and photographed the function. Varsha and Rati hovered around her. Two newspaper reporters had also showed up, asking questions and taking notes.

After the late lunch, some people went home. Children loitered in the *mandap*, and Balbir served them ice cream. The Health Minister left in his car and the consultants from the city packed into their bus and waved good-bye. When the sun set, the family and overnight guests lingered in the *mandap*. Balbir and

Mohan brought trays filled with tea and refreshments and passed them around.

Bhajanma sipped her tea and looked happily around at her family. "I can see you all are exhausted. For the next couple days you must rest. Kuldip and I will manage the kitchen. I want you to enjoy each other's company."

"Aren't you tired, Bhajanma?" Charan asked.

"No, I'm not," she said. "I can't tell you how happy I am to have the entire family under one roof."

Everyone slept late the next morning and had a late breakfast. The Delhi relatives and other overnight guests packed their bags and left. Devaki interviewed Rajkumari and Balavant Singh and bid them good-bye. At Varsha's insistence, her friend Rati stayed on.

After the other guests had gone, the younger crowd was free to play cards, carom board, badminton and walk the fields.

As afternoon approached, Charan pulled his cousin Varsha into his room. "I know Rati is your friend," he said, "but am I right that there's something going on between her and your brother?"

Varsha winked. "How should I know? If you're so curious, why don't you ask her yourself?"

"No way. I'm not that brave. But come on, why don't you just tell me?"

"Just wait a few years, and maybe you'll see a wedding….."

"I thought so!" He looked at her seriously then. "I'm fine with it, but Balbir…"

"Balbir what?"

"He doesn't approve."

"So? Who needs his approval?"

"I didn't say anybody asked him. He just volunteered his opinion. He says Rati's a Hindu."

Varsha had been lounging on a chair. Now she got to her feet. "So is my mother," she said defiantly.

"Balbir says times have changed."

Balbir appeared in the doorway. "What's going on?

Varsha strutted across the room, mock-shaking her hips. "I

was just asking Charan if you have a girlfriend."

Balbir replied, "I have no intention of ever getting married."

"Why?" Charan and Varsha asked simultaneously.

"Because I want to be a politician."

Varsha giggled, "So? Most politicians I know are married. Dad's friend, Uncle Bhushan, the big fat U. P. Minister is married."

"Politics can be dangerous," said Balbir.

"So? Get bodyguards like uncle Bhushan," Varsha said.

Balbir tried to change the topic. "What about you? What are your plans?"

"After I finish college, I plan to do social work," said Varsha. "I'm not interested in marriage."

She crossed her arms. "How can you be a politician, Balbir? You're so hot-tempered!"

"My kind of politics requires a hot-tempered person," said Balbir.

Mohan came in followed by Rati.

"Mohan," said Balbir, "your sister says she plans a life of social work. Is that true?"

Mohan sat down on a bed. "So she says," he replied. "She's crazy."

"What about you, Charan?" asked Varsha. "What are your plans?"

"I don't know. I have to decide between medical school and agricultural college."

"You should go to agricultural school," Varsha advised. "Then you can marry a woman doctor to run the hospital when your mother retires."

"Brilliant, Varsha. And where am I going to find a doctor wife?"

"I'll find you one. Rati will help me."

Mohan turned to Balbir, "What about you, Balbir?"

But it was Charan who responded. "It used to be farming for me and medical school for him, but now he says he wants to go into politics. And he says he doesn't want a family because his politics will be dangerous."

"That's right," said Varsha. "He says his politics require a hot-tempered man."

Mohan looked alarmed. Silence filled the room.

Rati turned to Charan. "You promised me a ride in a tractor."

"I'm coming, too!" squealed Varsha.

Giggling, the girls dragged Charan outside.

"Good riddance," Mohan said. He studied Balbir with concern. "Brother, are you planning to play regular politics or…" he stopped.

Balbir laughed, "Or what?"

"You're not thinking of joining the Khalistan Movement – the militancy – are you?"

Balbir smiled. "You know me well. Yes – I was thinking about it."

Mohan was incredulous. "You know what our family went through at the time of the partition. Do you really want Punjab to burn again?"

"Don't get so upset. I haven't done anything yet."

"Good thing. Breaking away to form a separate Sikh state is crazy. You'd have to fight the whole government of India and its army."

"Revolutions always face a powerful opposition. Even if our generation pays a price, it will be worth it if future generations can be free."

Mohan shook his head.

"Don't worry," said Balbir. "If I join the Movement, it won't affect the rest of the family. I'll just vanish. The family won't have any contact with me."

"But a family is like a human body, Balbir. If one arm is cut off, the whole body suffers."

Balbir laughed. "Now you're talking like a doctor, Mohan." He stood up. "Please just promise me you won't say anything."

"I won't say a word," Mohan sighed.

"Snacks are served," called Maya from the living room.

The young men joined her, giving no hint of the

conversation that had just taken place in the bedroom.

The family spent two more happy days together.

For once, Rajkumari let other doctors manage her practice and spent time with her family.

When everyone was ready to leave, Bhajanma had tears in her eyes. When, she wondered, would the family ever spend such a happy time together again?

CHAPTER 11

Maya sat on the front steps of her bungalow, waiting for Darashan. Mohan and Varsha had already had their dinner.

"Mommy, please join us," pleaded Mohan. "Don't wait for Dad. He's always late nowadays." But Maya refused.

The night grew darker and quieter. Household noises from the neighborhood subsided. Maya wrapped herself in a shawl and waited. Eventually, she fell asleep, her head leaning against the door.

"Maya, wake up." Darashan was shaking her. "Why are you sleeping on the steps? I told you not to wait for me." Maya couldn't see his face, but she could hear the irritation in his voice.

She went into the dining room, blinking in the bright light, and began serving dinner. She had set the plates out hours earlier.

"I had my dinner. You should have had your dinner with Varsha and Mohan."

Maya looked up. The expression in her eyes melted Darashan's heart.

"You go ahead and eat. I'll have a glass of buttermilk." Maya poured it for him.

"Darashan, what's wrong with you these days?" She cast about for words. "Why are you always..." But before she could even finish her question, Darashan had left the room.

Maya watched him go with a sinking feeling. Darashan had changed. He was not the man she had loved and married.

After their wedding nineteen years ago they'd moved to Indore and started two businesses, a shop selling clothing material and a new business selling tractors. Both had prospered, and they'd been able to buy a plot of land and build the kind of bungalow Maya had always dreamed of.

Until Darashan had started acting so strangely, her life had been happy.

In the old days, he would engage in daily chats with Mohan: "What did you study in college today? Can I help you with your studies?"

Mohan would laugh. "How can you help me? You're not a doctor."

"Just try me," Darashan would say, picking up Mohan's textbook and pretending to read it.

Now if Varsha or Mohan so much as approached Darashan with a question, he would be dismissive. "Go ask your mother," he would snap.

Mohan hadn't complained, but just the other day, Varsha had asked, "What's wrong with Dad these days? He's so cranky."

Maya groped for an explanation for Darashan's behavior. Had the business suffered a financial loss? Could he be involved with another woman? Was he gambling?

Until recently, Maya had helped Darashan run his business. But now that the business was prospering and Darashan could afford help, she had withdrawn from her bookkeeping duties and started to focus on a hobby she'd come to love: writing short stories and poems. She had signed up for a Masters in English and Hindi at a local college. There she had met Devaki, a woman who lectured occasionally at the college and published a monthly magazine, *Janani*, devoted to women's issues. Devaki had asked Maya to help edit short stories and poems for the magazine, and Maya had happily agreed.

But now, just as Maya was discovering what she wanted to do with the rest of her life, these unexpected changes in her husband were threatening to upend her world.

A few days later, Darashan returned home early and frantically began rummaging through his files. "What are you trying to find?" Maya asked. "Can I help?"

"No," he said tersely, and turned his back.

For several days, he ransacked the house, looking for the mysterious item. Eventually he gave up, packed his bags, and headed out the door, saying only, "I'll be back soon."

The morning after he left, Maya decided to cancel her appointment with Devaki and skip her classes. She needed time to think.

After Mohan and Varsha left for school, she restlessly

125

walked in her garden. It was a space she had meticulously designed herself, and it rarely failed to soothe her.

Red and orange roses climbed the fence surrounding the bungalow, while pink, white and yellow flowers put on a display of riotous colors around the yard's perimeter. A marble fountain sprayed continuous jets of water in the center of the yard. Maya stood by the fountain, gazing into the spray. Drops of water hung in the air, brilliantly refracting the sunlight. She breathed deeply and tried to shake off the tension.

Feeling marginally better, she sighed and went back into the house.

No sooner had the door closed behind her when the phone rang. "Hello?" Maya said. She heard only a click. She'd received several such calls in the last few months. Varsha had also complained, "Someone calls and hangs up on me."

She went into the kitchen. "Do you want some tea?" the cook asked.

"No," Maya answered, opening the closet.

"Can I help you?" the cook asked.

"I'm going to dust the furniture," Maya said.

"The maid already dusted it this morning," the cook told her. Ignoring her, Maya pulled out a dust cloth. The cook shook her head and went back to kneading dough for Parathas.

Maya began dusting the living room, grateful for this straightforward task into which to direct her nervous energy.

When she got to the sofa she picked up a cushion and discovered a piece of paper wedged below. It appeared to be an envelope, already opened. Recalling Darashan's frantic search for a mysterious missing item, she pulled the paper from the envelope and, her hands shaking, started to read. She got through a few lines and then crumpled onto the sofa, trying to regain her equilibrium.

The doorbell rang. Maya rushed into her room and hid the letter in her closet, between her folded saris. By the time she got to the door, the cook had washed her hands and was rushing out of the kitchen. "I'll get it," Maya called.

Gopal, carrying his little suitcase, stood on the step. He

gazed at Maya. In his eyes was the same inscrutable expression she had seen in college.

"Someday I will describe the expression in a poem," Maya had promised herself years ago. Now, at this inopportune time, the promise came back to her. On the heels of that thought another flickered in her mind: "My protector is here. I need him right now."

"Is Darashan home?" Gopal asked.

"No," she replied, then added quickly, "He went to Delhi," though in fact she had no idea where he was.

"Are you all right?" Gopal asked, looking at her quizzically.

Maya wanted to cry. To avoid Gopal's gaze, she said, "Why are we standing in the hallway? Wash up. I'll fix you some breakfast." She vanished into the kitchen.

Gopal sighed, picked up his little suitcase and headed into the guest room to wash up.

His thoughts revolved around Maya. "What does she know?" he wondered.

She was waiting for him in the dining room. "Please have a seat," she said. By now she had collected herself.

Gopal had visited Maya and Darashan at least twice every year since they'd moved to Indore. Even in the old days, when Darashan had sometimes lost money and had financial problems, Maya had never been disheartened. "We must be brave and face life's ups and downs," had been her motto.

But Maya had appeared almost despairing, when she'd come to the door.

"Does she know what Darashan and his father are up to?" Gopal wondered. "She can't possibly…" he thought. "Surely Darashan is honoring the code of secrecy."

Maya brought out a tray with tea, toast and omelets. Gopal started to butter the toast, avoiding the temptation to gaze at Maya.

"When will Darashan be back?" he asked.

Maya hesitated, and then decided to be truthful. "I have no idea where Darashan is and I don't know when he'll be back."

Words failed Gopal, and for a change, Maya was quiet.

She wondered about the true purpose of Gopal's visit.

Usually he called ahead to let them know he was coming, and workers from the communist party or his social work projects would call the house to set up appointments. But Maya hadn't received a single call this time.

"Does he know about Darashan?" she wondered.

But neither Gopal nor Maya broached the topic of her husband's activities.

In the afternoon, Gopal headed out, saying he was going to visit the party office and the clinic.

Not long afterwards, the doorbell rang again. Maya recognized the man at the door as Gopal's unofficial bodyguard in Indore. Usually he escorted Gopal around the city during his visits.

When he asked to see Gopal, Maya told him he'd gone out. The man was surprised.

"By himself?" he asked.

"Yes. Didn't he inform you he was coming?"

"No. His driver called and told me he dropped him at your house. Did he say where he was going?"

"No."

"Don't worry. I'll find him," said the man, and set off.

The exchange confirmed her suspicion: whatever had brought Gopal here was not a routine work visit.

She picked up the dust cloth and got back to work on the living room. "Just work," she told herself. "Don't think. Whatever happens, there's nothing I can do about it."

CHAPTER 12

Indore had endured a hot summer, but now light breezes cooled the autumn evenings. As Mohan walked Rati home, golden sunlight lit the street.

"If I marry you," Mohan teased, "our children will be less than five feet tall."

"If you want tall children, marry Kiran," Rati retorted. "She's five foot seven."

Mohan laughed, "No. It's ok — I'm willing to sacrifice my children's height for love."

"If you think it's such a sacrifice, we should break up," said Rati picking up her pace.

Mohan caught up to her. "You can't outrun me," he teased. "Listen; don't be angry, you know love is blind."

"Am I really so ugly?"

"Stand still." Mohan circled Rati twice, pretending to judge her, taking in her curly hair, dimpled smile, and big brown eyes.

"My love isn't blind," concluded Mohan. "It just ignores height."

Mohan stood still. "Now my turn," he said.

Rati laughed. "I don't even know what you look like. Your beard and moustache cover more than half of your face."

They had reached Rati's home. "Do you want to come in for a cup of tea?" she asked.

"No. I'd better go home. I have to study tonight."

Back home, Varsha opened the door. "Where's Rati today?"

"She went home."

Maya called from the kitchen, "Gopal will be here for dinner."

Varsha clapped her hands with delight.

She loved going with Gopal to visit his schools and clinics. Whenever he held a fundraiser or arranged lectures, Varsha and Maya attended with him, and he would introduce Varsha as his niece.

Through him, she had met many political leaders and social

workers.

Darashan had complained once, "Maya trusts Gopal more than she trusts me. She happily sends Varsha into the slums with Gopal."

"The people Uncle Gopal works with are not slummy!" Varsha had protested. "They treat me with the utmost respect."

"Why wouldn't they?" Darashan had teased. "After all, you are Gopal's niece."

"At least those people are real – not fakes like your business associates."

"Do I really trust Gopal more than Darashan?" Maya had wondered. "Yes," she thought. "Why, I trust Gopal more than I trust myself." Darashan's insight astonished her.

While Varsha loved to talk with Gopal about his social work projects, Mohan loved discussing political ideology with him.

When the bell rang a bit later that evening, both Varsha and Mohan rushed to the door.

Before Gopal could come in, Varsha asked, "Uncle, can I come with you tomorrow wherever you're going?"

Mohan elbowed her, "You can skip school and join him tomorrow. Tonight, *I* want to talk to him." Gopal settled down on the sofa.

"Varsha, please fix Uncle Gopal a cup of tea and a plate of biscuits," said Maya, stepping into the living room. She took a seat across from Gopal.

Varsha bustled into the kitchen and emerged balancing a plate overflowing with biscuits. She stuffed one in her mouth and headed back into the kitchen.

"Uncle Gopal–" Mohan began. But Maya cut him off.

"Mohan, Uncle Gopal traveled all night. He must be exhausted. Please don't hound him with political questions."

She sighed. "I don't know when these two will mature."

"I like them the way they are," said Gopal. "I'll feel like an old man when Varsha and Mohan start behaving like adults."

"What brings you to town?" Maya asked.

"To see Darashan," Gopal blurted. Immediately he regretted

his mistake.

"Why?" Maya demanded.

Gopal sensed that Maya suspected the real reason for his unplanned visit.

"It's nothing important," Gopal replied uncomfortably. "It's just that I haven't seen him in a long time. He visited Bombay last month, but I was in Nasik. If he doesn't show up in a couple days, I'll have to fly back."

Maya sighed and asked no more questions, but Gopal knew he had failed to convince her.

Detecting his discomfort, Maya sought to reassure him. "Gopal, we're happy you're here."

He smiled gratefully.

"Devaki wants to interview you," said Maya. "She wants to write a piece about your life. Are you free tomorrow evening?"

"I've lived an ordinary life," said Gopal. "But if she's interested, I'd be happy to answer her questions."

"All Devakiaunti ever talks about is women and women's liberation," said Mohan. "Why would she want to interview a man?"

Everyone ignored him.

The next day, Varsha accompanied Gopal to his school and clinic. The following evening, Devaki came by to interview Gopal for her magazine.

Gopal, who rarely spoke of past events in his life, discussed them openly now, in response to Devaki's thoughtful questioning. Maya, Mohan, and Varsha, who had known little of Gopal's past, learned of Gopal's sister's death. They heard how a mob had invaded his village and looted and burned his home after Mahatma Gandhi's murder. They learned that he'd been sent away from his mother, and that his family had faced a food shortage in Pune. They heard about his having to visit wealthy homes to ask for alms and how insults had been heaped upon him. They discovered how it was that he'd ended up in Delhi and that Arun wasn't really his cousin.

The story astounded and shocked the family and riveted

131

Mohan and Varsha, who listened wordlessly. "I never knew," Maya murmured, looking at Gopal in wonder. "I had no idea."

Gopal explained why he had turned to communism and how, later on, disappointed with the politics, he had switched to social work. Though he was no longer an active communist, he said, the party still provided him with valuable services, as his work was beneficial to them.

When Devaki announced that the interview was over, Gopal asked Devaki, "No more questions?"

Devaki said, "I'm done. Your life is unique. Thank you."

That night Maya couldn't sleep, thinking about Gopal's life and pondering her own and her children's future. She wondered what a liberated woman like the ones Devaki always talked about would do in her situation.

CHAPTER 13

The phone rang and Mohan picked up. "Hello, it's Uncle Ikbal," said the voice on the other end of the line. "Is your father home?"

"No, he's out of town," said Mohan, "but Uncle Gopal is here."

"I'm a lucky man, then!" exclaimed Ikbal. "Bhushan dropped by for a visit just last week. He's a big shot and travels with bodyguards. And now I'll get to see Gopal, the famous social worker and ex-Communist leader."

Mohan heard someone hurrying Ikbal in the background. "Mohan, I should go, but please ask Gopal and Darashan to see me for dinner tonight." He read off an address, "It's a wedding hall — I'm here for a wedding."

Mohan promised to pass the message along and then headed off to school for the day.

When he got home, he found Devaki enthroned in a chair, busy talking to Gopal, Maya and Varsha. It was clear that his father still hadn't returned. He put his books away and joined the group in the living room. "Uncle Ikbal is in Indore for a wedding," he announced. "He's invited Daddy and Uncle Gopal for dinner tonight."

"I don't think your father will be back by then," said Maya. She avoided Mohan's eyes.

"It's ok – I can go by myself," said Gopal. "I'd like to see Ikbal."

"Can I join you, Uncle Gopal?" asked Mohan.

"You can't invite yourself to a wedding!" said Varsha.

"No – its fine," said Gopal. "I'm sure Ikbal's family and friends would be happy to have him."

That night, in the wedding hall, a crowd surrounded Ikbal, who was now a renowned *Shayar* and had composed many popular movie songs. When Gopal and Mohan entered, a few people promptly recognized Gopal and encircled him, too, asking him for his autograph and a photograph with their family members. Ikbal noticed the commotion and made his way over to join him. Questions and comments flew through the air about Ikbal's poetry and Gopal's social work. Mohan watched in awe, wondering if he would ever achieve the stature of his father's famous friends.

A group of giggly teenagers approached.

"Can we take our picture with you two?"

"We'd be honored," Ikbal said.

"Is that young Sardarji with you?" one of the girls asked, pointing to Mohan.

"Yes, he's my friend's son," Ikbal said.

"We want him, too, then. Come on." She motioned for Mohan to stand next to Gopal in the picture.

A photo session with a group of young men followed.

The evening went on in that vein, with Ikbal and Gopal swarmed by admirers, and Mohan basking in their reflected glory.

Before they parted ways for the night, Gopal had a word with Ikbal. "There's no privacy here. Come see me at Darashan's tomorrow morning so we can really talk." Ikbal promised he would.

When Mohan and Gopal arrived home, Maya was waiting for them. "Why are you so late?" she asked.

Mohan, intoxicated with the evening, couldn't stop talking. Gopal and Maya watched him with affection, each thinking wistfully back to their younger days.

"I had the time of my life," Mohan said finally, his eyes glowing.

Gopal laughed. "I noticed."

Maya was falling asleep. "I'm going to bed," she said. "You two can carry on."

After Maya had gone to her room, Gopal turned to Mohan. "I must ask you to skip class tomorrow morning. Ikbal is coming and I need to talk to both of you."

Mohan was perplexed, but he didn't ask questions.

Early the next morning, when Ikbal rang the bell, Maya welcomed him in.

"I have a class this morning," she said, but the cook can fix breakfast and lunch for you two." Noticing Mohan, she asked, "Why are you home this morning?"

"Class is cancelled," he lied.

She looked skeptical, but didn't argue. Not wanting to be late, she gathered up her books and hurried out the door.

Mohan poured tea and pushed cups around. Gopal and Ikbal cast meaningful glances at each other. Finally, Ikbal broke the silence. "Bhushan has learned from a reliable source that Darashan has joined or is planning to join the Khalistan movement."

Mohan's jaw dropped. Just a half hour earlier, he had been laughing and teasing Varsha, before she left for school, and until this moment, he had still been in a playful mood. Now all the joy vanished from his face. He stared wordlessly at Ikbal.

"He's already donated money to the cause," Ikbal want on. "Apparently his father – your grandfather, Mohan – is pushing him to get involved. Your grandfather and one of Darashan's nephews are already involved in it."

"I have similar information," Gopal said. "George has a list of names, and Darashan, his father and his nephew are on it."

"Bhushan wanted me to talk to Darashan," said Ikbal, "to see if I can make him change his mind."

"I came to Indore to talk Darashan out of his plan, too," said Gopal. "His involvement would be disastrous for the family." He was silent for a moment, then added, "I suspect Maya knows."

"Really?" asked Mohan, shocked out of his silence. "What makes you think that?"

"She's not herself," Gopal answered.

Mohan pushed back his chair. "Daddy always opposed the notion of Khalistan," he said. "I heard him say so just a few months back."

His voice shook as he continued. "But he's been so secretive lately, and out of sorts. And Mommy's been on edge. It devastates me to believe it, but I think you may be right."

Suddenly angry, Gopal said, "How did we reach this point? Our leaders who dreamed of a united India would have wept at the notion of Khalistan. When will we learn?"

"Calm down, Gopal," Ikbal said. "Just think, two friends–one Muslim and one Hindu– are here to talk to their Sikh friend's son about the separatist movement. Isn't that hope for the future?"

Mohan stood up. "Yes. Uncle Ikbal is right. The world is changing. Maybe scientific breakthroughs and a new spirit of collaboration will bridge the gap between peoples and nations. The world will be smaller."

"That's possible," mused Gopal. "Science can revolutionize the world. Printing machines, for example –"

Ikbal cut in. "We don't have time to philosophize. I don't understand politics, but I know we can't afford to let this nation get carved into little pieces. Just look at what's happened to Pakistan, a nation created with bloodshed and mayhem. It's already split again into Bangladesh and Pakistan with more bloodshed. It's time we learned to get along."

"That's true," said Gopal. "But obviously the situation is spiraling out of control."

Mohan finished his cold tea and said, "I have to go now. I can't afford to miss clinic today. Will I see you two tonight?"

Gopal and Ikbal looked at each other. "Go on," said Gopal. "Your schooling is important. We won't resolve the issue today. We'll get hold of your father sooner or later."

Mohan collected his books and headed out. Ikbal and Gopal watched him leave. "Should we ask Maya to send him to Canada?" asked Ikbal. "Sooner or later his grandfather is going to try to drag him into the movement, too."

"But that would mean interrupting his education. Surely the movement will leave him alone until he graduates. Doctors are valuable to violent revolutions."

Ikbal was unconvinced. "I think it's imperative to get him away from here. He can always return after the movement falters."

"Do you really think this movement will die out? Ikbal, we have to face reality. India's going to be unstable for the rest of our lives. We can't just run away."

"Whatever happens, we have to protect our families and friends," said Ikbal.

"But how can we protect Darashan from himself?" Gopal asked.

"We can at least talk to him," Ikbal murmured.

Both were quiet for few moments.

Gopal wandered over to the radio and switched it on. "Enough of this," he said. "We might as well at least lighten up and find out what's going on in the rest of the–" He trailed off as the announcer's voice froze his words in his mouth.

"I repeat – Prime Minister Indira Gandhi has been assassinated. The perpetrator, her bodyguard, is known to be a Sikh. Allegedly he was seeking revenge for Gandhi's decision to launch the army against the Sikhs' Golden Temple, where Sikh fighters had been based…"

Gopal struggled to adjust the volume dial. Ikbal sat stiff and erect, his eyes wide.

The news terrified Gopal. Childhood memories of the violence following Mahatma Gandhi's murder surfaced unbidden. "There are going to be riots," he thought. "Blood will flow in the streets."

Both Gopal and Ikbal sat motionless for a long time, listening intently to the report issuing from the radio.

Suddenly there were shouts in the street.

Gopal sprang to his feet and raced out the door. Ikbal followed close behind.

CHAPTER 14

As Gopal and Ikbal reached the garden gate, they spotted two Communist Party workers running toward them. "Where are you going?" one of them asked, addressing Gopal. "We're here to take you away. Riots have started. You're not safe in your Sikh friend's house."

"I'm not leaving," said Gopal. "No one will hurt me."

He pointed to the swarm of people in the street. "What's all the commotion?"

"The mob's surrounded a rickshaw," one of the party workers said. "They're demanding that the woman inside tell them where her husband is."

Gopal pushed the party workers out of his way and dashed toward the rickshaw. Superhuman strength seemed to possess him as he plunged into the crowd. As he had suspected, he could see that the terrified face inside the rickshaw was Maya's. Varsha was with her.

"We know where you live," an imposing man with wild eyes was shouting at her. "Tell us where your man is."

Gopal stepped between the man and the rickshaw. "The man you're looking for is out of town," he said firmly. "I suggest you leave this innocent woman alone."

The man tried to push Gopal out of the way, but one of the party workers yelled, "You don't know who you're dealing with. That's Gopal Sane, the famous communist leader."

The man hesitated.

"It's true," said the other worker.

The man, who seemed to be the ringleader of the mob, stepped back. He had no desire to tangle with a Communist Party figurehead. Gopal's gray eyes stared him down. "Let's go," said a smaller man standing next to the ringleader. The ringleader spat on the road, turned his back, and walked toward the main road. The rest of the crowd followed. A few neighbors, who until now had waited to see the outcome of the confrontation, emerged from their homes and thanked Gopal for driving away the wild mob. Then they retreated back into their homes, bolting their doors for protection.

Maya had been terrified more for Varsha than herself. She watched the departing crowd and turned her eyes to Gopal. "As soon as I heard the news, I went to Varsha's school to pick her up," she said breathlessly. "And then I hired a rickshaw to get us home. But the mob surrounded us when we were almost here."

She smiled at him gratefully. "You saved us from a disaster."

"I'm glad I was here," said Gopal, his heart pounding.

Now that the immediate danger had passed, Maya's thoughts turned to the rest of her family. "Mohan and Darashan—where are they?" she asked, worried.

"Darashan knows how to take care of himself," said Gopal. "Mohan can't be far away. We'll try to find him."

But even as Gopal tried to calm her, visions of the riots that had followed Mahatma Gandhi's murder gripped him.

The group went into the house and settled in the living room.

"Do you wish to stay here?" one of the party workers asked Gopal.

"Yes," said Gopal.

"We have orders to protect you," said the worker. "In that case, we'll stay here, too."

"No," said Gopal. "You're free to go. You needn't endanger yourselves for me."

"We'll wait outside the front door," said one of the workers. "We can camp here until tempers calm down. Others from the party will arrive soon to relieve us."

"Maya, there's someone's knocking at the back," said Ikbal.

Everyone rushed to the kitchen, where a young man was knocking on a window. When Maya caught his eye he pointed to the back door, jumped over the fence and disappeared.

Gopal opened the door. "Mohan!" Maya exclaimed. Mohan, his face bloodied, stepped in. Gopal closed the door.

"Don't worry, Mommy. It's not as bad as it looks. Head wounds always bleed like this."

Maya collected herself. She recalled Bhajanma's actions when Darashan had thrown the rock that hit her eyebrow. "Varsha, bring a freshly washed towel," she called.

Varsha complied, and Maya gently wiped the blood off Mohan's face just as Bhajanma had once wiped her own face. She washed the wound on his forehead, applied antiseptic and bandaged it.

"Do you have any other injuries?" she asked.

"No," said Mohan. "A young man who works in the hospital kitchen helped me get away. A rock hit my head while we were running."

Soon the power failed and the phones stopped working. A few more party workers arrived. Gopal, Ikbal and the party workers stood outside the locked front door. Throngs of men, mostly carrying sticks and cricket bats appeared from time to time at the front gate, but Gopal and his party workers warded them off.

Maya spent the whole day cooking to occupy her mind. For once, Varsha quietly helped her.

No one slept that night. Gopal sat by the front window and Ikbal by the back window, watching the empty street.

The next morning, a policeman appeared on the street. He said that a curfew had been imposed to control the citywide riots. That evening, the streets were deserted except for a few stray cats and dogs.

Maya's and Ikbal's efforts to contact their families failed. Phones were out of order. Batteries in the sole transistor in the house ran out and the group in Maya's home began to feel as though they'd been stranded on an island.

The following day someone knocked at the back door. "Who is it?" called Ikbal.

"Rati," answered a frightened voice.

Gopal opened the door and Rati rushed in.

"Where's Mohan? I heard that he…" She started to cry.

Mohan hurried into the kitchen, with Varsha trailing behind.

Rati hugged Maya with relief and started to sob.

"Rati, how did you get here?" asked Maya.

"Through backyards, crossing streets when nobody was watching."

"Rati, you fool!" exclaimed Mohan. "A policeman could have shot and killed you."

"Did you ask your parents' permission?" asked Maya.

"No. A friend who lives next door told me Mohan was hurt, so I snuck out while everyone was occupied."

"I'm afraid we must send you home," said Maya.

Varsha caught Maya's arm, "No—don't force her to go. Please."

"But her family will worry about her."

"Worry doesn't kill anyone."

Rati went to the door. "It's ok. I'll go back the way I came."

Maya pulled her back. "No. I can't let you do that."

"When the policeman patrolling the street returns, I'll ask him to take her back," said Gopal. "I'll go with her."

"Can I come along?" Varsha asked.

"Not on a day like today, Varsha," Gopal told her.

Everybody watched as Rati and Gopal headed off with the policeman. Maya sighed.

It was obvious that Mohan and Rati were in love. She had tried to warn Mohan against falling for a Hindu, just as Bhajanma had once warned Darashan. But she knew better than anyone that such admonitions would be hopeless in the face of young people in love.

When the phone rang the next day, Maya answered. "This is Ninad, Arun's son," said the voice on the other end of the line. "My father wants to talk to you."

Maya's heart raced.

"Hello, Maya," said Arun. "Darashan is with me. He's worried about you. How is everybody?"

Maya summarized the events of the last few days, then asked, "How is everyone at Bhajanma's?"

"We don't know. The phones are out of order. The roads are–" But the line went dead before he could finish. Maya was left holding the receiver.

Maya struggled to compose herself. Darashan was safe. She wanted to laugh and then cry. She didn't move for a long time.

When power was finally restored, a few days later, the group learned that widespread riots were still ongoing – the result of the majority's rage directed against the minority Sikh community.

Everyone wondered anxiously what had happened to Darashan and the rest of the family. As the tension grew, an uneasy silence gripped the house. Even Varsha, who normally chattered continuously, was quiet.

After a few days, the city calmed down. Shops opened under police supervision, and electric power was fully restored.

Ikbal had an important appointment. "I must go home," he said. "But I'll try to contact Arun and send a message."

"Delhi is a big city," said Maya. "The streets may be dangerous. Don't risk your life for us, Ikbal."

Maya tried to dial Bhajanma and Arun several times a day in vain.

Finally, early one morning, the phone rang. Arun was on the line. "Maya, I have sad news. Darashan and his grandfather were caught in the riots. Darashan is fine, but his grandfather was stabbed and is in critical condition."

Maya gasped, and tears flooded her eyes. "Where is Darashan?" She asked.

"He's with his grandfather."

"I'll come to Delhi."

"Maya, these aren't normal times. The Delhi streets and railroads aren't safe. Think of your children and stay put."

"How is Bhajanma?"

"I have no words to describe her courage. Take care, Maya. May I speak to Gopal if he's still there?"

Maya handed the phone to Gopal who, still in his pajamas, had rushed to the phone. Arun and Gopal talked for a long time, but Maya didn't hear a single word. She fell into the chair next to the phone and wept silently. She could visualize her father-in-law, Gurumukh Singh, with his tall, dignified, slightly bent bearing, his gray beard and the unworldly expression in his eyes. He reminded her of a sage in mythological stories. A cruel stroke of fate had displaced him and his family once, and he and Bhajanma had managed to make a new life for themselves and their family in an unknown land. Now fate had ruthlessly punished him and his family again. Tears rolled down her cheeks.

Bhajanma's charisma had charmed Maya when she was a little girl. When Maya met her again as an adult, she loved and respected her, and felt that if she ever needed help, she would turn to Bhajanma. Lately, as her world had spiraled out of control, Bhajanma had been on her mind continuously. She desperately craved the older woman's advice and comfort.

Gopal finished talking to Arun and sat down on the sofa, shaking his head. "This firestorm has engulfed the entire country," he said. He turned to Maya, "I'm sorry about your father-in law," he said quietly. "My condolences."

"Your presence has been helpful," said Maya.

He smiled sorrowfully at her, wishing there were more he could do.

When Gopal left the next day, the party workers left with him.

A few days later, Ranjit Singh called. In a dry voice, devoid of emotion, he informed Maya that Gurumukh Singh had passed away. "Darashan wants you to stay where you are," he said. Before Maya could ask a single question, he disconnected the phone.

"Why didn't Darashan call me?" Maya wondered. "Is he so busy that he can't find a minute to call?"

Gurumukh Singh's death didn't shock Maya. He had suffered from so many chronic conditions that his passing had seemed only a matter of time.

Nonetheless, she grieved terribly. His quiet presence had always buoyed and protected the family. And he had exerted a degree of control over his angry son. Now that control was gone and she didn't know what Ranjit Singh, set free, would do, or how his actions might affect her family and her children. Maya had lost her parents in a traffic accident, and now the only remaining father figure in her life was gone. She felt like an orphan.

Darashan returned two weeks later. Maya was thrilled to see him, but her elation didn't last long.

He had lost weight, and spent most of his time sitting on the sofa or lying on the bed, staring listlessly out the window.

Mohan and Varsha avoided their father and withdrew into themselves. Maya felt that her home had turned into a boarding house where unrelated men and women lived in their own worlds.

Loneliness engulfed her. When she was young she had imagined that love could overcome any obstacle. She had thought she and Darashan would walk through fire and across flooded rivers for one another. Even now, she thought, she would gladly step into fire if Darashan asked her to. But he hardly seemed to think of her.

"What if I were Sikh?" she wondered. "Would he be treating me differently? Who can I turn to for help if Darashan rejects me?"

One afternoon, the doorbell rang. Maya half opened the door and peeked out. There on the doorstep were Ranjit Singh, Kuldipma and Bhajanma. Dressed in white, Bhajanma held a cane in her right hand to support herself.

Maya's heart jumped with joy. She felt as though a goddess had descended from the heavens just for her.

But then a dark doubt surfaced. "Will Bhajanma still accept me, even though I'm Hindu, like the mob that killed her husband? Will she reject me like Darashan has?" Collecting her strength, she opened the door wide and stood still, her eyes lowered and her hand on the door frame.

Bhajanma lifted her free hand, put it on Maya's back and said gently, "Beti." At that one word, Maya's emotions exploded. She hugged Bhajanma and started to cry.

CHAPTER 15

For the last year, Darashan had been pulled in opposite directions. On one side were Maya, his children, his mother and grandmother and his own thoughts. On the other was his father, relentlessly pushing him toward the Khalistan movement.

"Darashan," Ranjit Singh reminded him, "We Sikhs don't have a homeland. We're like the Jews before Israel, a minority scattered in many nations. Don't forget—the Sikhs once ruled part of India. We had our own kingdom. Then the British took over, and when India gained its independence, we were ruthlessly driven from our ancestral homes. You lost your great-grandfather and granduncle in the mayhem. And when we arrived in India, we were homeless refugees. This is why we need our own country. I don't care if we have to shed our blood and die for the Khalistan revolution. Partitions are always bloody. You must help me. Don't you remember the promise you made when I first returned to the family all those years back? It's time to fulfill it. I want to die in my own country. India is not my country."

Darashan had plenty of Sikh acquaintances. But there was no one close to him with whom he could discuss his dilemma.

Many of his friends liked the notion of an independent Sikh homeland: they talked resentfully about the Indian government's unfair policies toward the Sikh minority. But they weren't willing to fight an army for the cause. As for Darashan's best friends from college, they weren't Sikhs, and couldn't understand. He knew that Maya, in deference to him as his wife, would never oppose his decisions or reveal her true feelings on the subject. As for Varsha and Mohan, they simply laughed at the notion of Khalistan – vowing that they would never move out of their beloved Indore. Even Rajkumari, living in Punjab, considered the idea of Khalistan wrong. "Let's fight for our rights democratically," she said. "We don't need more violence."

He did try to talk to his grandfather and Balavant Singh. "It's not worth the price," they said.

"I don't want any more bloodshed in my life," Grandfather

said. "I want peace. I want to see my great-grandchildren."

Balavant Singh looked sad. "I lost my entire family at the time of partition," he reminded Darashan. "We've paid a heavy price for India's independence. I don't want to lose more family members for any cause."

But joining the movement was all Darashan's father had ever asked of him. As a son, didn't he have an obligation to fulfill his father's wishes?

He was wracked with indecision.

"We could be jailed or killed," he told his father. "Who will care for Bhajanma, Kuldipma and Gurumukh Bauji then?"

"Rajkumari," replied his father, without the slightest hesitation.

Darashan knew Rajkumari would do just that, but the assumption seemed unfair. "Sons are supposed to care for their parents, not daughters," he said.

"Maybe so, but this situation is different," said Ranjit Singh. "Normal rules don't apply."

His father's hypocrisy rankled. He had refused to let Rajkumari study medicine because she was a girl, but was happy to let her shoulder his responsibility when it suited him.

"And who will look after Maya?" Darashan asked.

Ranjit Singh merely shrugged his shoulders. For his father, his beloved wife – one of the reviled Hindu majority – didn't count. Stung, Darashan lapsed into silence.

"Maya's educated and she's a member of the Hindu ruling class," said Ranjit Singh. "She'll be fine."

Tormented and hopelessly conflicted, Darashan became testy and withdrawn. His wife and children started to tiptoe around him.

Gurumukh Singh's eyesight had begun to fail, so for the last six months Darashan had traveled to Delhi once a month to help him with his bookkeeping work. But his father kept dragging him to secret meetings for the Khalistan movement. The bookkeeping was delayed again and again.

In the past it had been Ranjit Singh who had helped

Gurumukh Singh. But lately he had ignored the chore.

When Darashan finally looked at the scope of the backlog, he realized that he would need an entire day to get through it. He and Gurumukh Singh set out for the store early one morning to get started. They decided not to open the shop that day so Darashan could focus on the task at hand. He planned to finish the work that day then get back to Indore. All morning, he added and subtracted numbers. Kuldip had packed a lunch. When they finished the food, they went right back to work. By the afternoon, they were feeling weary. "I'm exhausted," said Gurumukh Singh. "We've spent the whole day in this airless room. I have a headache. A cup of tea and fresh air will revive me."

"I need a break too," said Darashan. "Let's go."

The moment they stepped out of the shop, Darashan could see that something was very wrong. All the nearby shops were closed, and the normally busy thoroughfare was nearly deserted. The few men they saw on the street seemed tense and in a hurry. From somewhere came the sound of screams. Darashan tried to waylay a man who was hurrying past. But the man only glanced at Darashan, and sprinted away, vanishing down an alley. With growing concern, Darashan decided to lock Gurumukh Singh and himself inside the shop and try to find out what was going on. He had just turned to open the door when a mob appeared, seemingly from nowhere, and surrounded them.

"Murderers!" the mob yelled, and started to hit them with cricket bats and sticks. Darashan grabbed hold of his grandfather, trying to shield him from the angry blows, but the mob pulled him away. A switchblade glinted in the sunlight. As he fell to the ground, he became conscious of a widening pool of blood. Someone was dragging him away from the mob. Then total darkness enveloped him.

When he awoke, he was in an unfamiliar room. His head throbbed. The light hurt his eyes. The figure of a woman sitting on a chair by his bed floated before him. He moaned and lost consciousness again.

When he awoke again, he tried to focus on the figure.

147

"Maya…." He mumbled.

The woman stood up, moved closer, and said softly, "I'm not Maya. I'm Usha, your friend Arun's wife."

Darashan closed his eyes but someone shook him. "Darashan, can you hear me? It's me – Arun. You're with me."

Slowly Darashan regained his senses. Vaguely recollecting what had happened, he asked, "Where's Bauji, my grandfather?" As he asked the question, a feeling of doom descended on him.

"Were you with your grandfather?" Arun asked.

"Yes. Where is he?" Darashan tried to get up, but Arun gently pushed him back. "You're in no condition to get up," he said. Darashan tried to fight him. "Darashan, don't be a fool," he said. "You need to rest." As Arun spoke, the room vibrated. Darashan collapsed back onto the bed. He closed his eyes and fell asleep.

The next morning, he was more himself. He managed to slowly stand up and walk to the bathroom attached to his bedroom. He looked at his bandaged head in the mirror, washed his face as best he could, wiped it on the towel, and slowly returned to his bed. Arun came in. "You look better today," he remarked. "We've been worried about you."

He helped Darashan to the dining room, and when settled down in a chair, Usha poured him a cup of tea. "What happened to me?" Darashan asked.

"A mob attacked you right outside your shop," said Arun. "My gardener, Sameer, and his brother, Pratap, were in that mob. They recognized you and managed to pull you away, but by the time they got to you, you'd received some blows to your head. They carried you to Pratap's home and then phoned me. Luckily the phone worked. I sent a military van to pick you up. A doctor friend who lives nearby examined you and thought you were all right. He said your turban protected your head. You were restless so he sedated you."

"But what's going on?" Darashan asked. "Why did the mob come after us?"

"You don't know?" Arun looked surprised.

"No."

"Indira Gandhi's Sikh bodyguards shot and killed her. People are angry, and they're taking it out on any Sikhs they can find."

The news hit Darashan like lightning. His head spun as he thought of the consequences of Indira Gandhi's murder. The feeling of impending doom worsened.

"Bauji was with me," he said, suddenly remembering. "I tried to hold onto him, but I fell and someone pulled me away.

"Darashan," said Arun softly, "Sameer and his brother did what they could to save you. They begged the crowd to have mercy on your Bauji. But in the end they needed to get help for you, so they rushed you away. They did say that as they left, they saw another man intervening to save your Bauji. They went back later to help him but he wasn't there. Many people hid Sikhs in their homes and did what they could to help."

Darashan was despondent. "My grandfather paid a heavy price for my life. I have to find him." He struggled to his feet and tried to make for the door, but Arun blocked his way. "I won't let you go outside. There are rioters in the street. My men are searching for your grandfather."

Darashan put his head in his hands.

"Darashan, what could you do?" asked Arun gently. "Even God couldn't have saved your grandfather in that situation. You can't fight a whole crowd by yourself."

"How can I face Bhajanma and Rajkumari?" Darashan asked tearfully.

Usha had been quietly listening. "I can speak for the women," she said. "They will thank God you survived."

Darashan thought then of the rest of the family. "What's happening in Indore?" he asked anxiously.

"Riots have engulfed the country. Travel isn't safe. Phones are out of order."

Darashan was seized with concern. "Maya, Varsha and Mohan are by themselves."

"I have word that Gopal is with them. He had gone to Indore

149

to see you."

"Gopal's there?" Relief washed over Darashan.

"Yes, I'm sure they'll be all right."

"And what about Bhajanma, Kuldipma…?"

"They're safe," said Arun. "My men visited them to let them know you're with me. They informed my men that your grandfather was with you. My men are now trying to find your grandfather. So far they've searched hospitals and haven't found him."

"Bhajanma must be frantic. I should get home."

Usha spoke up again. "You can't even walk a straight line right now. Please regain your strength here and then go home."

Arun's son Ninad rushed in. "Uncle Bhushan is here," he announced.

"He's in town for Indira Gandhi's funeral," said Arun. "How could a politician miss it?"

A moment later, Bhushan appeared in the doorway. "Stand up, Darashan," he bellowed.

Taken aback, Darashan did as he was told. Bhushan enveloped him in a hug. Then Bhushan stepped back and surveyed Darashan's bandaged head. "Bastards!" he exclaimed, shaking his head.

"Apparently my people aren't welcome in this country anymore," muttered Darashan.

Usha approached and gently patted Darashan's shoulder. "Jijaji, of course you're welcome in this country. Your wife is Hindu, the men who saved your life were Hindu, we are Hindu, and we want you." Then she turned to Arun and Bhushan, "He's not himself. He's had a head injury."

Bhushan seated himself beside Darashan and sipped the tea Usha had poured him. "It's true that Hindus have hurt innocent Sikhs," he said. "And I apologize on behalf of all Hindus. We must make valiant efforts to find the hoodlums who committed these atrocities and punish them."

Usha asked the cook to fix tea for everyone.

Trying to lighten the mood, Bhushan looked at Usha.

"Bhabiji," he said, "you're as slim as you were at the time of your wedding. You should see Bindi. Her size has doubled and she walks like an elephant."

Arun laughed aloud, "Never mind, BindiBhabiji. Look at yourself." He patted Bhushan's bulging tummy. "The size of a watermelon! Looks like you need to cut down on the ghee and sweets, and start getting some exercise."

"I can't help having a slow metabolism," Bhushan protested.

"So you say. The fact is, you eat like a pig," teased Arun.

"MayaBhabiji is also slim," said Bhushan, looking over at Darashan, hoping to draw him into the conversation.

"It's because she eats vegetables, vegetables and more vegetables," said Darashan distractedly.

The cook brought out a tray bearing a teapot and cups, biscuits, and sugar. Usha poured the tea, and everyone sipped it quietly.

Darashan turned on the radio, and the three of them listened to the news for a bit. The reports stunned Darashan. "How can I call this country mine?" he wondered.

Arun read the despair on his face. "I'll try to have a doctor see you today," he said. "As long as he agrees, you can go home tomorrow. I'll drive you myself, since the streets aren't safe."

Darashan's friends were treating him with such kindness, but still he was on the verge of tears. "How can the majority be so cruel to the innocent minority?" he wondered. Maybe his father was right. Perhaps they should fight for a homeland of their own.

It was as if Arun could read his thoughts. "Darashan," he said. "When Nathuram Godase, a Marathi Brahmin, shot and killed Mahatma Gandhi, mobs attacked Brahmins. They were beaten and their homes were burned. Even so, Brahmins didn't renounce India as their country."

Darashan sat in silence, his head bowed.

"You know, when we visited Gopal's village," Arun went on, "his mother told me about something that happened to Gopal when he was young."

Darashan turned to look at him.

"She said that a mob forced his family out of their home after Mahatma Gandhi's murder. Everything they owned was stolen, and their home was burned. The family had to send Gopal away to live with his uncle in Pune, but his uncle didn't have enough to support him, so Gopal was sent door to door to ask for alms."

"He had to beg for food?" Darashan couldn't imagine proud Gopal begging for anything.

"Brahmins are allowed to ask for alms, and others have an obligation to fulfill their request. People did offer alms, but only grudgingly. Sometimes they insulted him. Gopal's mother says the experience scarred him for life. He was never the same afterwards."

Darashan tried to imagine himself begging for food. His own family had lost their home, but he had always been well fed

Bhushan looked thoughtful. "In a diverse nation like ours, one group is always fighting another. Think of the untouchables and all they've suffered."

"But partition isn't the solution," he went on. "Has partition made for a happy Pakistan? It's already split into two more nations, Bangladesh and West Pakistan. And now there are separatist movements in West Pakistan. Years back, when one king like Ashoka or Vikramaditya, ruled us as a united country, Indians were prosperous and lived in peace." He sat back and folded his arms. "We must be tolerant and learn to live together."

"Your philosophy won't bring dead Sikhs back," said Darashan.

Usha sighed. "Now isn't the time for pontification." She turned to Darashan, "Jijaji, please try to rest. You're not well." She retrieved the pain medication they'd given him earlier and offered him two pills.

"No. No more pills. They knock me out. These are nightmare pills." Everyone laughed. "I'll lie down for a short time and then I must go home."

Back in the guest room, he tried to rest, but sleep eluded him.

He tossed and turned fitfully for more than hour, then gave up and returned to the living room. Arun looked up as he entered,

Gurumukh Singh

worry clouding his face. "I'm afraid there's been some bad news," he said, holding up a note. "Your grandfather is in critical condition in a Rathor hospital."

Darashan's heart raced. "I must go see him!" He rushed to the door.

"Jijaji, your clothes!" exclaimed Usha.

Realizing he was still in pajamas, Darashan went to his room and quickly changed. The crisis had energized him. Arun was waiting by the door. Together they ran to the waiting car.

At the hospital, they found Gurumukh Singh semi-conscious and incoherent.

Arun had also sent a car to fetch the rest of the family. They arrived soon after Darashan. Even in this dire situation, Bhajanma, Kuldipma and Ranjit Singh were overjoyed to see Darashan.

Darashan recollected Usha's words: "I can speak for the women. They will thank God that you survived."

Over the next few days, Gurumukh Singh's condition worsened. Arun and Usha visited every day. Bhushan dropped by before flying to U.P., and Ikbal came by as well.

When death seemed inevitable, Bhajanma asked Gurumukh Singh's doctor to stop the treatment. "We're only prolonging his suffering," she said. Darashan, sitting on a bench outside Gurumukh Singh's room, wept.

Distraught, Kuldip and Darashan were in no condition to make decisions. In their grief, they turned to Bhajanma for direction. She asked for a simple funeral. Her courage astonished them all.

When the funeral rites were over, they phoned their other relatives and told them to forgo the customary condolence visits, because the streets weren't safe yet.

Overwhelmed with sadness, Darashan and Kuldip mechanically busied themselves in routine chores. But Ranjit Singh began to come to life. He pulled Darashan aside. "Revenge!" he whispered, his eyes glowing. "Khalistan must be the revenge for Bauji's brutal murder. Let Bauji be a martyr who died for Khalistan.

Many more Sikhs like us may have to lay down our lives. But it's a price well worth paying if it earns us a nation of our own…"

CHAPTER 16

A few days after the funeral, Ranjit Singh decided to open the shop. He asked Darashan to join him later and left.

Bhajanma watched him go, then handed Darashan a piece of paper. It was inscribed with a pair of names and addresses. "Please sit down," she said. "I want to talk to you."

When they had seated themselves, she went on. "Please invite these men to our home. I want to thank them."

"What for?" asked Darashan.

"They intervened and begged the mob to stop beating an old man. And when the mob left, they drove your Bauji to the hospital."

Darashan cast a glance of surprise and admiration at Bhajanma.

He himself had been crazed since that fatal day. After his uneasy rest at Arun's home, he had felt like a man swirling in a hurricane. Sometimes he was seized with fury and hatred; other times he felt so dejected he wanted to end his life or go crawling off alone. He could barely recollect who'd come by to offer condolences to the family or what conversations he'd had.

And yet, through all this, Bhajanma hadn't forgotten the people who'd helped her husband. He felt proud of her and at the same time ashamed of himself.

Bhajanma watched him with concern. "Darashan, you need to accept reality and move on. You have responsibilities."

Her words shook him from his musings. "How did you find these names and addresses?" he asked.

"I asked at the hospital. They kept a record."

Again, he marveled at her presence of mind.

"We can't ever repay them for what they did for us," Bhajanma said. "But I want to thank them and give them a small gift as a token of appreciation. I also want to learn what happened that day."

"What about the hooligans who hurt Bauji?" Darashan asked, bitterness creeping into his voice. "Shouldn't we find them, too? They deserve to be shot."

Bhajan was appalled. "Don't talk like your father. You're the sole support of this family now. Let the police deal with murderers. You need to control your anger."

She softened her tone. "Your grandfather was old. He had a weak heart. He had told his doctor that he planned to stop taking his medications soon. He was going to talk to you first, but he passed away before he had a chance."

The tranquility of Bhajanma's voice and her serene face pacified Darashan.

"I'm tired too," she went on. "And I want to be with your grandfather. But first I want to see you and Maya recover from this trauma. And I want to spend my last days with Rajkumari, even though she's the daughter of the family. Her farm resembles my childhood home. I'm happy there."

"Whatever you wish," said Darashan.

"But there is one unresolved issue in my life," she continued.

He looked at her questioningly

"It's Ranjit," she said. "The Khalistan movement has relit the smoldering fire in your father's heart, and I'm afraid your grandfather's murder will only fuel it. I know him – he'll try to use this unfortunate event to induce the men in the family to join his cause."

Darashan was astonished at Bhajanma's awareness. "How do you know RanjitBauji is involved in the movement?"

She gave him a penetrating look. "Does she know I know?" Darashan wondered.

"Darashan, every mother knows her son. The moment I heard the word "Khalistan," I knew Ranjit would be drawn to it. I've watched him for the last six months. Secretive phone calls, late nights with friends… He had no friends, and then suddenly they've sprouted like grass blades."

He looked at her curiously. "What is your opinion about Khalistan, Bhajanma?"

She heaved a sigh.

"Darashan, when Pakistan was carved out of India, we were

forced out of our ancestral home in Pakistan. As Sikhs, we had to evacuate – just like so many Hindus had to. We raised our children in the new country. Our children belong to India now. Do you really want to leave your home and business, move to another country and start all over again? Surely there would be bloodshed. I don't care what happens to me, but I don't want a disaster like that to befall my grandchildren and great-grandchildren."

"Besides," she continued, "Khalistan would have to be a small nation. Undoubtedly it would only end up subjugated by more powerful countries around it."

"Whatever the facts," she went on, "a new storm is approaching fast and Ranjit is caught up in it. I know he'll try to push you – along with Balbir, Charan and Mohan – into the movement."

She looked Darashan in the eye. "Don't let him talk you into joining him. You decide the course of your own actions."

"Yes, Bhajanma." He lowered his head. "I will decide the course of my own actions."

"One more thing. I know you're upset that you were with your grandfather when he was injured. It's not your fault. If you had tried to fight the mob when it surrounded you, you would have died too."

She stood up. "Now, I want you to return to Indore as soon as possible. Your family needs you. Find those men and then go back."

She headed into the kitchen, leaving Darashan alone to ponder their conversation.

The next day, Ranjit Singh invited Darashan to another Khalistan meeting.

Darashan saw the same old faces, along with a sprinkling of new ones among the attendees. As for his father, he was a transformed man – animated now by his outrage over his father's killing.

Darashan stared in awe at this charismatic figure up on the stage. He radiated vigor, strength and energy and his voice boomed throughout the room.

"We must prepare to sacrifice and suffer deprivation for our new homeland. I lost my grandfather and uncle at the time of partition. I stayed back to save our home and lost my hand." He held up his stump, which was now his badge of honor. "Many like me survived the partition physically, but ended up as crushed, lost men. This fight will revive us; we must avenge our loss of honor. We must fight for our homeland."

Bhajan used to describe how spirited her son had been prior to the partition. Darashan and Rajkumari hadn't believed her. Now Darashan saw that she hadn't been exaggerating.

After the meeting, Darashan phoned Arun. "You've already helped me once. Now I need to ask for help again."

"Of course," said Arun warmly. "I know you would help me if the situation were reversed."

"Two men helped my grandfather when he was lying wounded on the road. My grandmother has their names and addresses. She wants to meet them. Do you think you could find them? If you do, I'll visit them and bring them over to see her." He read Arun the names and addresses.

Arun called the next evening.

"I managed to contact those men you asked about. Unfortunately, they're afraid it wouldn't be safe for them to visit a Sikh home. But they say they'll come to my home. Could you come over tomorrow evening?"

Darashan groaned. "So now Hindus won't visit Sikhs?"

"Time," said Arun, gently. "Time will heal these wounds."

Darashan sighed. "I'll be at your house tomorrow."

"Good. Bhushan is visiting Delhi. He'll be here tomorrow, too. He wants to see you."

Darashan had to face Bhajanma next. Fearing her reaction, he said, "Bhajanma, Arun did find the two men you wish to see, but they won't visit a Sikh family."

"Darashan, we must admit we're partially responsible for the situation," she replied wearily. "India welcomed us when we were forced out of Pakistan. We've prospered, but now here we are, looking to carve up India again."

Darashan looked away.

"Those men helped a Sikh man in need. They endangered their own lives to do it. I just want to thank them. You go see them and tell them we can't possibly repay them for their act of kindness. The least we can do is thank them and offer a token of our appreciation."

Bhajanma handed Darashan a few pieces of her jewelry and some cash.

When Darashan reached Arun's home the next day, Ninad opened the door. "Mommy and Daddy will be back soon. Uncle Bhushan is here. Please have a seat."

Bhushan was sitting on a sofa scribbling on a note pad. He smiled at Darashan as he entered, then went back to his scribbling.

Darashan's mind flew back to the old days when Bhushan and Ikbal had spent hours composing poetry. They would read it aloud, but George, Arun and Darashan had mostly mocked their efforts with flippant wisecracks.

The memory briefly made Darashan forget his current troubles as he watched Bhushan at work. "Life was so simple back then," he thought.

Arun and Usha showed up. "What are you writing? A speech?" Arun asked Bhushan. He took a seat beside him and peeked at the paper. "Good God – poetry!" Arun exclaimed.

"Yes. It's called 'Mother India Laments.' I'll read it to you when I'm done."

"Hell, no. I had hoped not to suffer any more of your poetry after college! When Ikbal visits he reads his latest work and we have to listen to him. At least he's a famous *shayar*. I'm not ready to submit to ministerial nonsense! What's this poetry about, anyway? You and Ikbal used to write about love and heartbreak. Are you chasing other women? I must inform BindiBhabiji."

Arun's mockery never failed to aggravate Bhushan. "Arun, you are so ignorant! A poet is a poet for life, and love isn't the only theme for poetry. There are other topics – nature, death, a mother's love, hunger…"

Arun interrupted him again, "…corruption, blackmail,

159

smuggling, racketeering, influence-peddling…"

"Arun!" Bhushan exclaimed. "You haven't changed a bit. Be serious for once."

Darashan laughed. He couldn't stop himself.

"Okay. I'm sorry. Please read your poem." Arun moved to the floor and sat in a lotus position with fake somberness on his face.

Bhushan stammered, "The poem…it's an English poem."

"Are you crazy?" Arun asked. "Can you write literary English?"

"No, but I'm planning to send it to George for publication. He can correct it. His newspaper is in English."

Arun laughed. "Just because George is your friend and you're a Prime Minister, you want to make him to publish your poem? He'll feel obliged to print it – probably on the last page, which no one reads." Arun collapsed into laughter, and Darashan, transported to old times, joined him.

"The poem is devoted to India and the present turmoil," said Bhushan, ignoring them.

That failed to impress Arun. "So?"

"I wish Gopal were here. He doesn't make fun of my poems."

"Gopal doesn't understand your poems. He only pretends to appreciate them."

"That's not true!"

"I give up. Read your poem," said Arun.

But before Bhushan could proceed, Ninad came in. "Security called. Two men are here to see Uncle Darashan."

"They can come in," Arun told Ninad. "Your poem will have to wait, Bhushan." Bhushan went back to his writing.

"Do you want us to leave you alone, Darashan?" Arun asked.

"No – please stay," Darashan said. Everyone watched the door.

Two men hesitantly entered the living room. Their escort let them in, saluted and left. The two men were obviously impressed

160

by the escort, the security and Arun's lavishly decorated living room.

The younger man, skinny, dressed in blue pants and a checkered red-and-blue shirt, held an unlit cigarette between his fingers. His black hair was heavily oiled and combed so that every hair was in place. He seemed to be making a deliberate effort to appear unaffected by the riches surrounding him.

Darashan came forward and touched the old man's feet. Arun and Bhushan followed suit. The gesture seemed to overwhelm the old man.

"Please, sit down," Arun said.

The old man had gray hair and wore a dhoti and a shirt. Unused to receiving such attention, he sat anxiously on the edge of his seat. The younger man spread out comfortably in a chair. Silence filled the room.

A servant appeared carrying a tray of teacups and snacks, which Usha passed around.

"You must be Jairam and Chiragmal," said Darashan.

"Yes, I'm Jairam, and this is my grandson, Chiragmal. You don't know me, but I know your family. I didn't recognize your wounded grandfather at the time of the riots. Later on, when I visited the hospital, I read his name and guessed who he was."

"You know my family?" Darashan asked, surprised.

"I'm Ramlal's nephew. Ramlal worked for your grandmother's parents, Bijibai and Gobind Singh. As a young boy I helped my uncle with farm chores. I knew your great-grandparents and your grandmother's brother who, along with his father, was killed at the time of the partition."

Darashan slowly grasped the connection. "So you lived in my grandparents' and parents' village?"

"Yes. Like your family, we left Pakistan after my Uncle Ramlal was murdered. Recently I started to work in a shop close to yours. There I heard your grandfather's name and wondered whether he was the Gurumukh Singh that I knew. I stopped by, and your father and grandfather immediately knew who I was. Your grandfather was happy to see me and invited me to visit the family. I wanted to meet Bhajanma and also to see you and your sister. You were little kids then. I was planning to visit your family, but before I could…" Jairam stopped.

"I understand," Darashan said, misery filling his heart.

"How is Bhajandidee?"

"She's brave – braver than me. She's dealt with the situation better than all of us. She faced one calamity at the time of partition, and now she's facing another." Darashan stopped, wondering if he had said too much.

"We understand," said Jairam. "Amrutchachee, my Uncle Ramlal's wife, didn't cry when her husband was murdered. And mentally, she continued to live in her old home. Sometimes she would weep for her husband for days." He addressed Darashan. "I have a request for you…" Everyone could hear the anguish in his voice.

"Go on," Darashan murmured.

"Please give up the notion of Khalistan. I can't tolerate the idea of Hindus and Sikhs spilling each other's blood."

"Many Sikhs are already dead," Darashan responded, his voice unemotional.

"I'm sorry," Jairam said. "Let's stop it right here. Let's not ruin more lives. Chiragmal says India must be a Hindu country. But that's impossible. We're a complex mosaic." He paused and looked around at everyone. "I'm sorry. I'm an old man. I can't control my emotions. You all are educated people. You understand the situation better."

Darashan spoke, his voice soft, "No – that's not true. You suffered at the time of the partition. You had to run away from home. Experience is the best teacher."

"We all feel it," said Bhushan.

"Please visit Bhajanma sometime soon," Darashan said.

"We'll come as soon as we can, but I don't know when that will be. Our neighbors are so angry with Sikhs right now."

"It doesn't have to be now. Whenever you feel it's safe."

"I will," Jairam promised.

"We are grateful. Thank you," said Darashan, wiping tears.

"Bhajanma often spoke about Ramlal and his family. I know she'd like to see his children and grandchildren."

Jairam stood up. "We must go now. Chiragmal has a job."

Bhushan stood up. "Jairam, you're a very courageous man. We all admire you. If I can do anything for you please let me know."

Arun added, "You know where I live. Our country needs people like you."

Darashan had with him a bag containing gifts for the two men. But he couldn't bring himself to offer them. "Bhajanma will offer them to Jairam when he visits," he decided. "That would be more appropriate." He walked the men to the door, then returned and settled back down on his seat. Everyone was engrossed quietly in their own thoughts.

Usha's voice broke the spell, "I'm still waiting to hear the poem." She stood in the hallway, watching the gloomy trio.

Bhushan lifted the pad he had dumped on the floor and began to read.

BHARATMATA LAMENTS

For centuries
with few exceptions,
because of internal dissension.
I have been dismembered,
and suffered the humiliation,
of foreign rule and domination,
because
my beloved children
never seem to learn.
They fight, burn and slaughter
their very own brothers.
They help a foreigner
who ultimately conquers
and tramples
them and their brothers.

My beloved children
never seem to learn:
a brutal blood-soaked partition
leaves a part of the population
in the mainland
and in the partitioned country.
They are now considered outsiders
in their homeland
of a thousand years.
They are now eternal
enemies of their neighbors.
My children, you are Indians first,
and must learn to live with each other.
Amalgam of diversity,
you share a powerful bond.
If severed, it will bleed,
and destroy you all.
My children,
many times in the past,
with a blood bath
I have been ripped apart.
A divine force then unleashes a fury
and unites me again and again,
for I am indivisible.

After he finished reading the poem, everyone was quiet.

At last Bhushan spoke. "Jairam expressed my feelings much
better than I ever could. I can never match the intense emotion in
his voice and the expression in his eyes."

"I think you have," said Darashan, surprising himself and
others. He smiled and looked at Bhushan. "Jairam's talk and your
poem have been very educational."

CHAPTER 17

The upheaval following the Prime Minister's assassination had ruined Mohan's sense of security. A curtain had descended between his carefree past life and his current troubled state.

Superficially, his life had returned to normal. He woke up, had breakfast, went to college and tried to study.

But everyone was transformed. His whole family seemed anxious and on edge, though no one talked about it.

He'd been thrilled to have his father back home. But since his arrival, he'd existed as a man apart – as if he weren't related to the rest of the family. Mohan had begun to have nightmares in which his mother would call plaintively, "Darashan…. Darashan!" But his father would only glance at her, turn his back, and walk away.

Only Varsha seemed to be unchanged, laughing, joking, and arguing with Mohan as if nothing had changed.

Mohan recalled that Uncle Gopal had wanted to see his father. Soon after his father's return, he'd asked his mother to phone him.

But Maya had already tried. "He says he can't travel," she reported. "He fractured his leg in a car crash. He'll visit us as soon as he can walk. He did try to phone Daddy, but Daddy's never home." She looked pained. "I asked your father to call Gopal, but he ignores me."

"I've been trying to talk to Daddy, too," said Mohan." But he's always in a bad mood – and anyway, Ranjit Bauji is always with him."

It was true: since his arrival, Ranjit Singh had followed Darashan like a shadow. These days it was almost impossible to find Darashan alone.

One evening Maya told Mohan that Rati had dropped by.

"While I was at school?" Mohan asked, surprised.

"Yes. She wanted to talk to me," said Maya. "She met Bhajanma, too. She told me you asked her to forget you and move on because of your religious differences."

"It's true," said Mohan.

"She was very upset," said Maya. "She says she loves only you, and that religion is immaterial to her. She pointed out that I myself am a Hindu, married to a Sikh man."

"What did you tell her?" Mohan asked, anxiously.

"I'm not a wise woman. I didn't know what to say. I explained that when I married your father, the political situation was different. And if you and she decide to marry, she's more than welcome in our family."

"And what did Bhajanma say?"

"She liked Rati. She said she'd like to forget politics and accept her with open arms.'"

"What do you think I should do, Mommy?"

"I'm sorry, Mohan – I don't have answers. At this point in my life I have only questions." She sighed. "I suggest that you wait. The political storm may blow over."

Mohan resolved to ask his father's advice.

The next night, Devaki invited Maya, Bhajanma and Varsha for an overnight stay at her home.

"This is my chance," thought Mohan. "I'll talk to Daddy tonight even if I have to wake him up."

After dinner, he studied in his room for a while, then tiptoed to his father's room. From the dark hallway he could hear low voices. As he moved closer, he realized that his father and grandfather were in deep discussion. Putting his ear to the door, he made out his grandfather's voice. "When the British left we should have fought for our own country like the Muslims did. If we had, we wouldn't be in the situation we are now. I want you to join me. People will remember us as a father-son team. You've come to our meetings. Now it's time for you to commit. Be one of the leaders."

"But…Bhajanma…," Mohan could imagine the look on his father's face.

Ranjit Singh didn't let his father finish his sentence. "Yes, I know– She'll try to stop you. Bhajanma and mothers like her want their families home. They love their children and their grandchildren above all else. It's not that I don't love my family.

But I'm willing to sacrifice everything on the altar of Khalistan. We need to act now. A delay will only add to our difficulties. Balbir is with me. I'm trying to get Charan involved."

Mohan's heart started to race. Had his cousin joined his grandfather? And was he after Charan, too?

His grandfather was speaking again. "I know Rajkumari is opposed to the notion of Khalistan. But I want you to know that I didn't have to drag Balbir. He's a fighter. He joined the movement on his own. Darashan, you too must renounce your family obligations."

Mohan held his hand on his mouth to stop himself from uttering a sound. The firestorm of Khalistan had not only engulfed his family, but was splitting them into opposing groups.

"But Mohan – What about Mohan?" Mohan heard his father's question and caught his breath at the sound of his own name.

"We need doctors to help us," said his grandfather. "So we'll want him to finish his education. In the meantime, he needs to be won over to the cause. It won't be easy. He loves his mother; we'll have to help him break that bond."

Mohan swallowed hard, appalled by his grandfather's words.

"You, too, Darashan – you must break your bond with your wife. She can't be trusted. Her friend Devaki routinely publishes anti-Khalistan articles. The movement holds that against her. You must leave her – preferably get a divorce."

Mohan started to shake. He couldn't control his sob. He tiptoed to his room and wept.

"How casually my grandfather dismisses my mother! She's his grandchildren's mother and his son's wife. But he dismisses her like a servant."

When he had collected himself, he wiped his tears, switched on the light and picked up an old family photo displayed on his desk. In it, Maya held Varsha while little Mohan stood by her side. All three of them were smiling. Mohan hugged the picture. Whatever the future might bring, he vowed, he would never abandon his mother.

Then he thought about Varsha. She needed to know what was going on.

The next evening he offered to take her to her favorite restaurant.

"You? Asking me out?" Varsha asked, surprised.

"Yes."

"Can I call Rati? I bet she'd like to join us."

"No. I want to talk to you."

For once Varsha didn't ask questions.

Over dahi vada Mohan slowly recited the conversation he'd heard the night before.

Varsha laughed. "So, what else is new? You are so naive. Why did you think our grandfather's been visiting us? You know what he thinks of women and that Auntie Rajkumari hates him. Ignore him, Mohan. He doesn't count."

Varsha's reaction astonished Mohan. He'd been oblivious to his grandfather's involvement in the Khalistan movement, yet his little sister had guessed long ago.

"If our grandfather thinks he and his cronies can fight the Indian army, they're out of their minds," said Varsha. "And if our father joins him, he's out of his mind too."

"Varsha!" Mohan exclaimed.

"It's the truth, my dear brother."

Mohan thought for a moment. "I'm afraid Daddy may join him out of a sense of loyalty."

"Loyalty? To whom? What about us?" Varsha spat.

"Varsha, calm down."

"I feel like screaming," she said. "Nobody except our grandfather is for Khalistan. We live in India. Our homes and businesses are in India. If we pack up and move to so-called Khalistan, we'll have to start all over again. Our mother and her family is Hindu. If, despite this reality, Daddy decides to join the cause, let him. What can we do? We can't stop him."

"But Mommy...she'll be devastated."

"Yes, but she'll live. She has us. Now stop worrying about a situation you can't control and eat."

Mohan saw that Varsha had already finished her food.

"Now I have a piece of advice for you," said Varsha. Mohan looked up from his plate to his sister's calm face.

"Don't dump Rati. Don't throw away a jewel for the sake of stupid politics. You would be submitting to a cause you don't even believe in."

Mohan looked up from his plate and grinned.

"Varsha, you're amazing! Mommy's right. You're like Auntie Rajkumari!"

"Maybe I am," Varsha said. "Now please order me some chocolate ice cream."

Late that evening the doorbell rang, and Mohan and Varsha both rushed to the door. There was Gopal, on crutches. Beside him was his driver, holding his little suitcase.

"Uncle Gopal!" Varsha and Mohan shouted in unison. Mohan hugged Gopal, who lost his balance, sending his crutches crashing to the floor. The driver dropped the suitcase as he tried to steady Mohan and Gopal. Darashan came out of the guest room to see what the commotion was. Varsha clapped and laughed. Maya smiled as she watched the scene unfold. Even Darashan laughed aloud. Bhajanma emerged from her room and observed Maya's, Mohan's and Varsha's reactions. She noticed that Ranjit Singh, too, was in the hallway. His face was blank, but his fist, she saw, was clenched. He couldn't be happy about the intrusion.

Gopal, now smiling, entered and asked, "Did Brian let you know I was coming?"

"No," Maya answered.

"I'm sorry. He always forgets. We're late. Our car broke down."

Noticing Ranjit Singh and Bhajanma, he hobbled over to Bhajanma and curtseyed. "Namaskar Mataji." Then he went to Ranjit Singh and tried to offer a curtsey, but Ranjit Singh stepped back.

"No need for that," he said curtly.

Gopal managed to sit down on the sofa. Varsha and Mohan

immediately positioned themselves on either side of him and started to chatter simultaneously, each vying for Gopal's attention. Maya came in with a tray full of cups of tea. She smiled as she offered one to Gopal and sent out a cup with Mohan for the driver, who was waiting in the car.

Bhajanma looked on approvingly "Darashan," she said, "your friend has restored laughter to this home."

CHAPTER 18

Winter was almost over, and the weather was getting warmer. Balavant relaxed in the early morning sun on a chair in his little flower garden. Newspapers lay across his lap. Having felt some discomfort in his chest that morning, he'd decided to rest. Though he remained physically immobile, his thoughts raced backward in time.

After Balbir's birth, life had moved so swiftly that he'd hardly had time to reflect.

Moving to Punjab, he'd been well aware of the struggles he would face as a farmer, but he'd had little concept of what it would take to run a busy maternity home.

He'd found construction workers and had managed to get the hospital and dispensary built for Rajkumari, and then had breathed a sigh of relief, thinking the hard work was done.

But two weeks after Rajkumari started admitting patients for delivery, he had learned his first lesson when she she woke him in the middle of the night, saying, "I need O positive or A positive blood right away!"

"What?" Balavant had tried to open his eyes.

"I need blood donors. I'll test them."

"Where am I supposed to find donors?" he'd asked groggily.

"Wake up our farm workers, anyone – and bring them to the maternity home."

Balavant had gone off to track down some farm workers, while Rajkumari had sent her patient's husband to collect his relatives and bring them to the maternity home.

Rajkumari's technician collected a few blood drops from each person.

"What are you doing to us?" they'd asked, terrified.

"I need bottles of blood from matching donors."

"What will happen to us? We'll die if you take our blood."

"Nonsense. This won't hurt you," Rajkumari had said sternly. "Two lives depend upon your cooperation. If your blood group is the same as our patient's, I'll take a bottle of your blood."

Some of the women had started to cry, and the men had looked scared.

"I'll bring a lamb. Take the lamb's blood, instead," one woman had begged.

Rajkumari was unyielding. "Humans need human blood."

Two of the donors matched, one of which happened to be the patient's husband. His mother wept aloud, "My son is going to die."

Rajkumari's nurse was well trained. "Your son's blood will save your daughter-in-law and grandchild. Stop crying."

A pair of nurses dragged the two men to a small donor room, shoved them down on narrow beds and pushed needles into their veins. The terrified men had watched the blood draining from their bodies into a bottle. When the bottle was full, the nurses clamped it, and, to the men's relief, pulled the needles out of their bodies. To their surprise, the men realized that they were fine. The nurses offered them lemonade. When the men emerged from the donor room, those in the waiting area were amazed that the bloodletting hadn't killed them.

After what seemed an eternity, Rajkumari had stepped out of the operating room with an eight-pound howling baby boy wrapped in a white sheet. The patient's husband and mother-in-law rushed to touch her feet.

Word of that night had spread along with Rajkumari's fame. Women had traveled from nearby villages to Rajkumari's maternity home and her practice had flourished.

Balavant started recording the names, addresses and blood groups of all potential donors in the area, and hired two night guards. Whenever the need arose, one of those guards would round up the donors at their homes.

Soon Balavant had had to buy a car because Rajkumari sometimes had to send infants to the city for intensive care. Balavant hired a driver, who could bring the infant to the hospital. But Rajkumari wanted a nurse to accompany the baby and the nurses wouldn't travel with a strange man. So Balavant had had to travel to the city in the middle of the night with tiny babies. Finally

Rajkumari had hired several male nurses to accompany the driver, so that Balavant wouldn't have to chaperone nurses caring for the baby in the car. Until recently, though, he'd had to substitute when the male nurses were unavailable.

While helping Rajkumari as best he could, Balavant had also had to tend to his farm and animals. And he'd willingly shared the childcare responsibility. He loved his boys and lived for them.

During the day, Balavant and Rajkumari were busy with their work. They had reserved their evenings and dinnertime for the children. By bedtime they were exhausted.

Over the years the question of Rajkumari's love had continued to haunt him.

He knew Rajkumari had had an ulterior motive in marrying him. He'd been well aware at the time that she hadn't loved him. But he'd told himself that in due course she would come around. He knew of plenty of arranged marriages where the couples had come to love each other. "I'll do everything in my power to help her fall in love with me," he'd vowed.

Through the years, though, he'd wondered, "Does she really love me, or does she merely go through the motions of a dutiful wife? Her personality is so solemn! Is she even capable of true affection?" She never asked for clothing or jewelry. She wanted instruments, modern laboratory facilities and oxygen cylinders.

He knew she must love her children, but she wasn't warm like other mothers. She smiled occasionally, laughed rarely and teased and joked only once in a great while.

Balavant noticed that when Darashan and Maya visited, Rajkumari would relax and laugh aloud. She didn't seem to mind Darashan's incessant teasing. And she clearly enjoyed Maya's company. She had a special bond with Maya and would sometimes talk with her for hours.

Seeing this, Balavant would feel lonely, wondering why true intimacy had failed to develop between Rajkumari and himself.

He did take satisfaction in the fact that people were impressed with their achievements and often pointed to them as an ideal, successful couple.

Rajkumari's little maternity home truly was something to be proud of. It had grown over the years. She had added more rooms around a central courtyard with a garden and slides and swings for young children. She now had a nursery, minor surgical suite, a delivery room and an isolation room. She had built kitchen facilities, too, with a separate laundry room and a small laboratory where emergency blood tests could be done.

The architecture was light and airy. A tile-roofed veranda lined the courtyard with potted plants and benches for visitors. Pictures of newborn babies covered the walls of the dispensary and the patient's rooms.

She'd hired more doctors to help her and had developed an affiliation with the medical school in a nearby city. Some of the professors there were so impressed with Rajkumari's facility that they started having their house surgeons do rotations in her maternity home and offered a free consultation service to her poorer patients.

From the beginning, Rajkumari had insisted that the maternity home's financial accounts be kept separate from Balavant's farming accounts. Initially, she'd borrowed money from him to build and staff her maternity home. She'd borrowed money from Darashan, too, for equipment. She'd returned Darashan's funds as soon as she could, and in time had refunded Balavant's money as well.

As far as Balavant was concerned, a marriage meant that all assets were shared. He hadn't intended for her to refund him the money he'd lent her. And he couldn't understand her need to make a point of the fact that she'd paid for her maternity home herself.

Once, when Maya heard Rajkumari proudly telling guests, "My own income supports my maternity home," she'd watched Balavant's reaction and saw that Rajkumari's words hurt him.

Later, Maya pulled Balavant aside. "Rajkumari's father belittled her when she was young, and wouldn't let her go to medical school. He always ignored her achievements and said women are incapable of earning a living. Don't take it personally if she wants the world to know that her success is her own and she's financially independent."

Balavant understood. But it bothered him that he hadn't picked up on this himself. "My sister-in-law knows my wife better than I do," he'd mused.

Balavant had been successful in his own ventures as well. He'd experimented with new varieties of crops, and had started a cooperative with neighboring farmers, selling grains, produce and milk. He'd also established a successful poultry operation and sold chickens and eggs.

His ventures impressed Bhajanma and Gurumukh Singh, who had once known farming life themselves.

"You work very hard, Balavant," Bhajanma would say approvingly.

Balavant would laugh. "Trying to keep up with your granddaughter, Bhajanma!"

Then, last year he'd suffered a heart attack.

Rajkumari had diagnosed it immediately. She'd set up a sickroom in the house and consulted a cardiologist, who examined Balavant and decided he could be treated at home, as long as he agreed to rest. Rajkumari, with her usual efficiency, now dealt with both the farm and medical practice by herself, to allow Balavant time to recover.

Now, sitting in the Garden, Balavant felt pain stabbing in his chest again. He held his breath and closed his eyes until it abated. Eventually, he fell asleep. When he awoke, Rajkumari was standing over his chair, studying him with concern. "Are you sick?" she asked.

"No, just tired."

Balavant knew that she wouldn't accept this answer. "Why are you tired so early in the morning?"

"I couldn't sleep last night," he said, hoping she would believe him and leave him alone. But she ignored his explanation.

"I'll have Dr. Dhandha check your heart. You need a cardiogram."

To her, he knew, he was he was simply a patient right now.

"I think you need more help," Rajkumari continued.

"Farming is hard physical labor."

"I know what I can and can't do," Balavant retorted.

"You had a heart attack," Rajkumari persisted. "Your blood pressure is erratic."

"I don't want to live like a dead man."

She looked at him sharply. "What do you mean?"

"If living means lying on a bed all day, it's not worth it."

"I'm not asking you to rest all the time. I just don't want you to overextend yourself."

"I've already cut down my workload. If I have to stop doing what I'm doing now, I might as well stop living."

"That's absurd," exclaimed Rajkumari. "I need you. Your sons need you. We don't care if you spend your days and nights in bed. We want you with us."

"You're strong," said Balavant. "You'll be tired of a sick husband before long."

Rajkumari threw up her hands. "I can't argue with you. But my friend Jayanti knows a reliable farm hand. Please at least talk to her."

Her habit of resolving issues without bothering to consult him irritated Balavant. Often her decisions were right, but he couldn't help wishing she would seek his opinion.

Until recently, though, she had never crossed over into his domain of farming. But with the excuse of his illness, she was starting to meddle in his affairs.

"I can find my own help."

"Just make sure you do it." She gathered herself to go. "Charan will be done with agriculture school soon. Then he can help."

Balavant watched her hurrying off to her dispensary, and then, worn out by the conversation, he dozed off.

Sometime later, he awoke with a start. Sharp noises were sounding in the distance. "Firecrackers? At this time of day?" he mumbled, and closed his eyes again, only to be jolted wide awake a moment later as a group of maternity home and farm workers went racing by. Balavant stood up to follow, but was overcome with exhaustion and settled back onto his chair. "I'll find out what's going on soon," he muttered.

Sure enough, a few moments later, his trusted farm manager, Rohan, approached his chair.

"I've been looking for you all over, Sardarji," he exclaimed, panting as he spoke. "Someone rode a scooter to the farm's entrance, and fired shots in the air. All the workers are terrified. Everyone's saying it was meant as a threat against the Hindus working on your farm."

Rohan looked shaken.

"You think it's a serious threat?"

"I think they mean business, Sardarji."

"I'll go see the police and hire guards," said Balavant.

"You'll need an army battalion to protect a big spread like this."

"I'll hire six guards then."

"Guards won't calm fears. I suspect your Hindu workers won't last long here."

Balavant studied Rohan's face. "How about you? Does this make you want to leave?"

Rohan was a powerfully built man with wild hair and bushy eyebrows. Despite his fierce looks, he was a kind man. Balavant saw fear flickering in his eyes, but his voice was resolute. "I won't let them drive me off just yet."

He looked at Balavant cautiously. "May I ask you a question?"

"Anything."

"Did you receive a threatening letter demanding money?"

Balavant was taken aback. How did Rohan know?

He had indeed discovered such a letter on his doorstep early one morning a few weeks back. After reading it over, he had simply shredded it, along with the envelope, and thrown it away.

"Who would write me a letter like that?"

"People in the Khalistan movement. A lot of townspeople have received letters, especially the well-off ones."

"I'm not afraid of threats," said Balavant. "A bullet is better

177

than another heart attack that would confine me to my room."

"You're not bed-ridden, Sardarji. You may not have another heart attack for years."

Rohan hesitated, then went on. "Some people are saying it's your wife's medical practice that's kept your farm safe until now."

Balavant was unperturbed. "I believe it. Even Khalistanis need medical care." He knew that Rajkumari had recently sutured one man's stab wound and dug a bullet out of another's arm. She never asked questions and never turned a patient away.

"So why are they coming after us now?"

"I'm not sure," said Rohan. "Outsiders are in town. Word has it the revolutionaries are gearing up for action." He sighed. "I fear we may all get burned in this fire."

Rohan eyed Balavant uncertainly, then continued. "Some people are saying Balbir has joined the movement."

Balavant stifled a gasp. His heart was pounding, but he tried to feign nonchalance.

"Has he? I'll talk to him. Thank you for letting me know."

Rohan studied him with concern. "I hope I haven't upset you with this news. I just thought you'd want to know."

He turned to go. "These are difficult times. Please let me know if there's anything I can do."

Left alone on his chair, Balavant sat bewildered. How could he have been so ignorant of his son's activities, he wondered? He would have a word with Balbir, he decided, and talk sense into him before it was too late.

But a week went by, and still Balavant hadn't been able to bring himself to confront his son. Then one morning he was in the dining room drinking his morning tea when once again he heard gunshots. For a moment he froze in his chair, his legs refusing to move. Then he struggled to his feet and ventured out. A nurse met him at the front door. "Rohan's been shot!" she exclaimed breathlessly. "He needs medical attention."

Quickly he wakened Rajkumari, who raced to the maternity home where Rohan was being prepared for surgery.

Balavant sat on the front step, anxiously thinking back to the threatening letter he'd so blithely ignored.

"If we don't receive 15,000 RS. within 15 days, someone will be hurt."

A phone number had been printed at the bottom.

"If I start handing out money, they'll only demand more," Balavant had thought.

He'd assumed the threat had been directed at him. His own safety was of little concern to him. Yet it was Rohan who had paid the price.

He walked over to the maternity home and camped out in the waiting room, anxious for word.

At last Rajkumari emerged from the surgical suite. "It was a shoulder wound," she said, "and a superficial one at that. He's going to be ok."

Balavant was overwhelmed with relief. He couldn't have forgiven himself if his actions had resulted in permanent injury to his loyal worker and friend. He resolved to send Rohan away for his own safety. "He can go to Delhi," he thought. "I'll ask Darashan to find him a job."

When Balavant tried to interrogate Rohan about the shooting the next morning, he got nowhere.

"You have no idea who shot you?"

"I couldn't see his face," Rohan said evasively. "He was on a scooter."

"And you didn't get a look at him at all?"

"No."

Rohan wouldn't meet Balavant's eyes.

"I want you to get away from here," said Balavant. "If you go to Delhi, Rajkumari's brother can find you work."

"That's kind of you," said Rohan. "But I have an uncle in Bombay. He's offered to help get me established there."

"We'll miss you," said Balavant.

"I had hoped to work for you for the rest of my life," said Rohan sadly. "But it seems the forces of revolution prefer to see me go."

"I'll make a police report."

"No," said Rohan quickly. "Please don't. They'll only harass our workers and they won't find the culprit."

Balavant suddenly wondered if his own son had been involved in this incident. Was Rohan trying to protect Balbir, in spite of everything?

Rohan sighed and said nothing further.

When the day came for him to depart, Rohan wept like a child at the train station. The farm workers seeing him off cried too. Balavant watched, struggling to control his own tears.

Things got worse for Balavant and Rajkumari from there.

Balavant began handing cash over to the unknown letter writers, hoping to forestall further attacks. Balbir began disappearing for long stretches, coming home for just a day or two at a time before taking off again. Balavant hoped that some of the cash he forked over to the movement was in some way reaching Balbir and helping him to survive.

One by one, their Hindu workers resigned to move to safety, away from Punjab.

Balavant and Rajkumari carried on mechanically. The farming and medical work went on as always. Their remaining staff managed to eat, sleep, joke and celebrate special occasions, despite the pervasive tension. But everyone's nerves were perpetually raw, and even the smallest stimulus, like a firecracker or a wisp of smoke, could set off a panic.

When word came of Gurumukh Singh's death, Rajkumari was devastated. The shell that the proud adolescent Rajkumari had built around herself shattered. She cursed her pride, and regretted never returning home for a visit.

As for Balavant, he struggled to keep the farm running. He talked of selling his beloved cows and water buffalos.

Rajkumari wrote a letter of apology to Bhajanma.

"I long to visit you, but the maternity home is short-staffed and Balavant isn't well. I'll come as soon as possible."

She controlled herself when she had to work, but at home her tears wouldn't stop. Balavant comforted her as best he could, but he was astonished. Rarely had he seen his wife shed a tear.

She was frightened. She didn't know where her older son was. The life she and Balavant had built up was threatened. Her family outside Punjab was insecure. At night she clung to Balavant and wept.

"I have many acquaintances," she thought, "but no real friends except Maya."

Before Gurumukh Singh's death, Rajkumari had phoned Maya often to talk. Discussing her problems with Maya had calmed Rajkumari, but now Maya was not in the mood to talk. "Darashan is not himself," Maya would say, and keep quiet. Rajkumari, who had been seeking solace from Maya, was disconcerted. "Has Darashan joined the movement too?" she wondered.

Her beloved grandfather lay dead. Her grandmother, who had sustained the family in difficult situations, was old and a widow. Meanwhile, the men in her family were being inexorably pulled into a movement she believed would fail, after destroying many lives and property, while her sick husband was withdrawing from the world.

The family she had so vehemently renounced, she suddenly realized, had been helping her all along. Yet it was only now that their support was teetering that she finally recognized all that they had done.

CHAPTER 19

Gopal arrived in Indore to spend a week with Darashan and Maya. Rankled by Gopal's presence, Ranjit Singh packed his bags the next day and decamped for Delhi by himself.

Gopal's and Bhajanma's presence, and Ranjit Singh's departure, lifted the mood of the household. Mohan and Varsha laughed and talked, and even Darashan's temperament improved. "Darashan," said Bhajanma. "Your friend is no ordinary person. He has the demeanor of a saint."

"Your judgment is always accurate," said Darashan. "Years back, Gopal visited our home in Delhi," he reminded her.

"I don't remember him," said Bhajanma, running through Darashan's college friends in her mind. "You had so many friends."

"That's true," said Darashan wistfully.

"He really seems to care for you and your family."

"He used to walk Maya home when I couldn't do it. He's always looked out for her. And he loves Varsha and Mohan, too, and they love and admire him. Maya seems to trust him totally. I almost think I trust him more than I trust myself."

"You're lucky to have a friend like him," said Bhajanma. She looked at Darashan appraisingly. "Your family may need his help someday."

All week long, Gopal spoke privately with Darashan in the evenings. At the end of the week, he had to go. "I'll visit again soon," he promised.

Not long afterwards, Darashan told Mohan that he had sold the family's business. He brought Mohan to the bank and opened an account for him. "The money in this account should be more than enough for the rest of medical school and your four years of specialty training," he said.

Mohan was taken aback. "I don't need a separate account," he protested. "I've always asked you or mommy when I needed money. Why can't we keep it that way?"

"You're old enough to deal with your own finances," said Darashan. "I've opened another account for your mother and

Varsha. You won't have to worry about them."

Mohan was perturbed. "Why would I have to worry about them?"

The look on his father's face was inscrutable.

When Ranjit Singh returned a week later, he sat down for a serious discussion with Bhajanma. "Kuldip plans to go stay with Rajkumari," he said. "You have a choice. Do you want to stay here in Indore, or go to Punjab with Kuldip?"

"If returning to our home in Delhi isn't an option," she said, giving Ranjit Singh a penetrating look, "then I think I'd like to go to Rajkumari's. Her farm reminds me of our old home in Pakistan."

Maya overheard the conversation and cast a sad glance at her beloved Bhajanma. She wanted to plead with her, "Please, stay with me! Rajkumari's strong. I'm not. I need your support." But she controlled herself. "Bhajanma will be happy with Rajkumari," she told herself.

A day later, Ranjit Singh approached Bhajanma and Kuldip. "Are you two ready to go?" he asked. "Rajkumari has lots of help. She can easily care for you two."

Varsha, who happened to be in the room, exploded. "They can live here if they want to! Mom, Dad, Mohan and I are just as able to take care of them as Auntie Rajkumari. And Mohan will be a doctor soon."

Varsha's outburst shocked Ranjit Singh. Nobody – except Rajkumari once, long ago – ever talked to him like that. He was speechless.

"Varsha, you can't speak to your grandfather like that," said Maya. "Apologize."

Bhajanma stepped forward and patted Varsha. "Your family takes wonderful care of us here, Varsha. But Kuldip and I do want to visit your aunt and her family, too. We haven't seen them for a while."

"All right, but please promise you'll come back soon," said Varsha, ignoring Maya's directive to apologize.

"I hope to," said Bhajanma. "But you must remember that your great-grandmother is old. I may not–"

Varsha cut in. "We want you to live forever, Bhajanma."

Bhajanma patted Varsha and smiled.

Kuldipma and Bhajanma packed their bags. The entire family went to the railroad station to see them off. Bhajanma hugged Maya and whispered, "I'm sorry to leave you. You must endure and sustain yourself."

That night, Maya and Darashan held each other. "One question haunts me," Maya murmured. "If I ask, will you answer truthfully?"

Empathy for his beloved Maya flooded Darashan's heart. "I'll try." He hugged her more tightly until, realizing she could hardly breathe, he loosened his hold.

"Why did you let go?" Maya asked.

"You couldn't breathe, Maya."

"I *want* to stop breathing," she said, with anguish. "But I have responsibilities... Varsha."

Darashan stroked her hair. "We should have heeded Bhajanma's words. Our marriage was a mistake."

Maya wiped a tear. "Not for me. I've had a wonderful life with the man I love. I'm lucky."

Darashan held her tightly again. "Now the question," he murmured.

She looked at him with apprehension. "Is Balbir in the movement?"

He let her go. "Maya, you know the answer."

She sighed heavily. "Ok, then. In that case then I want a promise."

Darashan knew what she wanted – assurances that her son wouldn't be dragged into the movement too. But what control over events did anyone have in times like these?

"I'm sorry," he whispered. "I can't make any promises."

She looked away.

"Now I have a question," Darashan said.

"Yes?"

"Do you want a divorce?"

She looked at him sharply. "No."

"I...I thought...maybe Gopal..."

Maya pushed Darashan away. She sat up. Darashan could see that she was furious. Her eyes flashed. "Don't drag Gopal into the mess we created. The relationship I have with him is different."

"I know that, Maya. I've sensed that since our college days."

"Then why did you ask?"

"I'm sorry, Maya. Please don't be angry..." But Maya stormed out of the room.

A week later, Darashan left.

Maya wanted to go to the train station to bid him good-bye, but Darashan wouldn't let her.

She stood at the gate and watched him walk to the rickshaw stand. Prepared for his departure, she was composed.

That night, she told the children that their father had gone.

Mohan was distraught, wanting to track Darashan down and make him change his mind. But Varsha was unfazed. "It's his life," she said. "Let him live it the way he wants to."

"Don't you even care?" asked Mohan

"He's doing what he wants," said Varsha. "We should be happy for him."

"I don't understand her!" exclaimed Mohan.

Maya shook her head. "She's like her aunt: independent and strong-willed."

But Maya dreaded telling Rajkumari that her father and brother had forsaken the family for Khalistan. She especially hated the thought of Bhajanma having to absorb this news after all she'd been through – and so soon after her husband's death.

She thought of traveling to Punjab to break the news in person but she was reluctant to leave Varsha by herself.

Finally, late one night she resolved to write a letter. She had just settled down with paper and pen when the phone rang.

Rajkumari was on the line. It was clear she'd been crying.

"What's wrong, Raj?" Maya asked.

"Has someone told her about Darashan and Bauji?" she wondered

"I need to speak to Bauji," choked Rajkumari, through sobs.

So she didn't know. But in that case, what new disaster had precipitated Rajkumari's tears? Maya's heart started to race.

"Bauji's not here," she stammered. "Why are you crying?"

"Bhajanma's sick," said Rajkumari.

"It's pneumonia, and the treatment's failing. Please tell Bauji and Darashan they must come to Punjab right away."

Maya started to shake. She recalled Bhajanma's parting words, "You must endure and sustain yourself."

Maya had lost her parents years ago, and Darashan had left her. Yet none of that had seized her with as much terror and panic as Bhajanma's impending death now. She felt like a vine wildly swaying in a storm.

"Are you there? Speak, Maya!" Rajkumari pleaded.

"I'm sorry – Darashan and Bauji aren't home," Maya managed.

"Can you find them?"

"I'll – I'll call you back." She disconnected the phone and collapsed on the sofa.

That night, Maya tossed and turned, unable to quiet her racing thoughts.

Bhajanma must have suspected that her son and grandson would join the movement. But why should she have to learn of their desertion on her deathbed? Why not let her go peacefully?

Early the next morning, the phone rang. Rajkumari was beside herself. "Bhajanma's not with us."

Maya gasped.

Rajkumari went on. "In her last moments, she asked me to look after you and Kuldipma. Why would she say that, Maya? Kuldipma is Bauji's responsibility, and you have Darashan."

Maya struggled to find the right words. "Bauji and Darashan are gone," she finally blurted. "You can...guess why."

"What? I knew what Bauji was up to, but I didn't think Darashan would join him. I can't believe it! Bauji must have forced him."

But then her anger seemed to subside. She wept as she spoke. "Maya, we're orphans now. We'll have to look out for each other."

CHAPTER 20

Every day, Maya repeated a mantra to herself: "Bhajanma is my role model. My children need me. I must not wallow in the past. I must go on."

Rajkumari phoned often. "I live in Punjab," she assured Maya. "If I learn anything, I'll let you know."

"But, Raj, you're so busy," Maya told her. "I love to talk to you, but please call me only when you have time."

"It's ok – I need to talk to you," Rajkumari said.

Rajkumari had always seemed so strong. But now Maya could no longer be sure in her frequent conversations with Rajkumari who was more balanced and who sustained the other.

"I didn't recognize how much Bhajanma's existence buoyed me through hard times until she was gone," Rajkumari lamented.

Maya tried to help. "Rajkumari, you're doing your best and you still have your maternity home to keep you busy."

Rajkumari sounded disconsolate. "I wish I could talk to you in person."

"Me too," said Maya. Their wish for face to face conversation was more than just emotional; both suspected their phones were being tapped.

Maya also faced another problem. Rati was visiting every day. "I love Mohan and he loves me," she said. "But he avoids me now because I'm Hindu. He says I should forget him and marry someone else. My family agrees with him, and they're trying to arrange a marriage for me." She began to plead. "Please ask Mohan to marry me. I promise I won't create any problems for you."

Maya looked at her sadly. "Rati, I'm Hindu and I married a Sikh. And I'm afraid I can't tell you it's been a success. You're a sweet girl. I don't want to see you get dragged into a political mess."

She went on. "Right now I don't think Mohan should be marrying anyone – Hindu or Sikh. Let's wait."

Rati sighed. "I'm not a child anymore. I know what's best for me."

Varsha concurred with Rati. "Mommy, do you want Mohan and Rati to break up over a political movement? If so, you're giving in to a threat. Death is better than that kind of life. Let Mohan marry Rati. Mohan won't find another wife like her."

Mohan refused to discuss Rati at all. He avoided both the topic and Rati herself.

*   *   *   *   *   *   *   *

Late one night the doorbell rang. "Who is it?" asked Mohan. "Gopal."

Mohan opened the door. Gopal cast one glance at Maya's anxious face and hastened to assure her, "I'm not here with news about Darashan. I'm here for Mohan."

"Me?" asked Mohan. "Why?"

"I've heard from reliable sources that the movement is plotting to pull you in after graduation. They need doctors."

Maya gasped.

"The movement took my husband and now they want my son?"

"It's true," said Mohan. "People have been calling and leaving me notes. They say, 'Your father and grandfather want you with them.' They say they'll wait till I graduate and finish my internship, and then it's time for me to join."

"Why didn't you tell me, Mohan?" asked Maya.

"How would it have helped?" said Mohan. "You can't stop them. You would only have worried."

Maya's eyes brimmed with tears.

Gopal was matter-of-fact. "We can't afford to be emotional," he said. "Mohan, have you finished all your requirements for graduation? How soon can you leave?"

Mohan was taken aback. "My requirements are almost done, but I still have to pass the examination. What do you mean, 'How soon can I leave?' Leave to go where?"

"To Canada," said Gopal. "Time is short. I have a van with two guards waiting outside."

He addressed Maya. "Mohan can live with George. He'll be relatively safe there, although he'll have to cut off his hair and blend into the general population. George is already working to get the papers he'll need to get into Canada. He can finish his studies there. George has a friend in Canada who's willing to help."

Mohan straightened up. "I won't move away from Mommy and Varsha!"

Gopal was standing where he entered. Now he walked to the sofa and seated himself.

"Mohan, your sister and mother are safe in India. You are not. They can join you in Canada later. One way or another you'll have to leave them. Time is running out."

"I can fend off the callers," Mohan protested. "My place is here, in my home."

Maya had been quiet. Now she wiped her tears. "Mohan, Gopal is right. Pack your bags."

She went to her room and shut the door.

Mohan, holding his head, sat down on the sofa. Gopal watched him.

"If I go, Mommy will be so lonely! Varsha lives in her own world."

"She'll be lonely and worried about your safety if you get dragged into the movement."

"Uncle Gopal, may I ask a question?" asked Mohan. "Please don't be angry."

"Ask any question. Feel free."

"If I go away, will you protect my mother and my sister?"

"Of course. I'll do everything in my power to keep them safe. It would be improper for me to visit Maya with you and your father gone, but I can find a female guard to live here. And I'll phone often and come by when I can with a female social worker for a cup of tea."

"One more question," Mohan said.

"Ok, but quickly."

"What is Mommy's and your relationship?"

Gopal's expression changed. His mind seemed to wander as

though he were looking into the distant past. "When I met your mother she was already in love with your father, my best friend. Even then I could have loved her. She's beautiful. But we don't love each other that way."

He went on. "I had a little sister who died when I was young. I think that if she had lived, she would have resembled your mother. But it's not that my love for Maya is brotherly." He paused. "All I can say is that our relationship doesn't seem to fit into any standard human relationship the world defines."

Mohan was thoughtful. "Daddy seems to know that," he said.

Gopal glanced anxiously at his watch.

Mohan continued. "Mommy trusts you. She's ready to send me with you."

"Mohan, we must go"

Mohan took a deep breath. "I must live for Mommy," he said.

He knocked on Maya's door.

She stepped out, her eyes red and swollen, and ducked into Varsha's room.

Varsha's sleepy, drooping lids flew open when she heard what was going on. She hugged Mohan. "Go to Canada," she said. "Don't worry about Mommy and me. I'll look after Mommy and she'll look after me. Uncle Gopal, I promise I'll keep my mouth shut."

Mohan packed a bag. Maya handed him all the cash she had and her gold chain. She hugged him. "Be safe," she murmured.

Maya closed the door, and together she and Varsha watched the curtained van speed away.

The next day, Maya had to face Rati. Before Rati could speak, Maya said, "Mohan's out of town."

Rati was baffled. "But he's not finished with med school."

"That may be, but he's gone. Please don't say a word to anyone."

A frantic look came into Rati's eyes. "Where is he? When will he be back?"

"Please, no more questions, Rati." Maya's tears and bereft look quieted Rati.

Soon strangers started to call. They weren't easily put off. "Mohan owes us money," one man said ominously. "We must find him."

"His father wants to see him," another insisted.

When two strangers accosted Varsha on the street, Maya decided she had to act.

She called Gopal, who promptly sent a van to pick them up. The driver brought them directly to Rala, Gopal's old village.

In Rala, Gopal's family welcomed them warmly and made them feel at home. Varsha hit it off with Gopal's nephews and nieces, while Maya enjoyed getting to know Gopal's cousins and their wives, who treated her with utmost respect.

When, a week later, word arrived that Mohan had made it safely to Canada, Maya and Varsha were free to return home. They bid a tearful goodbye to Gopal's family, then set out from Rala, returning by van and train to Indore. Maya was grateful to see her little bungalow and garden.

Soon after they set foot in the house, the menacing phone calls began again. But Maya told the very first caller that Mohan was beyond reach in Canada, and soon the calls stopped.

The next morning Rati showed up. "Where were you?"

"We had to go away for a while."

"When will I see Mohan again?" The pleading look in her eyes touched Maya's heart.

"Please sit down, Rati," she said. Holding Rati's hands in her own, Maya said gently, "We had to send Mohan to Canada. He wasn't safe here."

Rati grasped the situation immediately. Her eyes widened in dismay, and she tried to control her tears.

"Rati, go back to college. You'll find someone."

"No." She threw back her head. "No marriage for me. I'll join Varsha. I'll help her with her social work."

"Rati, Varsha always wanted to be a social worker. You wanted a family. Don't force yourself into a life you didn't dream of."

191

"I don't want to be someone else's wife. If I can't marry Mohan, I won't marry at all." Rati spoke with such determination that Maya believed her.

When Rati had gone, Maya dialed Rajkumari's number.

"Where have you been?" Rajkumari exclaimed. "We were desperate and phoned everybody we could think of! We didn't know what had become of you."

"I'm sorry," said Maya. "I don't know how to explain what's happened. Mohan went to Canada and Varsha and I had to lay low for a while."

"Oh, Maya," said Rajkumari, "you're so alone now!"

Maya sighed. "Every day I think of Bhajanma's words, 'You must be your own support,' and carry on."

"Bhajanma was a visionary woman," said Rajkumari.

A few days later, a young man came by the house. "I live in Canada," he said. "Your son asked me to carry this letter to you." He slipped an envelope into Maya's hand before hurrying away again, promising to visit again before returning to Canada.

Her hands shaking, she tore the envelope open.

```
"My Dear Mommy,
     I live with a Sikh family and help them in
their shop.
     I think of us and India all the time. Now I
know how Bhajanma and Gurumukh Bauji and Kuldipma
must have felt when they had to flee to Delhi. I
feel like a refugee.
     I miss you terribly - and Varsha and Rati,
too.
     My love to everyone,
     Mohan"
```

Maya hugged the letter. "Refugee," she murmured, "refugee…"

CHAPTER 21

For Darashan, leaving his beloved Maya and the children had been wrenching. He'd lingered in Indore, postponing the inevitable as long as he could, while Ranjit Singh phoned every day, badgering him to leave his family and come join him. Finally, he'd threatened, "If you don't show up by the end of the week, I'm leaving without you."

The day he'd torn himself away from Maya and the children, he'd been in a state of shock. Resisting the urge to turn around and go right back home, he'd asked the rickshaw driver to take him to the train station, where he'd reserved a seat by the window in a first class compartment. His head hurt and his mind was in turmoil. He'd leaned back, closed his eyes and tried to sleep.

An issue that had tormented him for weeks started to haunt him again: before vanishing for good, shouldn't he visit Rajkumari, Bhajanma and Kuldipma to bid them good-bye?

Ranjit Singh had fought the idea. "Women don't comprehend concepts like revolution and liberty," he'd insisted. "They can't understand sacrificing family for independence. They're like crabs in a pot. If one tries to climb up and escape, the others pull him down. They're happy in their little pot. Rajkumari, Bhajanma and Kuldip would only try to stop us. Your mother's tears would flood the whole house."

"What do you expect?" shot Darashan. "We're deserting the family."

But Ranjit Singh ignored Darashan's outburst, and the idea of a visit was dropped.

"What of Maya and the children?" he wondered now. Would he ever see them again?

He thought back to the lengthy debates he'd had with Gopal recently.

Gopal had compared his predicament to that of Rama, hero of the epic Ramayana.

"Rama blindly obeyed his father's wishes, exiling himself and his wife to a jungle where his wife was kidnapped and he had to fight a war to rescue her," Gopal had pointed out. "Don't you think there's a lesson there?" he'd asked.

But in the end, it was Ranjit Singh's arguments and Darashan's sense of loyalty and obligation to his father that had won out.

Now Darashan's thoughts wandered yet again.

His college friends, Bhushan and Arun were rising through the ranks in India's power circles. Bhushan could even become Prime Minister one day, and Arun could become a General. The implications dismayed him. By taking up arms for Khalistan, Darashan would be warring with his best friends.

When he reached Delhi, Ranjit Singh was waiting for him at the station. "Tomorrow we go to Punjab," he told Darashan.

Balbir and Ranjit Singh had already rented a small apartment there. People in the movement visited endlessly, plotting strategy. Balbir was away, trying to find new recruits.

A month later there was a knock at the door. "Who is it?" Ranjit Singh demanded.

"It's your grandson," said a voice on the other side.

Ranjit Singh flung open the door.

There on the stoop stood Balbir, his face ashen.

"What's wrong?" Darashan asked.

"I have sad news," said Balbir. "I've had word…"

"What is it?"

"Bhajanma…" He stopped, his eyes downcast.

"What about Bhajanma?" Darashan asked, his heart starting to race. "Is she sick?"

Balbir shook his head.

Ranjit Singh couldn't stand such indirectness. "She's dead, isn't she?" he said flatly.

"Yes," Balbir whispered.

Darashan's stomach churned. He couldn't think.

He stood rooted, swaying, his eyes vacant.

"Are you Ok, Uncle Darashan?" asked Balbir.

He led Darashan to a chair and quickly fixed him a cup of tea.

Darashan swallowed a mouthful, then stammered, "We should have…I should have visited Raj."

"Your grandmother was old," said Ranjit Singh dismissively. "She had high blood pressure. She wanted to die. She probably didn't suffer very long – did she, Balbir?"

"I heard she was sick for a week. Mommy tried to save her."

"As she would. I know her," Darashan mumbled.

He gazed, unseeing, at the cup of tea on his lap. Then abruptly he looked up.

"I must visit Rajkumari," he declared.

"What's the point?" snapped Ranjit Singh. "Bhajanma's gone."

"You don't have to come with me. I'll go by myself." For the first time in his life, Darashan was firm with his father.

Ranjit Singh looked at him in surprise.

"All right. We'll go. Balbir, you stay here. If anyone in the movement comes looking for me, tell them your grandfather will be back soon."

They traveled to Rajkumari's by taxicab, deliberately arriving late in the evening. In the old days, the door to Rajkumari's home had stayed wide open until bedtime. But lately, Balavant Singh had begun locking it at sunset.

Darashan rang the bell and, after carefully ascertaining who was there, Balavant Singh opened the door. "This is a surprise," said Balavant Singh, ushering them into the house.

When Rajkumari saw her father and brother, she wordlessly went to the kitchen and sent the servants home. Then she heaped food on two plates, brought them into the dining room and set them on the table.

"Eat your dinner," she said matter of factly, "and then we can talk."

They picked at their food silently, until Darashan could stand the silence no longer and asked Rajkumari about Bhajanma's illness.

"She had pneumonia," Rajkumari replied. "But that's not what killed her. She wanted to die."

Ranjit Singh opened his mouth to say, "I told you so," but he swallowed his words. He merely glanced at his son.

"Did she have a message for us? What were her last words?" Darashan asked.

"If you really want to know, ask Maya. She knows."

Darashan felt bitterness radiating from his sister like a dark cloud. He couldn't blame her.

Rajkumari went on. "Even now it's not too late. You're alive. You can fight democratically for our rights."

Darashan and Ranjit Singh didn't respond.

"I'll tell you what *I* think," she continued. "India has plenty of young Sikh men. They'll hear your speeches, fall for your dream and lose their lives."

Darashan sat quietly, his eyes downcast.

"You may have dragged my older son into your war, but mark my words," she said, enunciating each word precisely. "If you try to recruit Charan, I will murder you both."

"Rajkumari, Balbir joined the movement on his own," Ranjit Singh began. "Besides, your children owe allegiance to the new nation and their grandfath—"

Rajkumari stood up, her eyes flaming. She banged her fists on the table. "I am your daughter. You treated me like a second-class citizen. You wouldn't allow me to study medicine. I married Balavant so I could do it in spite of you. You disowned me for my crime and didn't set foot in my home for years. You and Darashan were supposed to care for your mothers. In the end, your mother died under my roof and your wife lives with me. My children owe you nothing. If you approach Charan, I will forget you are my father and that Darashan is my brother. I have contacts in Punjab. You two will not live to fight your war."

Shaking with fury, Ranjit Singh struggled to formulate a response.

Kuldip, who had been silently crying until now, spoke up. "Raj is right. Please don't try to recruit Charan or Mohan to fight your war." She wiped her eyes and hurried upstairs. Rajkumari followed her.

"A woman turns into a lioness when her cub is threatened," Balavant Singh murmured.

Ranjit Singh had heard enough. He turned to Darashan. "Let's go."

Darashan hesitated. He desperately wanted to talk to his sister. But Ranjit Singh was at the door, glaring at him. Darashan looked to Balavant Singh, hoping he would ask them to stay.

But Balavant Singh ignored his glance and silently went to the door and opened it. They parted wordlessly.

Upstairs in her room, Rajkumari wept into her hands.

"How many generations of my family must suffer?" she cried. "When will these revolutions be over?"

But she was talking to herself.

She heard the front door close, and rushed to the window facing the front yard. In the moonlight, she could make out two figures walking away. She clutched her throat and watched as they grew smaller.

One of them turned for a moment to glance backward.

Now both of them stopped and appeared to be arguing. From her place at the window, Rajkumari could see wildly gesticulating arms and she faintly heard an angry voice.

Abruptly one of the figures tore itself away and stalked onward. The other stood motionless, watching his companion disappear into the darkness.

The lone remaining figure turned and walked back to the house.

AUTHOR'S NOTE:

I was born in British India. In 1947, when I was nine, the country was partitioned, and a flood of people fleeing Pakistan arrived. Many had suffered terrible atrocities. It was my first contact with refugees.

When Mahatma Gandhi was murdered in 1948, I was living in Pune. Because Gandhi's assassin was a Maharashtrian Brahmin, Brahmin homes were looted and burned. I saw this happen to some of my friends.

Over the years I continued to meet many refugees from Pakistan and hear their stories. Some I met were from divided Muslim families, like the parents I met in India who pined to see their grandchildren in Pakistan.

In 1963 I moved to Canada, and later to the United States. In both countries, I met many refugees — so-called "displaced persons" — from Europe, and later from Bangladesh.

Refugees' stories, I learned, have common themes. Refugees are not migrating by choice, and most never fully recover from the trauma of the loss of their homeland.

When the Khalistan movement started in India, I watched from afar, dreading another wave of refugees. I began writing this novel in 1985 in my mother tongue, Marathi. My father helped, filling me in from India on relevant news developments, and offering encouragement. I finished the book in 1988 and returned with it to Pune, my hometown. I had published a couple of books in Marathi by then, but when publishers learned what this book was about, they wanted nothing to do with it; they were afraid of militants. In 1986, a general had been assassinated in Pune for leading an attack on a Sikh temple.

My father passed in 1989, and I was devastated. The novel languished. Then I met Dinkar Gangal of Granthali Prakashan Books in the United States. He agreed to publish the novel, and it was eventually released on December 25, 2003. It won the Maharashtra Government award.

I have worked for several years on this English-language

version of the novel. The story is largely the same as the original, but the translation is not exact, and I have changed the ending.

I must thank several helpers. My father, Vithal Pundalik Rege, for his assistance and loving support, Dinkar Gangal for helping rewrite the Marathi version of the novel, and my friends who read it and advised me. I must also thank Amy Meeker, who edited the first few chapters, Sage Stossel, for editing the novel and helping me publish it, and Amit Kaikini for his cover design and illustrations.

I am also especially grateful to *Ekata*, a Marathi magazine published in Toronto, Canada. It is that magazine that inspired me to write.

All characters appearing in this novel are fictional. Any similarities to real persons are purely coincidental.

The book touches on many communities in India. In writing the story I did not wish to hurt or slight any group. If anyone feels maligned or unfairly portrayed, I apologize. That was not my intention.

FAMILY TREE

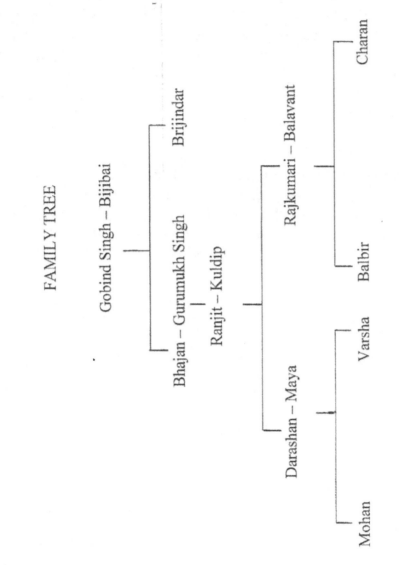

Gobind Singh – Bijibai

Bhajan – Gurumukh Singh   Brijindar

Ranjit – Kuldip

Darashan – Maya   Rajkumari – Balavant

Mohan   Varsha   Balbir   Charan

Characters List

Amrit - *Ramlal's wife*
Arun - *Gopal's friend and classmate and Darashan's friend*
Balavant - *Rajkumari's husband*
Balbir - *Rajkumari and Balvant's son*
Bhagawan - *Binnee's brother, Bimala's son*
Bhajan - *Ranjit's mother, Darashan and Rajkumari's grandmother, Gurumkh Singh's wife*
Bhushan - *Darashan's friend*
Bijibai - *Bhajan's mother*
Bimala - *Gurumukh Singh and Bhajan's neighbor*
Bindi - *Bhushan's wife*
Binnee - *Bimala daughter*
Brijindar - *Gobind Singh and Bijibai's son*
Charan - *Rajkumari and Balavant's son*
Chiragmal - *Jairam's grandson*
Darashan - *Ranjit and Kuldip's son*
Damayanti - *Kuldip's sister*
Devaki - *Maya's friend*
Ganga - *one of Gopal's girl cousins*
George - *Darashan's friend*
Gobind Singh - *Bhajan's father*
Gopal Sane - *Darashan's friend*
Gurumukh Singh - *Bhajan's husband, Ranjit's father, Darashan and Rajkumari's grandfather*
Hasan - *one of Gobind Singh and Bijibai's farm workers*
Ikbal - *Darashan's friend*
Jairam - *Ramlal's nephew*
Jashwant Singh - *Gurumukh Singh's cousin*
Jitendra - *Darashan's friend*
Jivan - *Veer Singh's friend*
Khandya - *Gopal's childhood friend*
Kuldip - *Ranjit's wife, Darashan and Rajkumari's mother*
Mani - *Gopal's sister*
Maya - *Darashan's childhood friend and wife*

Meenakumari - *Maya's mother*
Meera - *one of Gopal's girl cousins*
Mohammed - *Siraj Hasan's nephew*
Mohan - *Darashan and Maya's son*
Ninad - *Arun's son*
Pratap - *Sameer's brother*
Ragesh - *Ramlal's son*
Rajkumari - *Ranjit and Kuldip's daughter*
Ramlal - *one of Gobind Singh and Bijibai's farm workers*
Ranga - *one of Gobind Singh and Bijibai's farm workers*
Ranjit - *Bhajan and Gurumukh Singh's son, Darshan and Rajkumari's father*
Rati - *Mohan's girlfriend*
Rohan - *Balavant's farm worker*
Sameer - *Arun's gardener*
Savita - *Jivan's wife*
Siraj Hasan - *Gurumukh Singh's business associate and friend*
Usha - *Arun's wife*
Vijaya Varavadekar - *Arun's mother*
Mr. Varavadekar - *Arun's father*
Varsha - *Darashan and Maya's daughter*
Veer Singh - *Damayanti's husband*

Important Dates

1942	Darashan and Gopal are born
1945	Rajkumari is born
July 1947	Gurumukh Singh's family departs for Delhi
1947-52	Gurumukh Singh's family lives in a chawl
1952	Gurumukh Singh moves his family to a flat
1948	Gopal moves in with his uncle
1959	Gopal moves to Delhi for an education
1963	Rajkumari marries Balavant Singh
1963	Gopal, Bhushan, Darashan, Arun, Ikbal, Jitendranath graduate
1965	Darashan marries Maya
1966	Mohan is born
1969	Varsha is born
1984	Gurumukh Singh is murdered
1984	Darashan joins the Khalistan movement and moves away from home
1985	Bhajanma's death

Relevant History

India is a multi-religious, multiethnic, multiracial and multilingual country. Its traditions, customs, and even the types of food people eat vary widely. The weather, too, changes from region to region—being cold and snowy up north and very hot in the south.

Throughout its history, the Indian subcontinent was divided into multiple small princely states. Beginning in 600 B.C., a number of foreign powers, including Alexander the Great in 327 B.C., invaded India from the north. Periodically, a great prince would manage to unite India. During these times of unity, India would be prosperous and the nation would flourish.

In its early years, India's inhabitants practiced the Hindu, Buddhist and Jain religions. Because these religions preached tolerance, there were no religious conflicts.

Historically, whenever a foreign power has invaded India, an Indian ruler has helped that power to gain a foothold. This history was repeated when a Turk named Muhammad Ghori invaded India in 1192 A.D., defeating an Indian ruler, and founding a Muslim dynasty there. In the sixteenth century, Mongols defeated the power in Delhi, and the Mongol leader Babar crowned himself *Badshaha* (ruler). That victory marked the beginning of the Mongol Empire, another Muslim power.

The British first sailed to India in 1700 A.D. for purposes of trade. By this time, Mongol power had been weakened by revolts. Over time, the British appropriated territory and gradually consolidated power, defeating Indian states one by one. In 1857, Indian rulers joined forces to fight the British, but British forces defeated them and established their rule over the entire country. British India contained 565 princely states within its borders.

The British used India primarily for commerce. Indians chafed under Britain's colonial rule, and a few educated Indian citizens established a congress in 1885 to demand fairer laws for Indian citizens. In January 1915, Mahatma Gandhi, an Indian citizen, arrived on the scene from South Africa, where he had perfected his technique of non-violent civil disobedience. A charismatic leader, he spearheaded a movement for independence for India.

After World War II, the British partitioned India into two separate nations, India and Pakistan, and ceded power to the newly formed governments on August 15, 1947. Citizens of both countries rejoiced, but their joy was tainted by violence in the newly created nations.

Atrocities perpetrated in Pakistan against Hindus and Sikhs at the time of partition, and Mahatma Gandhi's policies of tolerance toward Muslims infuriated many Indian citizens. On January 30, 1948 Nathuram Godase, a Marathi Brahmin from the state of Maharashtra shot and killed Mahatma Gandhi to put an end to his influence on India's politics.

When news of the murder reached the masses, anti-Brahmin sentiments flared all over India. Riots engulfed Maharashtra, Godase's home state. Brahmin homes were looted, pillaged and burned, and many Brahmin men were beaten.

The Communist Party existed in India before independence, and remained as one of the political parties after independence. Communism appealed to many young, idealistic Indian men and women in the 1950s. But in 1962, communist China invaded India and annexed some of India's lands, and in 1969 a militant subgroup of India's Communist Party attempted an armed revolution in Bengal to upend the exploitation of landless laborers by the landowner class. The violent uprising started in Bengal and spread to Bihar, Andhrapradesh, and Orissa. The party split into factions, and the movement's influence and appeal in India waned, as communism lost its appeal for young people.

In 1971, Bengali-speaking East Pakistan resolved to secede from Punjabi- and Sindhi-speaking West Pakistan. With India's help, East Pakistan won a war of independence with West Pakistan and established a new nation of Bangladesh.

*　　*　　*　　*　　*　　*　　*　　*

In 1469, Guru Nanak was born to a Hindu family near Lahore. He traveled extensively and studied all the Indian religions. He abhorred the Hindu-Muslim religious conflicts that were raging in India. Around the turn of the 16th century, he founded the Sikh religion, dedicated to the worship of a single god, and attracted disciples from many backgrounds. In 1699, Sikh Guru Gobind Singh introduced a form of initiation into the Sikh religion called *Khalasa* (or "pure"), which prescribes a specific set of moral and physical behaviors. *Khalasa* requires Sikhs to wear certain symbols designed to express one's allegiance to the community. One such symbol is the *Kirpan*, a steel dagger to symbolize the defense of truth. Another is long, uncut hair, to symbolize the acceptance of God's will. Sikh men traditionally cover their heads with turbans. Sikhism today has approximately 20 million followers. A large majority live in India, with many concentrated in the Indian province of Punjab. Others are in the United States, Canada, the United Kingdom, or scattered all over the world.

In 1799, Maharajah Ranjit Singh, a Sikh born in Punjab, established a Sikh empire in the region. The kingdom flourished for half a century, but in 1849, the British defeated Ranjit Singh's descendants and won control. At the time of Partition, West Punjab became part of Pakistan while East Punjab remained in India.

Approximately 15 months after independence, Sikh political leader Master Tara Singh of the political party Akali Dal, demanded a separate Punjabi-speaking province within India. Prime Minister Jawaharlal Nehru opposed the idea.

A plebiscite was held in 1961 to resolve the issue. Many Hindu families who spoke Punjabi feared that Sikhs would dominate a Punjabi-speaking province. To prevent such a development, they claimed that their language was Hindi. This move strained Hindu-Sikh relations.

Then in 1966, during Indira Gandhi's prime ministership, Punjab was divided into three separate provinces: Haryana, Punjab, and Himachal Pradesh. Haryana and Himachal Pradesh were predominantly Hindu, while Punjab province was primarily Sikh. Nonetheless, Akali Dal, a Sikh-dominated party, was unable to win the elections in Punjab.

The creation of the three separate provinces failed to satisfy the Akali Dal party: the important city of Chandigarh was part of Haryana, and Akali Dal wanted it.

In 1973, Akali Dal passed a resolution officially establishing itself as a Sikh party. A few of its members also began to agitate for a separate Sikh homeland, which they referred to as Khalistan.

From here on, all attempts to resolve the Punjab issue diplomatically failed. Violence erupted in 1981 as those in the Khalistan movement began to take up arms on behalf of the cause. Serious diplomatic efforts failed again in 1983. The situation deteriorated and violence worsened.

In October of 1983, Prime Minister Indira Gandhi dissolved the Punjab province's government and declared President's rule there. But her efforts failed to stop the violence. Sant Jarnail Singh Bhindranwale, a militant Sikh leader, converted a revered Sikh holy site known as the Golden Temple into a military camp, though many Sikhs dispute this. In June 1984, Prime Minister Indira Gandhi ordered India's military to attack the Temple. The move succeeded in dislodging the militants, but it left the Sikh community with a lasting grudge.

Four months later, on October 31, 1984, Indira Gandhi's Sikh bodyguard shot and killed her to avenge the attack.

News of the Prime Minister's murder infuriated Hindus, sparking extensive rioting, looting and burning of Sikh property. Many Sikhs were caught totally unaware of the events and were injured in the ensuing upheaval.

*   *   *   *   *   *   *   *

NOTE: As with any complex, highly fraught history, some of these details are in dispute. But the chronicle above represents a good faith attempt to summarize as accurately as possible the outlines of India's history as pertains to the story.

Lalita Gandbhir's fiction, poetry, and non-fiction have been published in India, Canada and the United States, both in Marathi and in English, in such venues as *The South Asian Review, Ekata, Weber Studies, Her Mother's Ashes*, and *The Massachusetts Review*. She is a recipient of the 2003-2004 Maharashtra Government Award for Fiction for the Marathi-language version of this novel. A former physician, she now lives in Singer Island, Florida with her husband.

Made in the USA
Monee, IL
19 June 2020